HAMILTON

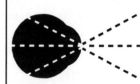

This Large Print Book carries the
Seal of Approval of N.A.V.H.

HAMILTON

CATHERINE COOKSON

THORNDIKE PRESS

An imprint of Thomson Gale, a part of The Thomson Corporation

Detroit • New York • San Francisco • New Haven, Conn. • Waterville, Maine • London

THOMSON

™

GALE

Thorndike Press® Large Print Basic.

The text of this Large Print edition is unabridged.

Other aspects of the book may vary from the original edition.

Set in 16 pt. Plantin.

LIBRARY OF CONGRESS CATALOGING-IN-PUBLICATION DATA

Cookson, Catherine.
  Hamilton / by Catherine Cookson.
    p. cm. — (The Hamiltons ; #1)
  ISBN-13: 978-0-7862-9272-1 (hardcover : alk. paper)
  ISBN-10: 0-7862-9272-5 (hardcover : alk. paper)
  1. Women authors — Fiction. 2. Horses — Fiction. 3. Human-animal
relationships — Fiction. 4. Large type books. I. Title.
PR6053.O525H3 2007
823'.914—dc22   2006038082

Published in 2007 by arrangement with Simon & Schuster, Inc.

Printed in the United States of America on permanent paper
10 9 8 7 6 5 4 3 2 1

HAMILTON

■ ■ ■ ■

PART ONE
THE CHRYSALIS

■ ■ ■ ■

CHAPTER 1

I've done it! I have really done it. After thirteen years I've done it. How long have I wanted to do it? Oh, for the whole of the thirteen years. Yes, all of that time. Now I don't care what happens to me. I don't. I don't.

I'm sitting here in this dreadful place wondering why it should have happened at all, and to me. I'm what you call inoffensive. Well, that's how most people see me. Some even think I'm odd; and, of course, that's without them knowing anything about Hamilton.

When did I first meet up with Hamilton? Oh, it must have been when I started talking to myself when I was seven years old. I didn't call him that then, though.

I remember very little before I was seven. Some people can go back to when they were two or three and recall instances as plainly as if they had happened yesterday. But there are only two I can recall before that time. One was my first day at school when the children stood me against the wall and measured my arms, making me hold them out straight in front of me when they would try to pull my left hand to meet my right, and when they couldn't, Katie Moore, who lived three doors down, explained to them that God had made my arms like that to get even with my mother who thought herself better than anybody in the terrace and she had no right after what had happened.

Long after I was seven I tried to get Katie to tell me what had happened to make my mother like she was, but she didn't seem to know.

The other event I can recall before that early age is of my mother knocking a book out of my hand, then sitting staring at me, and me sitting staring at her too frightened to speak, until she yelled, *"Why? Why?"* at the same time swiping with her hand a cup and saucer and jug off the kitchen table. And then she cried.

But from when I was seven I could give you almost a day to day report of things that happened. My first vivid memory is of George. Oh, I liked George. Oh, I did, because George was common. Funny, how soon I discovered that all the nice things were common, such as eating ice cream out in the street; or, when it was raining, running along a gutter and kicking the water up in sprays; or jumping in the garden and screaming as you jumped because of a wonderful feeling inside you which regrettably lasted only a second; or wiping your bacon dip up with your bread. But the most common thing was to say what you were thinking, especially if they were funny things. This wasn't only common, it was low; and George was both common and low in this respect, and his mother was even worse, and nicer.

Why did my mother marry George who was four years younger than her? I've never been able to fathom that one out. I understood that my own father popped off when I was two. I didn't know then whether it was popped off dead, or just popped off, because the only time I mentioned him I got my ears boxed.

Thinking he might have popped off dead I started to pray for him. That was when I became a sort of Catholic. You see George was a Catholic, a wooden one as he said. I couldn't understand that at first. But it wasn't the reason he couldn't marry my mother in the Catholic church but had to go to the Town Hall to have it done. He took me to church one Sunday. It was the very first time I had been in a church and my mother let me go for they had only been married a fortnight and she was still in a good temper. In spite of not understanding a word that was said, I liked that church very much. What with all the bobbing up and down, it was as good as the pictures.

George didn't go to church every Sunday, just now and again. Some Sundays he took me to see his mother, and she said to call her gran. But the first time I referred to her as gran at home my mother took me into the bedroom and, grabbing me by the shoulders, shook me as she said, "You're not to call that woman gran. She's an awful woman, common."

One thing I learned early, my mother was everything but common: she didn't talk common, she didn't act common, she didn't look common. She was about five foot four in height and had a lovely figure and was pretty. She had large grey eyes, dark hair with a deep wave in it, and a small mouth, and she always spoke nice, correctly. She was an only child and she had been born in this house, 7 Wellenmore Terrace, Fellburn. Her father had been a draughtsman, drawing ships' insides, so I understood from the few times she spoke about him. Her mother had been a music teacher. She didn't talk very much about her either. They had both died before I was born.

So why, her not being common at all, had she to marry a man like George, because you couldn't get anybody more common than George: he smoked and he drank, and he used language; he laughed a lot and very loudly; and then he wasn't a nice eater, he guzzled.

But George was nice. He altered my life . . . for a time. I always used to associate him with colours. When he came into the house it turned bright yellow; when he left, it dropped back into its extremely clean and extremely tidy, extremely well-furnished grey.

George travelled, that was, when he did the job he liked best which was driving a lorry. But he often lost his job because he didn't get the lorry to where it was going. When he got drunk on the way he just slept in it, and on one occasion when he was making for a port with some big crates, it was twenty-four hours after the boat had sailed when they found the lorry in a lay-by. He was still asleep in it.

Sometimes he worked digging ditches; other times he'd help knock buildings down. He didn't seem to mind any job that he did except the one that took him down man-holes, because then he smelt.

They began fighting towards the end of the first year because my mother knew by then she had let herself down in marrying George. But I was glad she had because I'd never had a companion like him. Whenever he met me outside he would always take hold of my short arm. And sometimes on a Sunday — this would be a Sunday when he hadn't a bad head first thing in the morning — he would take me to church with him and we would come home along a tree-lined path through the park which led to the field bordering our terrace. There he would say, "All right?" and I would look up at him and laugh and say, "Right ahead!" And then we would both hitch along, like Katie and I did. He was very big and bulky, and watching his feet leave the ground and flop down again seemed to me to be very funny, and always before the end of the path I would lean against him and laugh until my body shook. And then there was that memorable Sunday when he suddenly lifted me up until my face was level with his and he said, "Maisie Rochester, it's a bloody shame. All round, it's a bloody shame."

I couldn't make out why the laughter should suddenly cease and he was quiet on the way home. I only knew that in that moment I loved George Michael Carter and I loved his mother, and to me they were the most wonderful people in the world . . . my world.

I was thirteen years old when George left us, and there was no question about how he popped off because he came and told me that he was going. My mother had gone to a meeting of the Literary Circle. Apparently she had been a member for years before she married George, and then she stopped going, until six months ago when she started again.

It was on a Thursday night. We'd had our teas and I was washing up. I did most of the washing up and in spite of my short arm I rarely broke anything. There had been no conversation at the tea-table: Mother was talking less and less to George, and they weren't fighting openly any more like they had done when they were sleeping together in the big bedroom; for a long time now George had slept in the back room.

Our house was quite big. It had five bedrooms, the bathroom and a small store-room, with a long attic above; and downstairs there was a big kitchen, a sitting-room, a dining-room and a smaller room that my mother always referred to as the study, because her father's books were arrayed on shelves all round the room.

When my mother came downstairs this night she looked very pretty. She was dressed in pale blue and her face was made up, and as I looked at her I wished I loved her like I did Gran Carter.

"I'll be back at half past nine," she said. "You be in bed by then." She rarely looked at me when she gave me orders. When I come to think of it she rarely looked at me at all if she could avoid it.

She did not speak to George, but as soon as the door had closed on her he looked towards it for a moment, then went upstairs.

I finished the dishes; then I, too, went upstairs and into my room, because I had to do my homework and I always did it in my bedroom. But on that night I stood looking out of the window because the sun was still shining brightly. It was early September and it had been quite hot all day. As far as I could see there were deckchairs in most of the back gardens. I could see as far as the Stickles' garden and the top of Mr Stickle's head that came well above the back of the deck-chair.

The Stickles had only lived in the terrace for about six months. They rented their house, which in a way made them different, for most in the terrace owned their property. But the Stickles weren't common. Mr Stickle lived with his sister, and was looked upon as a sort of gentleman. He was a little old, being twenty-three, and he dressed very smartly. Katie Moore's mother said he'd have to because that was his job, being assistant manager in a high-class gentleman's shop, which Katie's mother said wouldn't last very long because men weren't wearing suits now.

It's funny about that, I mean the things that people say: men weren't wearing suits now. When Katie told me that, my mind did a funny little skip and I saw men going about in their shirts and underpants. It made me giggle inside. I had the habit of doing this, but nobody knew about it. Oh yes, they did, George knew. I had told him once and he had laughed and laughed.

I couldn't get down to my homework this night and I sat scribbling in my spare book — it was an exercise book that I wrote things in such as names and things I wanted to remember, and also sayings that sounded funny to me — when George's voice came from outside the door, saying, "Maisie."

I ran and opened it, and he came in and sat on the edge of the bed. He had his best suit on and his hair was wet and well combed back. His big face was shiny and somehow as I looked at him I thought he did resemble Oswald. That's what I called the bear he had bought me when he first married my mother.

I sat on the bed beside him and, when he didn't speak, I said, "What's the matter, George?"

He still didn't speak for a time, but then he muttered a blasphemy: "Christ Almighty!" he said.

I didn't flinch as my mother might have done because Gran Carter often said things like that. Gran Carter was always calling on God. She could do it in so many ways too. And now George turned to me and caught hold of both my hands, and I looked down on them as they became lost inside his, and he looked down on them too as he said, "I'm going, Maisie."

"Going where?" I said stupidly, knowing that there was only one place he would be going to and that would be his mother's. And he said this: "To me ma's." Then he looked into my face and his eyes were sad as he went on, "I can't stand it any more, Maisie. You know what I mean. This isn't life, this isn't living, it's hell. I suppose I'm to blame for part of it but not the main part. She's hopeless . . . your mother. Well, you

18

know that, I don't have to tell you, you've had her longer than me. And God help you from now on. You know something, Maisie?"

I gulped in my throat and told myself not to cry, but then I started to cry and he said, "Oh, pet, pet, come on. But look —" He brought my head towards his shoulder and as I sniffed I inhaled his particular smell of cigarette smoke, soap, and body sweat that was so comforting, and his voice came to me now, muffled as he said, "I might as well tell you, Maisie, I've stayed as long as I have just because of you. Me ma knows that an' all, 'cos as I said to her, that woman isn't human where you're concerned. I want to tell you something." He put his broad thumb under my chin and lifted my face up. "If she ever gets physically cruel, I mean with her hands, she's an expert with her tongue we know that, but if she should take up the other way, you come straight over to us. Now promise me?"

"Yes, George." My voice sounded like a squeak, and he smiled wryly now as he dried my eyes with his handkerchief, saying, "You've not only been unlucky with your mother, you've been unlucky with your fathers, although that poor bloke has my sympathy. Wherever he is, good luck to him, I say. He got away in time: he had only two

19

years, I've had six of 'em."

"He got away? You mean he isn't dead?"

"No. Well, I don't know, lass; he wasn't dead when he left her. Went to Australia, I understand. Well, now she'll be divorced for the second time. Oh, Maisie." He now stroked my hair back from my face as he said, "I wish to God I could take you along of me. I do. I do. You mightn't have the bloody cold elegance you've got here, but you'd know love, and appreciation, aye." He smiled widely now as he tapped my forehead, saying, "People don't know what goes on in there, do they? I think I must be the only one that's discovered what you've got up top. Anyway, what you've got to do, Maisie, at least for the next three or four years . . . What are you now? Thirteen? Aye, well until you're sixteen and you leave school, what you've got to do is don't answer her back, let her get on with it. But then you don't answer her back, do you? Perhaps it would be better if you did. Oh God, I don't know . . . Anyway try to make the best of it, because you can't do anything now as she's legally got the right over you."

We sat staring at each other. Then of a sudden he sprang up from the bed and pulled me into his arms and kissed me before going quickly out; and I turned to

20

the window, and the sun had gone in and the world had changed.

I sat down on the dressing-table stool and looked in the middle of the three mirrors. Because I was crying so much I could make out only the outline of my face But I knew what it looked like: two small round eyes, a nose that would have looked all right on anybody else's face but didn't seem to fit mine, and my mouth too, too big for the size of my face. My teeth weren't bucked, but still I had a job to keep my lips closed all the time. And my hair like tow, neither fair nor brown, mousy-coloured. Again it would have looked all right on somebody else's head because there was plenty of it, and it was thick and coarse, but there wasn't a kink in it. As for my figure, I was straight up and down. Gran Carter said it would be all right, I was a late developer and I'd have a bust like nobody's business in a couple of years' time. I wasn't troubled about having a bust, but my face troubled me even more than my arm, because I could keep my arm waist high and put my schoolbag on it and hardly anybody noticed it then. But you can't hide your face, and it was my face that my mother didn't like because no part of me resembled her. She was ashamed of me in so many ways. This thought was very clear in my mind as I blinked the tears away and dried my eyes. It was as if the six years that George had been in the house were as a tick of time, they had gone; and once again I was seeing my mother in a tantrum and hearing her voice saying, "God! To have to put up with you an' all and looking like you do. Why? Why?"

CHAPTER 2

I should really start from the time I was seventeen, and yet what happened between when I was thirteen and that time set the pattern for all the years following.

The effect on my mother of George leaving was varied. When she returned that night and read the note he had left, she laughed and laughed. I hadn't gone to bed as she had ordered, because I had felt in some strange way she would need comfort. But what she did was to throw herself on the couch in the sitting-room and laugh. In amazement I watched her lift her slim legs from the carpet until they were on a level with her hips, spread her arms wide, then throw her head back. Her small mouth was wide open and I could see her tongue wagging in the cavity. If she had cried and thrown things I'd have been less afraid. But this reaction of hers seemed to give me an insight into the complexity of her character.

Within days her reactions changed. Perhaps it was the neighbours that caused the different eruptions. Yet how could she know what they were thinking because she wouldn't let them into the house. I knew what they were thinking because of Katie. Katie said her mother said some folks thought it was the best thing that could have happened, because George was a big drunken slob. But others said that it was a wonder he had stuck to her so long, because they were oil and water.

I learned a lot from Katie on our journeys to and from school. I liked Katie. She was my best friend; in fact she was my only friend, and because of that I had to forgive her when she hurt me saying things about George and telling me what her mother said about me looking as I did. We quarrelled once and she said her mother said a pikestaff wasn't as plain as me.

It was on a Saturday about a week after George had left that my mother startled me by almost springing on me and taking me by the shoulders and shaking me with a strength that was out of all proportion to her size as she cried at me, "You go near his mother's and I'll murder you. Do you hear?

And if you see him in the street and speak to him I'll thrash the skin off you." Her voice and everything about her had ceased to be refined; in this moment she sounded as common as the people she despised for being so. She was thirty-four years old at this time and had no lines on her face. Yet such was her expression that she appeared older than Gran Carter who was very old, almost sixty.

"Speak!"

I couldn't speak.

"Do you hear? Promise me you'll never go near that house or go near him."

I couldn't promise.

When one hand left my shoulder and came in contact with the side of my head, my vision blurred. I heard a noise in my ear like a train choo-chooing in a station and I fell to the side and grabbed the kitchen table; and I stayed like that for some minutes. And when I pulled myself straight and looked slowly around, there was no one there.

George had said if she started with anything physical I had to go to him. Well, if I had taken him at his word, I would have run to him at least once a week during the next six months.

It was on my fourteenth birthday when I

received the card from George that she really did seem to go mad. It was a beautiful card, what I saw of it. It had a pretty girl on the front holding a bouquet of roses, and I had just opened it and read. "From George and Gran with love to Maisie", when it was snatched from my hand. As I watched her tear it into a dozen pieces and without uttering one word, it was then the voice became audible, but only to me.

Oh, you cruel thing. I hate you. Do you hear? I hate you. I'll go to Gran's, I'll go this very day. I will. I will.

I knew my mouth was opening and shutting as if I was saying the words, but, like her, I remained silent.

Gran Carter lived in the lower end of Fellburn, Bog's End where all the common people lived. She lived on a council estate. It was an old council estate. The houses looked like rows of rundown barracks, but inside Gran's house everything was bright, cheerful and cluttered. I knew the first time I saw the furniture that it was common; but it was comfortable, and she always had a fire on, a real fire not an electric one with artificial logs like we had. And she made toast at the fire and put dripping on it mixed with the sediment from the meat. I'd never tasted anything so wonderful as that first piece of toast and dripping. And on that Saturday morning I longed with a longing that was painful in its intensity to get into that house and to sit close to Gran Carter and perhaps see George. But my mother watched me like a hawk all day, silently, no word passing between us.

On Sunday morning when Katie called and asked if I could go for a walk with her, my mother said to her, "Where do you propose to go?" And Katie said, "Oh, as far as my cousin's at the bottom of Brampton Hill."

Brampton Hill was the real posh part of Fellburn. Most of the big houses had been turned into flats and Katie's cousin lived in one of them, but the name Brampton Hill was still a passport and so I was allowed to go. But no sooner were we outside the house than Katie said, "Will you do something for me?"

And I immediately said, "Yes," because I would do anything for Katie. "Well," said Katie, "I met a boy. He . . . he's nice. He goes to Paynton High School. But he's nearly seventeen and I daren't let Mam or Dad know 'cos he's so old, and he looks older. He's very tall." She smiled widely at me. "Anyway, I told him I'd try to meet him round by the lower park today. I told them

I was going out with you. You won't give me away, will you?"

I looked at her sadly: how could she say such a thing? She said quickly, "I know you won't, but . . . but I want to be alone with him for a while."

The idea sprang like a ray of light into my mind and I gabbled at her, "How long d'you want to be alone?"

"Well, I must be back for dinner-time, that's at one, and it's now quarter past ten. Say an hour and a half. Would you mind, I mean, being on your own?"

"No. No, I wouldn't. Look, there's . . . there's some place I want to go an' all, so let's meet back at the market place at half past twelve, eh?"

"Good. Yes, good."

We held hands and ran now towards the market, and from there my feet might have had wings on them, they moved so quickly, and I was gasping when, ten minutes later, I knocked on Gran Carter's door, and when she opened it she took a step backwards as she cried, "Why, pet! Why, pet! Well, you're a sight for sore eyes. Come on. Come on in. Georgie, look who's here!"

The front door led into a small hallway that gave off to a passage, and there at the far end, looking as if he had just got out of bed, was George, and he appeared beautiful to me.

"Why! Why, hello, lass!" He came slowly towards me, his hands outstretched. "You've flown the pigeon loft then?"

"Yes, George." I gazed up at him into his shaggy bear-like face, and he put his arm around my shoulder and led me into the sitting-room. It was rather untidy, but nice, and there was a smell of cooking and Gran Carter said, "Can you stay for a bite of dinner, hinny?"

"No, Gran. I'm very sorry. I'll have to get back."

"However did you manage to get out?" She bent over me as she spoke. She had a round face, not unlike George's, but her skin was softer. Her hair was a reddy brown; she had it touched up once a month; she was wearing a hair net. She flung out an arm now, saying, "You would catch us on the hop, wouldn't you? This is like Paddy's market. But it's Sunday an' we were both in late last night." She nodded towards George. "I was at the whist drive, an' I won again. I'm the luckiest so . . . body on this earth. They're tryin' to say I'm a card sharper." She put her head back and let out a laugh very like George's. "They're green. I won the lot last night, twelve pounds. What are you gona have, hinny? A cup of tea or cocoa? . . . Have we got any lemonade left?"

"We never have any lemonade left when there's beer in the house an' you want shandies, you know that." George plonked himself down on the sofa beside me and, pushing his mother with the flat of his hand, he said, "Go on, woman, this is a special occasion, give her coffee. You like coffee, don't you, Maisie?" And without waiting for an answer, he looked back at his mother and said, "She likes coffee. Of course" — he pulled a face at me now — "it isn't the real stuff, not like . . . well, in 7 Wellenmore."

His mother went into the kitchen laughing, and he turned towards me and, his face straight, he said, "How is she?"

I couldn't answer him.

"Like that, is it?" he said, and he jerked his chin. "Has she said anything about divorce?" He didn't wait for an answer but added, "Well, if she has or she hasn't, it makes no difference: if I have to wait I'll wait and gladly, and put in some practice for the next time." Then he added quickly, "Well, what I mean is, I'll shop around and not make the same mistake twice. Well, you know what I mean."

I knew what he had meant in the first

place and I knew that he thought I was too young to understand. And on the surface I was, but under it there was this other being that knew about some things without in a way having learned them.

"Did you get our card, pet?" Gran Carter's face came round the kitchen door and I looked towards her and opened my mouth twice but no sound came out. It was as if I was watching my mother tearing it into shreds again. And when I eventually did speak, I stammered, saying, "Ye . . . yes, thank you."

George must have noticed the effect the question had on me because he turned my face towards him and looked at me silently for a moment before he said softly, "You didn't get it, did you?" I nodded at him and muttered, "Yes. Ye . . . ye . . . yes I did."

"Well, she found out about it, eh? And what did she do, tear it up? Now, now, don't upset yourself." He was whispering now. "But say nothin' to her." He nodded towards the kitchen. "If she thought that had happened she would go round there and belt her face for her, she would that, 'cos she went into Smith's and took a long time to pick that card for you. I was with her." He smiled. "There was something in the little lass's face on the card that reminded me of you."

How kind, how kind George was. Suddenly I thought of the statues of the saints in his church. He was better than all the saints.

"Here you are, hinny. And have a chocolate biscuit."

As Gran Carter put the cup of coffee and a plate of biscuits to the side of me I knew for a certainty from where her son got his kindness. She now put her hand on my hair — I had taken off my school hat — and said, "You know, you could do something with that hair. You get that trimmed at the hairdresser's and it would look real bonny. It's strong hair. They always like strong hair. They have a devil of a job with mine." She now pulled the net upwards from her head. "Peggy Wicklow" — she nodded towards George now — "she says she can count me hairs on the top an' why did I pass on what hair I had to you. She said you should go to her and she'd trim you up."

"Aye, she'd do more than that, would Peggy Wicklow." They both laughed and he added, "See me goin' into a woman's hairdresser. I hate to go to the barber's; I'm gona be like the young chaps, let it grow down me back."

"You do if you dare! All them young bug

. . . people look lousy."

George became so doubled up with laughter that he spluttered as he said, "Why didn't you say it, Ma, she won't drop down dead? She's heard it afore an' she's had her bellyful of politeness. Haven't you, pet?" He pulled me towards him, and the voice inside me said, "More than me bellyful, George. Oh yes, more than me bellyful." At this moment all I wanted was to be like them, and be common. Oh, I did want to be common.

After I'd drunk the coffee and eaten three chocolate biscuits I said I'd have to be going, because I was to meet Katie at the market. Why, asked George, had I to meet Katie at the market? But I paused before telling them why, because I thought I was giving Katie away. I knew though I could trust these two people with Katie's secret. But I couldn't see what was so funny about it when George put his arm around his mother's shoulders and she put her arm around his waist and they hung together like that half over me while they laughed, and George said, "Eeh! the things that go on." Then he ended, "But you thank Katie for us. Thank her 'specially, and tell her you'll stand in for her every Sunday."

"I'll tell her."

At the doorstep they both kissed me, but

then walked down the short front garden to the gate, and when I reached the end of the row and turned, they were still there and they waved. But after turning the corner, all the joy left me and I was filled with such longing and a great urge to run back to them and be loved and be common.

That word common was coming into my mind more and more every day. And Katie was using it too. Such and such a girl was common. Such and such a thing was common. Such and such a place was common. But mostly she was saying nowadays that such and such a one talked common. How did one talk common? Perhaps she was meaning the people who talked in broad Geordie. But why were they common because they talked like that? This word common was in a way troubling me, because I knew that everything nice that had happened to me in my life had been common.

Katie was not at the market place. I waited until one o'clock and when the Town Hall clock struck, I turned in agitation and made for home, and as I neared the terrace and saw Mrs Moore leaving our door I knew what was in store for me.

I went in the back way and through the kitchen. She was standing in the middle of the hall, and what she said to me in a quiet voice was, "Where did you go when you left Katie to do her dirty work?" I didn't answer, but that voice inside me said, She's got a nasty mind; Katie wouldn't do anything bad.

"Where did you go? I'm asking you, girl."

The voice said, Speak. Say you went for a walk. Say something. If you don't, she'll hit you.

"You went along to them, didn't you?" She was standing close to me now. I hadn't seen her walk towards me; I think my fear had dimmed my vision.

When she did hit me it wasn't with the flat of her hand but with her fist. She had a small hand. It looked delicate but the bones seemed to go right through my skull. I was falling to one side when a blow came on the other side of my head. This time it was the flat of her hand. And now she was using both on me, flap-flap, flap-flap. I was crouched on the bottom stair, my face pressed tight now against the carpet on the third step and the fingers of one hand gripping the edge of the flat brass stair-rod.

I didn't hear her leave. The house was quiet, so quiet that I heard the sparrows chirping in the nest they had built above the cup of the drainpipe. I crawled up the rest of the stairs and then, bent double, made for my room. I knew I was crying a lot and yet I was making no sound, not outwardly at any rate, but inside the voice was yelling at me, Go to George's. Go to George's. He said you had to. I answered it, No, no; she'll get wrong; not only from him she'll get wrong, she'll get wrong from other people . . .

When I lay on top of the bed I shivered and for the first time I realized I hadn't my coat on. I remember my hat flying off my head but I couldn't remember her tearing my coat off me.

The next few hours became a blur. I must have fallen asleep, and I woke up with a dreadful dread on me because I felt I had gone blind. Something had happened to my face; it was stiff and I could scarcely open my eyes, but through their narrowed slits I saw her standing over me. The electric light was on so I knew it was night-time. As I shrank back into the bed her voice came to me soft and in a tone that she had never used to me before. "Sit up and drink this," she said.

It was a great effort to do as she told me, and she put her hand behind my back and it felt firm and gentle. And I found difficulty in sipping the tea because my lips were swollen.

When I couldn't manage any more she took the cup away, then stood looking down at me. Her hands were clasped tightly against the collar of her dress and her voice was a mutter now as she said, "You asked for it. You know you did, you asked for it. You shouldn't have done it. You asked for it." And as I peered at her I realized she was frightened, and the more this became clear in my mind the more my own fear of her ebbed away . . .

The following week is lost in mist because at times I knew I was in bed and yet at other times I felt I was some place else: sometimes at Gran Carter's; sometimes hitching along the park path with George; and more than once I seemed to be in a room that was lined with books and laughing at a man sitting across a desk. He was a nice man and I knew I liked him until he turned into a policeman, and he took my hand quite gently and led me into a cell-like room with bars on the door.

When everything else during that week turned into a misty blur, that last picture remained in my mind, foretelling the future.

My mother brought up meals and tried to make me eat, but my face was so stiff that I could only swallow liquids. She very rarely spoke to me and I never spoke to her at all, at least not during that first week. But sometimes during the second week, I said to her, "I . . . I must go to school. They'll be wondering." And she answered, "I've sent them a note and told them you've had a slight . . . a slight accident." She drooped her head now and turned to the side as she added, "You've got to say you toppled down the stairs. You understand?"

I understood, but I said nothing. "You brought it on yourself," she said again. And then she muttered, "I just couldn't bear it, the . . . the indignity, the . . . the . . ." When she turned away I knew she was almost crying and when she left the room I no longer hated her but felt sorry for her.

It was on the Monday of the second week that I saw my face for the first time. It was mottled blue and yellow. My eyes were black, my cheeks were swollen and my large mouth looked even larger. The voice said: No wonder she's frightened. She could have killed you.

Yet in some strange way I was glad it had happened because I had lost my fear of her and I knew also that she would never again raise her hand to me; she mightn't be able to stop her tongue, but the result of her rage had in a way entirely altered our relationship.

During the following days I sat by the back window, but not too close and my view only showed me the McVities' garden to the right of our house. The weather had turned colder so there was no one sitting outside. It was during these days that I first experienced aloneness. It wasn't exactly loneliness, it was if part of me was locked away and had no urge to get out. Yet this part of me seemed real, because nobody knew about it, not even George. I tried to put it into words in my exercise book but it didn't read right. Anyway, if I wanted to write in my book I had to keep alert in case my mother came in, for she would want to read what I had written. She had more than once torn out sheets from my book because she said she had never read anything so infantile in her life; a child of five could do better.

I always wanted to write down things that I thought when I was with Gran Carter, because everything she said sounded funny. Even when she was sad she sounded funny.

What I didn't write down was what had happened over the past few days, because that was beyond words; it was all feelings, feelings that couldn't be expressed.

Then on the Thursday night we had a visitor. When I heard his voice downstairs I clamped my hand over my mouth. The doorbell hadn't rung, so I knew he had come in the back way and he was yelling, "You try an' stop me."

When he burst into the room I was standing with my back to the window and he took only two steps before coming to a halt; then he shook his head as he whispered, "God Almighty!"

My mother was standing behind him and she was yelling at him, "She fell downstairs. She fell downstairs. I tell you, she fell downstairs."

I watched him turn slowly towards her and his voice now was low and his words slow as he said, "You're a bloody liar. Fell downstairs. Who do you think you're trying to hoodwink? It's me remember, George. I'll have you for this. By God, I'll have you for this. I warned you, I did. I warned you time an' time again when I saw what you meant to do. But you've done it. Well, it's the last time you'll lift your hand to her. By God, I'll see to that. Come on, hinny." He thrust out an arm towards me; but I didn't move from where I was standing, and he said again, "Come on, lass."

"I'm . . . I'm all right, George." I saw my mother's eyes on me, her lips were quivering, in fact her whole body was shaking, and then I was amazed to hear myself saying in a calm-like way, "I want to talk to George, Mother."

I saw her throat contract as she gulped, and I wasn't surprised when she turned about and left us alone.

George had hold of my hands, and as he stood looking down into my face his big head moved from side to side and when he muttered, "Poor bairn," I wanted to fall against him and cry. I wanted to feel his arms about me. I wanted to say, "I'll come with you now," but there was this other voice that seemed to belong to someone who had more knowledge and understanding than I had and it said to him, "I can't come, George. I can't leave her. She . . . she'll never do it again."

"By God! she won't. By God! she won't, lass."

"She's sorry. She's . . . well, she's frightened."

"An' well she should be. If this happened a week gone Sunday as I reckoned it did from what I've heard about you supposed to have fallen downstairs, she as near killed you as nothin'. Me ma only heard the day about your supposed fall. Some girl that goes to the same school told her mother, an' me ma soon put two and two together. I

. . . I didn't even stop to wash. Look at me!"
He held out his work-grimed hands; then
dropping down on to his hunkers, he said,
"If you came and she took the matter to
court and they saw a picture of your face as
it is now after all this time, she wouldn't
stand an earthly of keepin' you."

"She's lonely, she hasn't got anybody."

"Oh, hinny, you don't know her. She'll get
somebody; she'll have some other man in
here afore you can say Jack Robinson. But
he won't be like me." He smiled wryly now.
"A different type altogether. She's got over
my phase, digging in the dirt as she once
termed it. The next one will be some white
collar bloke with an interest in music and
such. You know the kind."

I didn't know the kind, but I understood
what he meant.

His hand came out and he gently touched
my still swollen face and all the time he was
muttering to himself; then he asked, "What
did the doctor say?"

"I . . . I haven't seen him."

"You haven't?" He screwed up his eyes.
"Well, it's about time you did then, isn't it?
Has anybody been from the school?"

"I . . . I don't know."

"Somebody must have been around, you
off school a fortnight . . . You're sure you

won't come?"

"I . . . I want to come, George, you know that. I want to come more than anything, but . . . but somehow I can't. If . . . if I came I would be thinking about her all the time."

"You're daft, do you know that? She's put an old head on young shoulders an' she's not worth your little finger, and she won't thank you for stayin' mind, she won't. I know her."

He was right. I knew that she wouldn't thank me for staying, not in the way I wanted, not by loving me. She was only afraid of me going because of what the neighbours would say and the publicity that might follow if she then took the matter to court. But as for thanking me; no, I knew that she would never even like me. I was, in a way, something that had spoiled her life. I . . . I was a sort of cross.

George stood up now and as he did so a sprinkling of light-coloured dust fell from his clothes: he was working on the buildings, knocking them down again. He now said, "I'm gona tell her that if you don't appear at our house within the next fortnight, when your face goes down that is, I'll be back again. And she won't like that because the neighbours' tongues will be waggin'. I passed two of them on the street as I came in. One was old Mrs Pratt and her lower jaw dropped so far her teeth nearly fell out."

I wanted to laugh but couldn't, and when he bent and put his cheek against mine the smell of lime and brick dust and sweat and cigarette smoke was like perfume to me.

At the door he turned and said, "You'll see a doctor an' all, yes you will." He nodded twice, and then he went out.

I sat down with my back to the window, my joined hands tight between my knees and my head on my chest, and my mind was crying: Oh, George, George, George . . .

My mother acted as if he had never been; but the following afternoon the doctor called. His name was Doctor Kane.

Over the years there were periods when my mother visited the doctor regularly, and at these times she took a lot of pills. I hadn't seen Doctor Kane for years and had only a faint memory of a man with a hairy face. I had never been really ill except with whooping cough and measles. The faint memory of him went back to a time when I fell on the elbow of my short arm and it swelled up and he stuck needles in it. After a time the swelling subsided but it continued to pain. And now here he was looking at me.

He looked at me for a long time before he

said, "Well, well, so you tumbled downstairs. When did this happen?"

"A . . . a few days . . ." His head seemed to snap round on his shoulders and he looked at my mother and said, "She's got a tongue, hasn't she? She can speak for herself . . . Now, when did this happen?"

"Over a week ago," I said.

"Precisely how long over a week ago?"

I daren't look at my mother. "A week gone Sunday," I said.

"A week gone Sunday. Well, well. And so I'm called in to see you now . . . Why?" He was looking at my mother again and her voice trembled as she answered, "She . . . she didn't seem to be recovering as she should."

"From the aftermath on her face I should say she's recovered remarkably well. She must have looked a pretty mess when she reached —" his eyebrows seemed to go up and his beard drooped down as he finished, "the bottom of the stairs."

There was a silence before my mother said, "She . . . she didn't look all that bad at first."

"You surprise me. But still, I'm used to surprises. Well, miss, how do you feel?"

How could I tell him how I felt. Could I say I feel lonely, unloved? But that would be a lie, because George loved me, and Gran Carter loved me. Could I say I feel lost and part of me feels I'm not grown up enough to know anything, and the other part of me feels I don't need to grow up to know? I know it all now, which, when I thought about it even then, was ridiculous.

"Come on, you must know how you feel."

"Not very good."

"Not very good," he repeated; then said, "Now we are getting somewhere. Where do you feel not very good?"

He was a difficult man to talk to and my other voice which I used only to myself now came out, saying tersely, "That's a difficult question to answer, because to tell the truth I don't know where to begin." His whiskered lips moved apart and he showed his teeth as he said, "Now we are really getting someplace, it's up to me to start eliminating, isn't it? By the way" — he turned and looked at my mother — "do you think there could be a cup of tea going?"

I saw her blink rapidly; then she looked at me. "Yes, yes; I'll make one," she said.

As soon as the door had closed on her he sat down on the edge of the bed and stared at me for a moment. "Well, now," he said, "let us use our horse sense, shall we? And I'm sure you've got quite a bit of it tucked away in that napper of yours."

I hadn't time to think that in a way he could be like a cross between George, Gran Carter, and a gentleman — for doctors were gentlemen — all mixed up, because the most strange thing happened at that precise moment, a weird surprising thing, for what did I see but a great horse which galloped right over him. I opened my eyes wider than I'd done since that particular Sunday morning when I'd come through the kitchen and saw my mother waiting for me. My mouth fell into a gape too, for although the creature was galloping, it had its head turned towards me; its eyes were full of knowledge and its lip was back as if it was laughing. It had a long white tail and two white front feet and a great flowing mane, a white spot on its nose, and its body was shining black and as sleekly as a seal's.

"I bet that's the first time you've tried to smile."

"What?"

"I said, miss, I bet that's the first time you've tried to smile. What were you thinking about? Do you find my face funny?"

"Yes, I do a little bit." The horse was galloping around him.

"Well, we are getting somewhere but not along the road I expected. Young ladies should learn to be tactful. You should have said, No, I think you're handsome."

That would have been stretching it . . . Eeh! my goodness, I had nearly said that, and the horse was laughing.

Was I going a bit funny? When mother punched me like that, had it done something to me? No, no, I wasn't going funny, because I'd always talked to myself, only I hadn't seen a horse before, a dog when I was younger, and there had been a little girl whom I called Jennie. She had gone when my mother married George.

I blinked my eyes a number of times and the horse faded away.

"Does your face still pain?" His voice was quiet now, no humour in it, and I said, "No, it's only a bit stiff."

"How did you manage to fall downstairs?"

I looked to the side before saying, "I tripped."

"Yes, you must have. Oh, yes you must have." He was nodding at me. "Do you get on with your mother? I mean do you argue and fight?"

I was staring unblinking at him and he at me and neither of my voices would give him an answer. Now he leant towards me and said, "If you should fall downstairs again with a kind of dizzy spell, which I suppose that's what it was, wasn't it? You must come straight to the surgery. Do you understand me?"

I understood him all right. His attitude was the same as George's, only he was using different words to express it. "I must tell your mother to come to the surgery," he said, "and I'll give her a prescription for a tonic. She's not looking too well herself . . . You still haven't told me which part of you feels the worst."

"I . . . I just feel low and tired."

"Do you have any trouble with your arm these days?" He reached out and took my hand and waggled it up and down as if he were weighing it, and I said, "No, none at all."

He now put his head on one side and surveyed me for some seconds. "You've grown a lot since I last saw you," he said. "But I think you could do with a little fat on your bones. Do you eat well?"

"Sometimes."

He now let go of my hand and stood up and, taking his case from a side table, he mumbled something before saying, "I'll have that cup of tea downstairs with your mother and I'll send you a bottle along that'll make you jump about a bit. Goodbye."

"Good-bye, Doctor . . ."

I don't know what passed between her and the doctor that day but almost until the day she died she visited him regularly every week. And from when I was fifteen I saw him regularly too.

CHAPTER 3

My mother had nerves, and I got them. They became evident when my left eyelid started to flutter and the corner of my mouth to twitch.

I had imagined the business of seeing the horse galloping across the doctor to have occurred because I was a little light-headed at the time, but I was to see him again on my first visit to the doctor and it was he who once more brought him into being.

I was to discover that Doctor Kane often used the term "horse sense", and on this day that he saw me . . . and alone, for he told his nurse to tell my mother to stay in the waiting-room, he said to me, "Now, miss, what's all this about? You haven't tripped and fallen downstairs this time. What's troubling you? And don't say you don't know, use your horse sense and tell me." And there it was again, this beautiful horse, galloping right across him, its white tail flying, its two fore-legs in the air, its head turned towards me, its upper lip back showing its big teeth in a grin; and it said, Tell him. Tell him that she doesn't hit you any more, but she talks at you. Tell him you've heard her story from when she was a pampered little girl to what she is now, a nerve-ridden hag, a hundred times.

Eeh! don't talk like that about her.

"What's that you say?"

"I . . . I said, it's my mother's nerves. She keeps talking."

"Yes, she keeps talking. And yes, it's her nerves." He nodded at me. "And her talking is getting on your nerves, isn't it? In fact, it's got. Well now . . . By the way, how old are you?" He looked at the open folder on his desk.

"Fifteen gone."

"How are you doing at school?"

"Not bad."

"What's your best subject?"

"English."

"What do you intend to do with yourself when you leave school? Going to try for university?"

"Oh no." I shook my head. "I'm not clever like that."

"You should leave that to others to say.

What makes you think you're not clever like that?"

"Well, I'm only good at English and drawing."

"Well, either of them should get you somewhere; and God knows, they want English, real English, because they've forgotten how to speak it in this country. If you want to hear English spoken correctly you've got to go abroad, because now and again out there you'll hear words pronounced as they should be. The English spoken today is like most doctors' writing, not understandable."

The whiskers on his face parted and I was looking at his lips: they seemed to be the only evident flesh on his face and I was surprised to see how many teeth he had and all large and white. He had always seemed to me to be pretty old. He was forty, but that, to me then, was as old as the Ancient Mariner. "Now" — he was leaning across the desk and wagging his finger almost in my face — "what you've got to do, miss, is to get out and about. Do you dance?"

"No."

"Can you dance?"

"No."

"Well then, you'll have to learn. Take dancing lessons. Join a club."

51

"I . . . I couldn't."

"Why not?"

"I don't make friends easily. It's . . . it's my arm."

"Nonsense." He pulled himself up straight and banged my case folder closed. "You've got two legs, haven't you? People don't dance with their arms. Come on, spit it out, get it off your chest. Tell me why you don't make friends; why you don't join clubs or go dancing."

Go on, tell him. The great black horse had stopped galloping and was looking at me. Its mouth was closed now, but its eyes were speaking. Go on, it said, tell him the truth. He's the only one you can talk to who will understand. You can't tell George because he would just bang about and tell you lies, because he doesn't want to hurt you. This man won't do that. Go on, right now, tell him. And tell him Katie hasn't spoken to you since the Sunday business because she blames you for splitting on her. And anyway, her mother has forbidden her to have anything more to do with you. Go on, tell him.

I didn't tell him that, what I said was, "It's my face."

"What!"

His eyebrows had moved upwards again;

his eyes looked huge round brown balls.

"I'm . . . I'm plain . . . very . . . not nice looking."

He sat well back in his chair now and let out a long sigh, pulled his beard onto his chest and nodded at me as he said, "Yes, it's true, you're plain, but as regards not nice looking, there's a difference. It's no use telling you that the ugly ducklings turn into swans, because I've found out already that you've got quite an amount of horse sense in that head of yours."

There! he had said it again, and the horse was at his antics once more and laughing now.

"But the last term, not nice looking, that doesn't apply," the doctor said. "Plain things can be nice. You will find that in life very few handsome men marry beautiful women. Some of the cleverest and most prominent women in the world are ugly. Do you know that?"

"No."

He paused and stared at me, and my lip began to twitch.

"The big fellow didn't come back?"

"No."

"Well, one can't blame him. But your mother was a fool there, that's the type she needed, not that she would admit it. Well now —" he rose from the desk and came round towards me and, putting his hand on my shoulder, he said, "you come and see me next week. And I want to see you looking . . . nicely plain. Do you understand? Nicely plain." He sighed now as he added, "Send your mother in . . ."

He was to say those four words to me a number of times during the following year. There were times when I had no fluttering of the eyelid and no twitching of the lip, but there were other times, generally following her bad bouts, when it seemed that the corner of my mouth was trying to reach my eye. But during this time I had one consolation, I acquired a companion. My horse came to stay and I christened him. It was funny how the christening came about, because in a way it was connected with real horses. Up till that day he had just come and gone at odd times, mostly when I was talking to the doctor. But then he began to appear when my mother kept talking at me while we were sitting eating a meal, one each side of the table, in the kitchen; or when I was feeling very lonely. At these times he would always try to cheer me up. Then this day I was coming from school and while passing the Bentley Street traffic lights that had turned red, there stood a horse box and almost on eye level with me were the words in small print: B. Hamilton, and immediately I said to myself, Hamilton. That's a nice name, Hamilton. Then there he was almost skipping over the crossing in front of me, as if he was pleased with the name. And so from then on he became Hamilton. It was as simple as that.

It was on my sixteenth birthday when I received the birthday card and a little parcel from George and Gran Carter that my mother had the first seizure.

I hadn't seen much of George during the last year. He was working again on the long-distance lorries, and whenever I managed to visit Gran's, he had just come or gone. Twice, when I saw him, he had the woman with him. She was the hairdresser that Gran had referred to that Sunday, that memorable Sunday, and from the beginning I didn't like her. Not that I was jealous of her. Yet I suppose I was a bit. But at the same time I wanted George to be happy and I knew that he had to have a woman in order to be happy. Right from the start though I thought that George should have a better woman than Peggy Wicklow because she was common, really common.

It was on my first acquaintance with Peggy

Wicklow that I realized all common things or all common people weren't nice. She was a different common from George and Gran, she was loudmouthed. Of course, Gran shouted when she talked, and so did George, but not in the same way as Peggy Wicklow.

Just as I didn't approve of her, so I knew she didn't approve of me. And I knew it was a mystery to her what George saw in me to make a fuss about, because at our first meeting he led me to her and said, "This is Maisie, Peggy, and she's my first girl." And at this Gran had cried, "There you are! After me bringin' him up he pushes me aside. I'm nothin' to him now."

It was all in fun but I wished they wouldn't do it because deep inside I knew they were putting a false value on me, a value that nobody else could see. I loved them for it, yet was sometimes irritated by it.

It was when I arrived home from school that I saw the parcel and the card. Neither had been opened, but she was there when I undid the sticky tape that was round the parcel. When I unwrapped the paper and revealed a little red box, I paused before lifting the lid and looked at her. She wasn't looking at me but at the box. I told myself not to open it, but my fingers wouldn't obey

56

me and when I lifted the lid there was a gold watch lying on a bed of red satin. I lifted it out and held it between my finger and thumb. The wrist band was gold linked and when slowly I pulled it over my fingers I found that it stretched. It was an amazing feeling that these small solid links could stretch. It was as if I was witnessing magic.

"Take it off!"

"But . . . but . . ."

"Take it off! Do as I say, take it off."

It was while I hesitated that it happened. She opened her small mouth wide and gasped at the air as her hands clutched at her throat. When they moved down to her chest she toppled over and fell to the floor. I tore the watch from my wrist and flung it on to the hall table, and bending down to her, I cried, "What is it? What is it?"

She rolled on to her side now and began to groan. The colour had gone from her face, her eyes were tightly shut, her mouth was open and she was gasping at the air.

I must get the doctor. Mrs Atkins had a phone three doors down. I rushed to the front door and out on to the path, and there I saw Mr Stickle and I grabbed at him, "My . . . my mother's taken ill. I . . . I've got to get the doctor. Mrs . . . Mrs Atkins has a phone."

"What is wrong with her?" His voice was cool and polite.

"I . . . I don't know. She's in a kind of seizure."

"Is she in bed?"

"No, no, she's in the hall." I jerked my head backwards.

"Well" — his voice was still cool — "you go and phone from Mrs Atkins's and I'll see what I can do." He passed me and went up the path, and I dashed down to Mrs Atkins and rang the bell three times. When she opened the door she looked surprised to see me. Again I was gabbling. She got the gist of what I was saying and said, "All right. All right. I'll phone him for you. You get back."

I dashed back and into the hall to see Mr Stickle putting a cushion under my mother's head. She was still on the floor, and he glanced at me and said, "It looks like she's had a heart attack. She'd better not be moved." Then straightening himself, he stood looking around the hall, his eyes lingering longest on the open door that led into the sitting room. After a while he spoke to me again, saying, "Has she had bad news . . . a shock?"

I didn't answer. But yes, she'd had bad news, a shock. Nine days ago she'd had her thirty-seventh birthday and the only thing she had received was a card from me. I'd written formally on the bottom of it: Happy Birthday, from Maisie. I couldn't say anything else. She hadn't received a present of any kind. I never had any money now to buy anything. Since George left the only money I handled was my bus fares, and at times the precise amount if I was going to the pictures. The exception was when I went to see Gran Carter. She often gave me a shilling, and George always put a half-crown in my pocket when we met, and I bought chocolates on the side with the money.

My mother, I knew, was quite well off; her parents, although not wealthy, had been saving people. How much my mother had been left I didn't know, only that she drew just so much out of the bank every week for the housekeeping. But on her birthday she hadn't received a present from anyone, and yet here was I, her nondescript daughter, her thorn in the flesh, as she called me, the recipient of a beautiful gold wrist-watch. It must have been too much for her.

When I didn't answer Mr Stickle he moved towards the front door, saying, "Well, I must get back to business," and he pulled the lapels of his coat together as he spoke, then adjusted his neat tie. I stared at him, wanting to say, Don't leave me. Before this I'd only glimpsed him, but now I was looking him full in the face. Without his trilby hat he didn't look so old as I imagined. He was tall and his face was round. The shape didn't suit his length. His skin was pale as if it had never seen the sun; his eyes I noticed were blue and his lashes quite long for a man; his nose was thin towards the tip, and his mouth small, like my mother's I thought; he spoke precisely, his words clipped. He paused on the doorstep and stood as if thinking for a moment; then turning to me, he said, "I'll go and tell my sister. She'll stay with you until the doctor comes."

"Thank you." I felt deeply grateful to him for his kind thought. I went back to my mother and knelt down by her side. She was moaning gently as if in pain and I asked her if she was: "Are you in pain, Mother?" I said, but she didn't answer.

Some minutes later when I heard the footsteps on the pathway I rose and went to meet Miss Stickle. I had never looked at her fully before either: she was as tall as her brother but twice as thick; she looked hefty, strong and much older than him. She seemed to bounce into the room. Her voice was loud: "Well, well," she said; "she's collapsed, has she? Dear, dear." And she bent over my mother and asked her, "Are you in pain?"

When she got no reply she straightened up and, looking at me, she said, "Looks like a heart attack. One thing sure, she won't be able to get upstairs for a while. Have you got a couch, I mean in your sitting-room?"

"Yes." I pointed, and she marched forward, right to the middle of the room, and there she stopped and stood looking about her, her eyes seeming to rest on one piece of furniture after another. I stood in the doorway watching her. Presently, she patted the chesterfield couch, saying, "This should do in the meantime. When the doctor comes we'll get her in here." And she again looked round the room before turning to me and saying, "Nice, nice. It's bigger than most rooms in the terrace. How's that?"

"I . . . I think it was two rooms at one time."

"Oh, yes, yes" — she nodded — "I can see now." Then she pointed to the windows. "Good idea, plenty of light." She came back into the hall now and, looking down at my mother and her voice low, she muttered, "Hasn't been well for some time, has she? Nerves, suffers from nerves?" She glanced towards me, and I said, "Yes."

"All nonsense really; lack of will power."

I was amazed at her talking like this and felt upset when I thought that the whole neighbourhood must know my mother had nerves. I wished the doctor would come . . .

It was fifteen minutes later when, seemingly reluctantly, he came through the open doorway and, after glancing first at Miss Stickle, turned to me and said, "What's this? What's this?"

"She's had a turn."

He knelt down by my mother's side and, taking her hand from her chest, he felt her pulse. Then quietly he said to her, "Mrs Carter, it's all right. It's all right," then rose and looked about him. Addressing me again, he said, "The couch in the sitting-room, we'll put her on there." And now turning abruptly to Miss Stickle, he went on, "You can give me a hand."

I was now surprised to hear Miss Stickle say, "She's had a heart attack; is it wise to move her?" especially after what she had previously said.

"What do you suggest, madam, leave her on the floor all night? Take hold of her legs and help me lift her."

Miss Stickle obeyed him, albeit somewhat slowly, and between them, with me hovering at the side, they managed to settle her on the couch in the sitting-room. And now he turned to me, saying, "Get some bedding and cover her up, then make a hot drink."

"Don't they usually send them to hospital in such cases?"

"What cases, madam?"

I stopped for a moment and looked at them. They were both bristling.

"I think she's had a heart attack."

"You're not paid to think about such matters, that's my job. Now, I'd be obliged if you would leave us."

As Miss Stickle marched from the room, I followed her, and in the hall I caught up with her and said, placatingly, "Thank you. Thank you, Miss Stickle, for your help." But all she said was, "That man! He's most unprofessional."

However on the doorstep, she turned and said quite kindly, "If you need me, you'll know where to find me."

"Thank you. Thank you, Miss Stickle." I sounded grateful, and indeed I was: neither Mrs Nelson nor Mrs McVitie would have come in and helped. I knew that.

Blankets. I dashed upstairs and brought some, and a top sheet, from the linen cupboard, and when I entered the sitting-room Doctor Kane was sitting by my mother's side talking to her. "Come on," he was saying. "Come on. There's nothing wrong, not what you think. The feeling will pass. I'm going to give you something to make you sleep, really sleep, then we'll have a talk. Now you are going to be all right."

Nothing wrong? Nothing wrong?

He turned to me and motioned me out of the room, and in the hall he said, "Don't look so worried, it's nothing."

"Nothing?"

"Hysteria."

"What?"

"Nervous hysteria." He nodded. "I'm not surprised; I've been expecting it."

"Hysteria?" I repeated.

"Yes, that's what I said, hysteria. Her nerves have got the better of her, causing her to show all the symptoms of a heart attack. It happens again and again: they think they're going to die, they don't. But one thing I do know." He wiped his fingers. "She should go away and have treatment. I've been telling her this for months past. What brought this on? Some climax, eh?"

"I . . . I got a present; it's my birthday. George had sent me a gold watch."

"Oh." His eyebrows made the usual effort to disappear into his thick brown wiry hair. "That would do it. Dear, dear. These

64

women." He shook his head. "Ah well, I'll be passing this way in a short while and I'll drop you in some tablets. See that she takes one at night; it'll make her sleep. But don't encourage her to stay on her back during the day, she'll be much better going about. And tomorrow make her a tasty light meal; and get her to eat it."

At the front door he turned and, looking at me, he said kindly, "No use wishing you a happy birthday, is it?"

I didn't answer, for, holding the door half closed, I was thinking: A tasty light meal. I knew nothing about cooking: she had never let me try my hand at anything in the cooking line. Dust and polish, yes, and clean brasses, especially the stair rods. She would see that I took them from their sockets every week. In fact every piece of furniture in the house was moved every week, especially those pieces standing on carpets, so the moths wouldn't get a chance to breed.

The sun coming through a narrow window near the front door fell on to the wrist-watch on the side table, and the glinting light drew me to it. I picked it up. It was beautiful; and yet it had been the means of causing her to have hysteria. On thinking about the word and its implications, it didn't surprise me because, looking back, I could see that she had always been hysterical. Yet what did surprise me was that the effect could resemble a heart attack.

I went back into the room and drew a chair to her side. After a while I realized she was awake but she didn't open her eyes, and so I said softly, "You are going to be all right. The doctor says you are going to be all right. He's bringing some medicine."

Her only response was to turn on her side, her back to me, and as she did so it came to me that she was not only wide awake now but had been so all along.

Chapter 4

It was from my sixteenth birthday that May Stickle became a regular visitor to the house. Strangely, my mother took to her. And it seemed natural that her brother Howard should at times call in too.

His manner towards my mother was very sympathetic: he spoke to her as if she was an invalid, and she seemed to enjoy this. I knew she looked forward to his visits but, as I put it naively to myself, she couldn't fall for him because he was only twenty-six and she was thirty-seven. But then, George had been younger too. Anyway she was still married to George and divorces took a long time. So this situation didn't worry me; in fact, I was pleased when he came in because he was always very nice to me. I say very nice, he was quietly polite, asking me how I was; and how was I progressing with my secretarial course which I'd taken up since leaving school. Looking at him as I often did now, I realized he could have been very good looking if he'd had a body like George, but he was too thin, weedy . . . scraggy.

During this time, as Gran Carter put it, George was going strong with Peggy Wicklow; and Gran Carter wasn't altogether too happy about it. Flibbertigibbet, she called Peggy Wicklow. What George wanted, in Gran's opinion, was a steady lass who would give him bairns, because he loved bairns. That was why, she said, he was so fond of me. And he was fond of me; she emphasized that he thought the world of me.

During the months that followed, my life seemed to enter a quiet period. I spent a lot of time up in my room; and I talked a lot to Hamilton. I'd had to have an understanding with Hamilton. He had sat on the foot of the bed one night, and he looked no bigger than myself, and this was strange about him because most times when he appeared, he did so as a full-sized stallion, and generally on the move, either galloping in front of people, or pawing the ground, or flashing his white tail from side to side. Yet this night, there he sat, his forelegs tucked under him, his back legs stretched out, his tail gently flicking the counterpane, and his face, his beautiful big strong face, looking fully at me. And when I said to him, "Now look here, Hamilton!" he said, Look where?

"Don't be silly," I replied.

Well if we can't be silly here, we can't be silly anywhere, can we?

That was right. I had to be on my guard when I was talking to people. If they were people I liked, then he rarely appeared, but if I didn't like them and I felt any animosity at all, he galloped like mad around them. Sometimes he kicked them in the bottom and let out a great neigh. And at these times I had to mumble and explain myself in some way or other. It was very disturbing. So I talked to him plain this night. "Look! it's all right for you," I said; "you haven't got to stand the racket."

You're talking like Gran Carter.

"All right. I could do worse," I answered.

True. True. He threw his head back and his mane bounced and a piece fell down between his eyes and covered the white spot on the top of his nose. I said now, "Promise me that you will keep your place when I meet strangers or someone I don't like."

Well now. Well now. He jerked his back legs out. That doesn't rest with me, it's up to you, isn't it?

He was right in a way. Yet I didn't seem to be able to do anything about it. Every time I thought contrary, there he was.

As I stared at him, I said, "I wonder if other people talk to horses . . . or . . . or things or . . . ?"

Yes; yes, if they're like you they will.

"I doubt if there are many people like me."

You'd be surprised. You can never judge anyone by their outside. Take your mother for instance. Everyone thinks she's such a refined creature, but you know she's not. Don't you?

"I don't want to talk about my mother."

Better if you did.

"Who would I talk to? There's only George and Gran and it's like giving her away to talk to them."

There's the doctor.

Yes, there was the doctor. I nodded my head, then added, "He knows all about her in any case."

But he doesn't know all about you, does he? Or about me.

I looked at him. His eyes were on me, great dark orbs, and after a moment he said,

That would be something, wouldn't it, if you told him about me. What do you think would happen then?

"He'd think I was up the pole. He'd likely want me to see a psychiatrist."

There's no doubt about it. But don't worry; if he does I'll go with you.

"Oh, Hamilton." I threw my notebook towards the bottom of the bed and it went through him and hit the wooden foot and he was gone.

That night I wrote about Hamilton for the first time. I filled ten closely written pages telling how I'd first made his acquaintance, and after I had finished it I saw him for a moment. He was standing near the bedroom door, full-sized now, and he said solemnly, I would tear that lot up if I were you; it's dangerous to leave it about. She's only got to see that and . . . well . . .

I knew he was right. So the next day, which was Saturday, I waited until she had gone out, then went up into the attic. I had a job to pull the swing ladder down, it was a tricky apparatus. Only once before had I been up here, and that time George had carried me up.

I tore the ten pages out of my notebook and put them in a brown envelope, then looked for a loose board under which to place them. I hadn't far to look, there were numbers of them, mostly where the roof sloped down sharply towards the floor. I chose one, prised it up and there, underneath, were the rafters and, about nine inches below, a layer of plaster.

I laid the first pages of Hamilton gently down on the plaster, replaced the floor board, then hurried towards the trapdoor; but on nearing it my eye was attracted to a trunk stuck in the corner to the left of me. It was covered with foreign labels. I lifted the rounded lid and saw it held clothes. Putting my hand down by the side, I felt the layers and layers of them. The material felt like soft silk, but in the dimness of the room I couldn't distinguish exactly what they were. I pulled down the lid again, telling myself that someday I would come up here and go through it. It would be exciting. When I eventually did, it was, and saddening, so saddening, that I cried for the torment my mother had created in herself.

CHAPTER 5

My mother died a fortnight before my seventeenth birthday and four days before her own. She'd had two pseudo heart attacks during the past months, the second

71

one occurring shortly after Miss Stickle told her that Howard had become engaged to be married. The third and final one occurred when there appeared on television one evening the smiling face of George being interviewed by a B.B.C. man and being praised for his bravery in rescuing a mother and two children from a burning building. He laughed about his hair being singed and his lack of eyebrows and made light of his bandaged hands. The interviewer had eulogized this man who had gone back into the blazing house again after bringing out the mother and one child. He had dropped the second child from an upper window into safe arms, then had, himself, been almost overcome by smoke and fumes but had somehow managed to get downstairs before collapsing. The woman he had saved had put her arms around him and kissed him and George had laughed his big hearty laugh.

I was sitting wide-eyed, my mouth agape and my heart beating rapidly with pleasure, and my mind was crying: Oh George, George. I knew you were a brave man, I always knew you were a brave man. Oh George, George.

The television screen went blank. My mother had turned it off, and she stood and stared at me before rushing from the room. I heard her run upstairs; then I heard her call. When I got into her bedroom she was writhing on the floor.

I didn't send for the doctor but helped her on to the bed, saying all the time, "It's all right. It's all right. It'll pass. You know it'll pass. Lie still now, lie still. I'll make you a cup of tea."

I wasn't long downstairs making the tea but when I brought it up she wasn't on the bed. The bathroom door was closed, so I put the tray down and waited. She was likely being sick. I waited for ten minutes before I knocked on the door, saying, "Are you all right, Mother?"

When I got no answer, I tried the door. It was locked.

For the first time in my life I experienced panic.

We had by now got the phone in and I rushed downstairs and phoned Doctor Kane. When the nurse said he was busy in the surgery with patients, I yelled at her, "It's important! I think my mother has done something silly."

At that she put me through to him, and after a moment he said, "Quiet. Quiet. Tell me what happened." And when I told him and finished, "She's been in there now over

73

a quarter of an hour, more," he said, "I'll be round directly."

He was as good as his word. He, too, tried the door but couldn't get it open. He called, but there was no answer. He told me to stand back, and then took his big foot and rammed it against the keyhole. There was a crunching of wood but the door didn't open. The third time he kicked at it, it sprang back.

She was lying on the floor. There were two empty bottles near her and one on the basin top. He said quietly, "Go and call an ambulance."

I rushed to do as he bade me. The ambulance was there within five minutes; within another five minutes she was in hospital. I went with her, and I know they worked on her for hours, but she died at eleven o'clock that night.

George and Gran Carter were with me. I don't know how they got to know but they reached the hospital about half past nine. I slept at their house that night.

At the inquest the verdict was suicide while the balance of her mind was disturbed.

After the funeral George and Gran sat with me in the sitting-room.

"Well, lass" — George looked at me —

"what you goin' to do? I know you're goin' to this typing school, but you can't live here on your own. My advice to you is to sell up and come and live with us. You were never one for fancy things. As you know, it's no palace, but you'll be happy."

I knew I would, but at the same time I also knew that somehow I didn't want to leave this house. Why? I couldn't explain. It wasn't only because I'd been born here; perhaps it was because I knew that this house was mine now, I actually had something of my own, I wasn't dependant on anyone. What money my mother had left would be mine too. I should know tomorrow when I went to the solicitor.

Gran Carter took my hand and said, "He's right, lass; you couldn't live here on your own."

I surprised them by saying, "Yes, I could, Gran. I . . . I could live here happily, comparatively happily anyway, now there's no one to . . . to . . ." I had almost said, torment me, but I replaced it with "look after"; then added, "In a few days time I'll be seventeen; and so I should be able to look after myself."

"You're still a bairn." George had his hand on my shoulder, rocking me gently.

"I don't feel a bairn, George. Well, I mean

part of me doesn't. And yet another part feels so simple, I sometimes think I haven't been born yet." I smiled at him.

"It isn't good for you to live on your own," he said.

"Well, I won't be on my own really. I shall be at the school most of the day, and then I could pop in on my way back to see you, that is when you're not off gallivanting." I nodded towards him even jovially. And he, taking it up, said, "Aw! now, now, don't be like me ma; let me have me fling when I'm young, I'll never be eighteen again."

Oh, George was funny.

Gran Carter now said to me, "Does that Stickle woman come in often?"

"Yes; she's been very good, very kind."

"Some piece that." George grinned. "A pickle of Stickle to handle, that one. Once round her, twice round Penshaw Monument."

"It was nice of them to come to the funeral," I said, and looked from one to the other.

Now they both nodded, saying, "Aye, yes, it was."

Apparently the manner of one's dying still affected many people and some in the terrace must have stayed away from the funeral because my mother had killed herself.

Then Gran said, "Does he pop in often, young Stickle?"

"Sometimes he did, to see Mother; that was until he became engaged."

"Oh, he's engaged to be married? That's good. That's good." Gran nodded at me, and I said now, "And he's not young, Gran, he's nearly twenty-eight I should say."

"Oh is he? Well, that's a terrible age, isn't it?" Gran pulled a face at me. "It makes our Georgie here old enough to be his father."

"Oh, hold your hand a bit, Ma. Hold your hand a bit."

And so went the talk in the sitting-room. Only when I persuaded them that I was quite all right and that I would be happy on my own, did they leave me; but not without qualms, I knew.

The door had hardly closed on them when Miss Stickle came in the back way. She had the habit of tapping on the door and at the same time opening it.

"How are you now, dear?" she said.

"Oh, I'm all right, Miss Stickle."

"You must call me May, dear. Miss Stickle sounds so stiff, so formal, and I'm your friend."

I didn't think I could ever call her May. She didn't look like a May. May trees bloomed and smelled nice, they were the harbingers of summer. Miss Stickle conjured up a thistle in my mind, proggly, not to everybody's taste. Yet she had been very kind to me.

She now walked through the kitchen, then through the hall and into the sitting-room.

She seemed to like our sitting-room. When she sat down on the couch, she put her hand out and drew me down beside her. It struck me for a moment as if it was she who was at home and I the visitor.

"Well, what are you going to do, dear? What are your plans?"

I answered calmly, "I mean to stay on here, Miss Stickle."

"You are not going to sell the house then?"

"No."

"It'll be very lonely for you."

"Oh, I don't mind that. I'm used to being alone."

"But you'll miss your mother."

I paused, "Yes," I said, "perhaps. But I . . . I know what I'm going to do. I'm going to finish my course at the typing school."

"Yes. Well, that's wise." And her head on one side, she added slowly, "I suppose you would like to be a secretary?"

She said this as if she thought there was very little chance of my ever becoming one. It had surprised the teacher at the school that I had taken to the typing so well. When I had first applied for the course she seemed dubious that I would be able to type at all. But all I did was sit slightly sidewards, draw my right arm in and stretch my left one to its full extent. It had been natural for me to do so many things this way, and I didn't feel awkward. In fact, she asked me if I had been practising at home. One of the pupils had said spitefully when she thought I was out of earshot, "She'll pass in shorthand without taking exams."

That was one of the times Hamilton had appeared and galloped all over her.

I answered Miss Stickle now by saying, "No, I have no intention of putting in for such a post, but I would like to set up a small business at home here." I looked about the room now. "Do typing for other people, writers and such."

"Oh, that's a very good idea. But . . . but in the meantime will you have enough to live on?"

It was a question and I said, "Yes; yes, I suppose so. I won't get details until tomorrow when I see the solicitor."

"Oh well, I hope everything works out as you would wish. Anyway, you know we are always at hand. Howard is very concerned for you."

"He is?"

"Yes; yes, he is. He was just saying yesterday that you've had a very sad life; that you never seem to have much fun or pleasure. Not that he thinks young girls should gad about. Oh, no, he's got very strict ideas, but as he said, there are limits, one must have a little recreation. We used to play tennis a lot when Father was alive. We lived in Gosforth then and our circumstances were so different from what they are now. Oh yes, so different." She sighed, then went on, "Howard wasn't intended for the tailoring, you know. Oh, no; it was rather a come down. But there, that's all in the past. As he says, life must be faced squarely. But my dear, I'm not at all in favour of the partner he's chosen to spend his future life with."

"You're not?"

"No. No, I'm not. Between you and me she isn't of the same class. You understand?"

I remained silent.

"Common. Utterly, utterly. She's in the office of the establishment. Proximity, you know. This is what it's all about, proximity. Half the people wouldn't be married today if they weren't thrown together haphazardly by fortune. Proximity."

Proximity, proximity, proximity. Hamilton was galloping round the couch. I followed his progress and when he stopped at the end of it, his head over Miss Stickle's, I looked at him imploringly and when he bared his teeth and took a strand of the top coil of her hair, I closed my eyes for a second, and opened them quickly again as Miss Stickle's hand came on mine saying, "You're tired, my dear, and slightly over-wrought. I can see that. I'll go and let you get to bed. You're sure you're not afraid to sleep alone?"

"No, no." I rose hastily from the couch, she more leisurely, but as she preceded me down the room there he was again right behind her, and he turned his back on her and kicked her, as George used to say, in the back of the front, because my mother had objected to his frequent use of the word backside. I saw her rise in the air and land in the middle of the hall.

In the hall she turned to me and said, "You're half asleep now, you're dropping on your feet; I'll say good-night, my dear. But don't forget, we are always near, we are always thinking of you. You need never be alone."

After bolting the door, I came back into the hall and I thought of Hamilton swivelling round on his forelegs and kicking our guest, and I started to laugh.

My mother had been buried that day and here I was laughing. Was there something wrong with me? Perhaps, because the fact that Hamilton didn't like Miss Stickle at all should have warned me. Yes, it should have warned me, but it didn't. I just thought it was that funny side of me that would emerge at the most odd moments. Some years were to pass before I realized there was more to my funny side than that, much more.

I look back on the months that followed as a happy time. And so many things happened. I passed my typing exam and got top marks; and as a result of this I put an advert in the paper:

Home typing done. First-class work.
(I thought I was qualified to say that.)
Grammatical corrections.

(That was a bit of a nerve; but still I'd been very good at English at school, especially essays, and seldom had red ticks against my punctuation or grammar.)

Paper provided. One and six per thousand words.

Gran Carter saw the advert and was highly delighted; especially, as she said, about the grammar bits. Professional like it sounded, she said. And I laughed at her and hugged her when she went on, "How about giving me a few lessons, 'cos eeh! I know I talk awful."

I knew she talked awful. Often when thinking about her, my thoughts would run as she was apt to talk: "What time it is!" she would say. I'd even said this out loud once or twice, only to hear my mother cry, "There you are! There you are! That's what comes of that association." And then there was her habit of interspersing the word "like" at the end of every sentence, or sticking it in the middle of one: "You know what I mean like. As I said like. Eeh! it was awful like. I nearly had a fit like."

I often wondered how this word came to be used as it was. However, my advert promised to do away with such deficiencies, at least in the writing of them. But when I saw the advert in print I went hot from head to toe. Who was I to say that I could correct people's writing when my own went rambling on, especially when I was writing about Hamilton. Sometimes I could do a full page on him without one dot or curl of punctuation.

During this time, too, my appearance changed a little but I don't think for the better. Gran had me go to Peggy Wicklow's to have my hair done. Peggy Wicklow had two assistants but she did me the honour of attending to me herself. The result was startling to say the least. She had cut my hair shoulder length, permed it and curled it, and the reflection from the mirror showed me a mass of frizz with a small face in the middle of it. And the face looked all eyes and mouth because they were both wide in astonishment.

"Now, how d'you like that?" she said.

What could I say? I said, "I look different."

"Yes, you do, you do, indeed. It's an improvement, I should say. What d'you think?"

"I . . . I'll have to get used to it." Once outside the shop I took my scarf from beneath my coat and put it over my head, pulling it tight in an effort to hide the corkscrews surrounding me.

When five minutes later I took off the scarf in Gran's kitchen, she looked at me without speaking for a moment, then said, "Aw, lass, I don't think that style suits you. She should have done something different."

"Can I wash it out, Gran?"

"You'll have a hard job, pet, it's a perm. Still if you get at it with one of those wiry brushes you might get it flattened a bit. Eeh! you know something?" She screwed up her face. "She's a bit of a bitch. And our Georgie is finding that out, for since he's got free, you know, since your mam died, she's been at him to get hooked . . . you know, married."

"Yes, I know. Doesn't he want to, I mean get married?"

"Not to her, lass, not to her. She was all right on the side. You know what I mean?"

Yes, I knew what she meant. I imagined I knew a lot of things by now. It was a pity that I had to learn later and painfully that I knew nothing about life or people; I was infantile, and an idiot as far as reading character was concerned.

"You know what?" Gran handed me a cup of tea now, then sat down on the black imitation leather couch fronting the fire. "He's for doin' a bunk."

"He . . . he hasn't done anything wrong? I mean . . ."

"No, no. That's me, not explainin' meself properly. Although mind, it wouldn't surprise me if afore long he hadn't to do a bunk . . . that kind of a bunk, because Peggy Wicklow's brother is on the fiddle in more ways than one — runs a bloody orchestra if you ask me — and they've pulled our Georgie in with them, things droppin' off lorries, you know."

It was I who now screwed up my face as I looked at her and repeated — I had a habit of repeating people's words; this is what I suppose caused many people to think I was dim — "You mean . . . dropping off lorries?"

"Aye, I mean just that, lass."

"Stolen goods?"

"Well, not exactly stolen. You know what I mean. Lightenin' the loads on lorries you know, a bit here an' there. Oh, the bosses can afford it. An' they're all at it, 'specially them drivin' stuff to the docks. Wicklow's brother is one. But he's got to have a lifter, somebody to pick up the stuff when it's dropped, if you get what I mean."

I got what she meant all right and I felt a bit sick. Fancy George doing that. But worse still, if he ever got caught and was sent to prison.

"Anyway, his heart's not in it. He's not that type, our Georgie: he'd give his boots off his feet then go an' buy a pair of laces an' find he had nothin' to put them in. That's how his mind works. He does things without thinkin' and then when he thinks after, he thinks what a bloody fool he's been and says it'll not happen again. It usually doesn't, not in the same way, but there are

lots of other ways left. Still, that's our Georgie. Anyway, it wouldn't surprise me if he
goes off down south and not afore long, and
oh God! lass, I'll miss him. But I'd rather
he go than get hooked up with Wicklow.
And he'll be killin' two birds with one stone,
getting out of her brother's clutches an' all.
As I said to him, fancy goin' along the line
for a box of safety razors. They thought they
were gettin' small radios, you know the kind
that the bairns carry round with them, but
no, hundreds of little safety razors, when
most men are using 'lectric ones! He
brought a box here" — she thumbed towards the back kitchen — "and I said to
him, 'You can get that lot out of here, an'
quick. Anyway, what the hell did you bring
them for? What can we do with safety
razors?' An' he said, 'I thought you might
want to shave your legs.' "

She pushed me and knocked me almost
sideways on the couch and we both laughed
as she cried, "Me, shave me legs! Look at
me varicose veins." She twisted her leg
towards me. "The knots are standing out
like plonkers. Shave me legs, my God!"

Her legs were a dreadful sight. Yet here I
was laughing at them, almost doubled up.
Then I happened to turn my head towards
the corner of the room where the sideboard

was, and there was Hamilton. He was sitting on it, looking like an enormous dog. His head was back, his mouth was open, and his lips were not only revealing his teeth but his gums, and, like me, he was shaking with laughter.

"What is it?" Gran said, following my gaze; then she exclaimed loudly, "Oh, don't look over in that corner; I'll get down to the sideboard sometime. There's no place to put anything, so everything gets pushed on there. Paddy's market isn't in it."

"Oh, I wasn't looking at the sideboard, Gran. Well, I wasn't thinking about it, just about you and your legs." I laid a gentle finger on her knee.

"Oh, don't worry about them; they'll be here as long as me. You know, I remember reading a story somewhere when I was young and it had a rhyme in it and it went: It wasn't the cough that carried her off, it was the coffin they carried her off in. I can never remember where I read it, but I often think of it an' laugh."

"Where's George now?" I asked.

"Oh, somewhere across the channel, as far as I can gather; he's taken on the long journeys. He enjoys them. Hissy on parlour francis. That's what he said when he came in that door last week. Eeh by! I hissy on parlour francised him, 'cos he was tight."

Ici . . . on . . . parle français. Oh, her granny was a scream. Better than going to the pictures.

When I left her on that particular day her last words to me were, "Does that woman still come in . . . big May?" And I said, "Yes; she often pops in."

"Does she ever try to borrow anything?"

"Oh no." I shook my head.

"Well, that's a good thing. I believe in the saying, never a lender or a borrower be." Then with a wicked grin on her face she leant towards me and whispered, "Have you got half a crown to spare until Monday, hinny?" before pushing me away . . .

Two things happened that week.

It was about nine o'clock on the Friday night and I was up in the attic hiding away some more bits I had done on Hamilton. I'd only asked myself once why I should hide scraps of writing, and the answer was that if I were to die through an accident or some such and anyone was to find them they would think I was nuts. Well, sometimes now I thought I must be nuts, because Hamilton was becoming more real to me than the people I met during the day; that was except Gran and George. May, although I saw more of her than of anyone else, was excluded for some reason or other; Hamilton didn't even take to her. Yet she continued to be so kind and thoughtful.

Anyway, I knew why I hid these bits of writing; I also knew why I didn't like going up into the attic at all now. I had been through the trunk that I'd looked into the night I had first hidden my writing on Hamilton and the condition of the contents told me more about my mother's life than a whole book could have done, for under the layers of silk underwear I found what remained of her wedding gown. I say what remained, the gown was all there. It was white satin and cream lace, but it was torn into shreds. There must have been at least a hundred pieces of it, but these had been meticulously laid out on tissue paper, one layer to form the skirt, another layer to form the bodice, and the third layer the long narrow sleeves.

Sitting on the floor with the evidence of despair around me, I cried and cried for her. Whether she had done it before my father left her or after I don't know. But she had done it, and systematically ripped the symbol of marriage into shreds.

Poor Mother. I had at one time hated her and felt I had reason to, for she had never given me any love, but now when she was no more I loved her with a deep compassionate love.

I had replaced everything in the trunk as I found it, but on my journeys up to the attic my eyes were always drawn to it and the sight made me sad, for in it lay a life of disillusionment that had led to despair.

But there I was, the floor board in my hand, stuffing some more Hamilton sheets down to join the others when I heard the doorbell. It was the front door bell, so I knew it wouldn't be May.

It rang four times before I reached the hall and opened the door, and there stood George.

"What's kept you so long?" he said, passing me. "I knew you were in; the light's on in the sitting-room. Where've you been?"

"Up in the attic."

"In the attic! What were you doing up there? . . . Can you pull the steps down?"

"Oh yes; I'm a big girl now." I grinned at him and he put out his hand and ruffled my hair, which still wasn't flat, and he remarked on it: "By, she made a mess of you, didn't she? Me ma was flaming mad. She didn't let you know that, but she was. She did it on purpose, I mean Peg. She's a bitch you know, a jealous bitch. Have you got the fire on? It's enough to freeze you out."

"Yes, the electric's on in the study. I'm using that as a kind of office now."

"Oh, aye. I hear you're in business. How's it goin'?"

"Up till now I've been swamped with silence."

"Aw, never you mind; it takes a time to get started."

When we were seated in the study, one each side of the electric fire, I looked at him and noticed he had on his best suit and overcoat. I said to him, "Aren't you going to take off your coat?" And he answered, "No, pet. I haven't much time. I'm meetin' a fellow round quarter past ten in the market."

"Oh, George." I lowered my head and he came at me now, saying, "What d'you mean, oh, George, like that?"

"Well, Gran told me. You'll get into trouble."

"Aw, lass." He reached out and took my hand. "He isn't that kind of fellow. He's just a man who's giving me a lift down south."

"You are going down south?"

"Yes. I'm popping off once again. People are always popping out of your life one way or another, aren't they, lass? And you know something, I hate to go for one thing, no two: I'm going to miss you and Ma. But

I've got to get away. You see, it's Peg. She's aiming to get me up the aisle. Now things weren't too bad when your mother was alive, there was a time limit afore I could get a divorce, but these last few months since she's gone, oh, my, the pressure's got so bad. It's funny what pressure does, it sort of pushes your eyes open, makes you see things. If the hand is light on you, so to speak, you can carry on happily, never trouble to work things out, come day go day, God send Sunday, so to speak. You know what I mean. But once the pressure starts it gets your old napper workin' " — he tapped his forehead — "and you ask yourself how you would look at this kind of life if it was legal like. An' that's what I've done, and I know I'm not up to it."

He leant towards me now, patting my hand. "I'm a bad lad. I ran out on your mother, now I'm runnin' out on another. I don't seem to pick 'em right. Now if I'd met a lass like you when I was young . . . well now, things would have been different, wouldn't they?"

I made no reply, my throat was full. Of all the people in the world, I loved George. He was all the fathers I had dreamed of; he was a protector; he was a knight in shining armour; he was the bulwark against all foes;

as long as George was at hand, nothing much could go wrong for me. If anyone really got at me I could go to George and he would . . . settle their hash. That's what he used to say during my schooldays: "You tell me if anybody gets at you in that school yard and I'll go and settle their hash for them."

"Ah, don't cry, pet; I'm not goin' to the ends of the earth. Look, I'll send you postcards, naughty ones with big fat women on." He pulled his chair closer to mine and put his arm around my shoulder, and I leant my head on his chest. He smelt nice tonight, soapy nice. But I noticed through my blinking tear-filled eyes that the bulge of his stomach was getting bigger. That was his beer drinking, added to which he was always eating chocolate. He said it helped to keep his strength up on the long runs. We sat quiet for a time; then he said, "You still all right for money?"

"Oh yes." I lifted my head and nodded at him. I was slightly puzzled. Then I said, "I still feel that you should have had it."

"Oh, no, no. She knew what she was doing all right." He pursed his lips. "And she was right, she put it in hard writing that you had to have everything."

"But you should have had something. You

could have claimed."

"I could have claimed nowt, lass. Well, I would have had to get a solicitor and by the time the case had gone through, he would have had the bulk of it. Anyway, I didn't want a penny of hers; I didn't feel I was entitled to it; and it was a mistake from the beginnin'. You were the only good thing that came out of it."

"Oh George. Look, will . . . will you let me . . . ?"

"No, no, not a dime. No, thank you, lass. Anyway, with the money I've been makin' lately I'm in clover. And the old dragon's kept half of it for me." He patted his chest pocket. "Me wallet's bulgin' an' I'm gona take care of it till I get set on somewhere. Oh, I'm gona be a reformed man, you'll see."

I was still puzzled that he had asked me if I was all right for money. My mother had left four thousand, three hundred and fifty pounds, besides the house and the furniture. Part of the money came through an insurance. George knew how much I had and he would know too that it would be impossible for me the way I lived to spend that money in so short a time. Anyway, I expected it to last me for years, even if I didn't earn anything. And then he gave me the answer,

"Don't mind me saying this, pet," he said, "but those two along the street, the Stickles, have they ever asked you for a loan or anything like that?"

"No, no, George. Gran asked me much the same question. What makes you think they would?"

"Oh, I don't know. To my mind they're a queer couple."

My voice was very low as I said, "They've been very kind to me, George. I know they are not like you and Gran. I don't get on with them like that, I . . . I feel awkward with them, but they've still been very kind, more so than anybody in the terrace. Do you know Katie Moore who I used to be so friendly with? She's married now, but she passed me in the street the other day as if she didn't know me; and her mother merely nods at me. Yet at one time I was always going in and out of their house. She . . . she was the only girl friend that I ever had. And those next door, the Nelsons and the McVities, they hardly speak."

"Oh, well, both of them are stiff-necks." He laughed now, saying, "Remember the time when McVitie's terrier jumped the wall and cocked his leg on Oswald, you remember that day?"

I did not smile or laugh for I did remember that day. My mother had picked Oswald up by the few hairs left on his cloth ear and, taking him into the kitchen, had lifted the boiler top and thrust him into the fire. George seemed to have forgotten the result of that incident. I had been almost dumb with sorrow for a week. And George had said, "Well, now, she couldn't have done anything else, not after the dog had widdled on it. Now could she?"

I remember my reply to this; "He could have been washed, and . . . and he looked like you," and the great roar he had let out. He had, I remember, bought me another bear, but it was never Oswald. I don't know what happened to it.

At the front door he stopped and kissed me, not on the cheek but on the mouth. It had the most strange effect upon me and I clung to him, crying, "George. George." He had to push me from him back into the hall; then he went out, pulling the door closed behind him . . .

The other thing that occurred that week was May almost bursting in the back door one evening when I was preparing my meal, and her first words were, "Sardines on toast again! You know this will never do; you must cook yourself a meal . . . or let me come and do it for you." This was the first time she had made such a suggestion, and she went on, "I'll give you lessons, for there's no doubt you need them." She laughed her exposed gum laugh. And then she told me the reason for her hurried visit. "Howard has broken off his engagement," she said. "You have no idea of my relief. She was so unsuitable; she was a person who would never have learned. As I told you, common wasn't the name for it. I was surprised he couldn't see it himself. But at last, fortunately, oh yes, fortunately, it has got through to him." And then she added, "Oh, you are pleased an' all. Howard's very fond of you, you know, very fond."

Was he? I hadn't noticed. He was polite to me. And was I looking pleased? I always used to think he was still serving customers after the shop had closed. Or perhaps it was just his height that made him bend slightly forward when he was talking to me. And sometimes he would raise his hands to his shoulders as if he was putting on an imaginary scarf. I was to learn he was adjusting his tape measure . . .

It was about a week later that I went to dinner at the Stickles'. Up till then I had never been further into their house than the hallway. But here I was, sitting in their dining-room and, to use May's own expression when speaking of most things and of people outside the house, the furniture looked common. It was what you would see in any of the shops on the main street that were always having sales. However, what the room lacked in refinement the meal made up for it.

I really did enjoy the meal. I couldn't say as much for the conversation that took place afterwards in the sitting-room, which by the way, like the dining-room, was very poorly furnished. Sitting there looking about me, I could understand why May considered our house . . . my house as I thought of it now, was so nice, because it was a palace compared with this.

The conversation ranged around Howard's hobby which was collecting bottles. May enthused wildly about it. Howard had little to say until May said, "Take her up and show her your collection, Howard." Then he looked at her and said, "Oh, she wouldn't be interested in bottles." Then he turned his head and looked at me and ended with, "Would you?"

"Oh, yes. Yes?" — I made my voice eager — "I would very much like to see them. I've heard about people collecting bottles."

For the first time I saw a look of bright animation in his face; my reply seemed to have changed him altogether, because, getting up quickly, he said, "Come along then. Come along." And I followed him up the stairs and into a room that was the same size as my bedroom. When he switched the light on there I saw the bottles for the first time. There were hundreds of them, arrayed on shelves all round the room, with more on a long narrow bench running under the window and even more on the floor.

I stood and gaped and said truthfully, "I've never seen so many different bottles in my life."

"They are lovely, aren't they?"

Like a man showing off some precious possession, he lifted a bottle from a shelf. It was square. It had a glass stopper and I watched his fingers stroking the glass as if it were the most delicate porcelain. "This is my favourite," he said. Then he pursed his small mouth and wagged his head and added, "But I really haven't got any favourites. She's lovely though, isn't she?" At this instant Hamilton peered over his shoulder and, his nose on the bottle, he turned his eyes towards me and there was a deep enquiry in them. He was asking the same question as I was: Are there male and female bottles?

"Oh." Howard had noticed my glance was

directed upwards. "Oh, you've got your eye on Bluey, have you?" he said. And reaching up, he took down from a shelf a large blue bottle with a glass stopper; then holding it out towards me, he said, "He's an old chemist's receptacle. I have a few dozen of his cousins."

Hamilton's head was at the other side of him now peering down on the bottle, one eye seeming to look at the bottle, the other eye turned in my direction: So they are male and female, he said. Not only that, there's families. My, my! What have we here?

"This" — Howard lifted another bottle from the shelf — "saucy thing has the maker's name in the glass. Look." He held it out towards me, saying, "Middle of last century, and she was a sauce bottle. Indeed, indeed, yes."

One thing that was revealed to me before we finally left the bottle room was that Howard Stickle was a different man when he was with his bottles: the shopwalker had disappeared; the assistant manager of Hempies' the high class tailor was lost under myriad pieces of glass and stone. Oh yes, there were stone bottles too, all shapes and sizes. Those on the table were ready for classification he informed me. The ones under needed to be washed and dressed, his own words, before they found their everlasting home on one of the shelves . . .

"There! What do you think?" May greeted us in the sitting-room sometime later. And I said, "It's most interesting. Unbelievable how many bottles there are about; I'm really surprised." But if I'd been truthful, my surprise, I would have added, was not so much about the number of different bottles, but with the discovery that Howard Stickle was just an ordinary fellow, and not someone superior who had once played tennis in Gosforth . . .

That evening was the beginning of a number of meals in their house and of an equal number in my own. Prior to the latter, May would come and supposedly show me how to prepare the meal while doing it mostly herself. There was one thing about May, she knew how to cook.

So things went on smoothly, progressing, I should say, as May intended for some months.

During this time I received a number of cards and one letter from George and generally showing different postmarks. The letter said he was enjoying himself, meeting different kinds of people that he never knew existed, and that the south wasn't as black as it was painted. No, not by a long chalk:

there were some decent fellows down there . . . and lasses an' all.

Gran missed her Georgie, mostly, she admitted, last thing at night before she went to bed because she had always waited up for him no matter how late he might come in, except, of course, when he was on the long lorry journeys. But she kept herself going all right during the day for she had a part-time job in a factory now, packing dresses.

I, too, managed to keep busy during the week but I hated Sundays. Sundays were interminable. I had discovered long ago that no matter what you did you couldn't change a Sunday. You could alter your pattern, go someplace, or stay at home, even be sick in bed, but you still knew it was Sunday. I always had the longing to talk to somebody on a Sunday: strangers in the park even; or to go and knock on May's door. And I might have done if it hadn't been for Hamilton; he was very attentive on Sundays . . .

The first invitation to go out with Howard came one evening in May. I had been to supper with them and he was walking me back to my door, and he looked out over the playing field towards the park and said, "It's a lovely evening. May is a lovely

month, a quiet month, it has so much promise."

He sounded so poetic that I stood looking
up at him, and as I did so, Mrs McVitie
passed us and Howard raised his hat to her.
He always wore a hat even on a short
journey. "Good evening, Mrs McVitie," he
said, and she mumbled something and went
into her gate.

We then walked on and he said, "May, as
you can imagine, was born in this month.
It's her birthday next Wednesday. I really
don't know what to get her. Perhaps you
would come and help me choose something?"

I was staggered by the invitation, and I
must have appeared so because he hesitated
in his step and, looking down at me, said,
"You will be too busy?"

"Oh, no, no." My voice was two tones
higher than usual. "I would love . . . I mean
I would like very much to come and help
you choose a present. And I must get her
something too."

He was standing at my door now as he
said, "It would be nice to end her birthday
at a play or something. They are putting on
H.M.S. Pinafore in the Town Hall on that
particular evening, it should so happen.
Would . . . would you like to come too?"

"Yes; thank you very much. Yes, I would."

I'd never been to a place of entertainment with a man in my life before. I'd never even been to the pictures with George. I thought the suggestion wonderful.

"Well, that's settled then. Now I must away because tempus fugit." Oh! that saying. How I came to loathe it. Tempus fugit, time flies. When years later I told Gran about it, she said, "Oh, that's an old one: tempus fugit, said the man as he threw the clock at his wife."

Nevertheless I thoroughly enjoyed that evening out; it was my first taste of Gilbert and Sullivan. The following day as I dusted, I skipped from one room to the other singing snatches of the songs.

This night out began a pattern of evenings out. At first May accompanied us; then one night — we had made arrangements to go to the pictures — she had a severe cold and insisted that Howard and I went alone. I must admit that I felt rather proud of being escorted to the pictures by this tall presentable man.

It was on a night in late August that Howard proposed to me. We had again been to the pictures and for the first time as we sat in the dark he had taken hold of my hand, and there flowed out from me to him a great wave of gratitude. That this man could find it in his heart to make this gesture towards me was so overwhelming that the tears poured silently down my cheeks. It happened to be a very sentimental picture, and when it was finished he chided me playfully about my concern for the heroine.

Later at home, I had just made some coffee and we were in the sitting-room. The electric logs were glowing and the pink shade on the standard lamp was adding to the warm radiance when once again he took my hand and this time said, "Do I have to tell you, Maisie, that I've become very fond of you?"

I was about to say, thank you very much, Howard, but I remained quiet, staring at him.

"You know I had a broken love affair some time ago?"

"Yes, Howard. I was very sorry about it."

"You needn't be." He pressed my hand. "I've got over that, entirely over it, and I know now it was a great mistake in asking that certain person to be my wife. But I also know now" — I watched his Adam's apple flicking up and down, as I imagined, with emotion — "that I'm making no mistake in saying to you, Maisie: Would you consider being my wife?"

I stared up into his face. There were small beads of sweat on his brow. That I was amazed by this offer was putting it mildly; yet at the same time I asked myself why I should be, because hadn't he in a way been courting me? But how silly. Just because he had taken me to the pictures once or twice and we had been to see some amateur theatricals, sometimes accompanied by May, was that a sign of courtship? From my point of view, they had both been kind to the extent of taking pity on me. But here he was, this presentable man, asking me to be his wife. Never in my wildest dreams had I expected to be married. I had thought the only romance that would come my way would be through the written word: once I began a love story I couldn't put it down, eager to know the heroine's desires, the fulfilment of her longings, the overcoming of her frustrations. And if the writer should explain that the heroine was no beauty I would glow as she did when at last the proposal came.

And now here was the proposal and I wanted to glow. I should be glowing, but there he was, that Hamilton with forefoot raised ready to kick Howard in the back of the front. In order to do that he would have had to bring his hoof underneath the couch; but Hamilton could do that, Hamilton was capable of doing anything disturbing.

From the back door of my mind I yelled at him, "Go away! I shall never get this chance again. All right, if it is a mistake I've got to make it. Who else do you know will ask me to marry him? Look at me."

"What did you say, dear?"

He called me dear, and I said, "Look at me. Well I suppose you don't really need to, you've already done so, but have you taken into account my arm?" I lifted up my shorter arm and then went on, "And what is more, I'm a very plain person. I . . . I mean my features, and they are not likely to improve."

"Oh, my dear, my dear" — he had a hold of both my hands now — "your humility does you credit."

Yes, he had a way of talking like that. I wasn't taken very much with it, but nevertheless at this moment I lapped it up.

"Plain women," he said, "are often the most interesting; and after all, beauty is only skin deep. There is a beautiful woman asleep in every plain one. And what's more, plain women are known to make lifelong companions, and that's what the partnership of marriage is all about to my way of thinking, companionship. What do you say, Maisie?"

It sounded too beautiful. In a daze I nodded: "Oh, yes I agree with you, companionship is important. Oh yes, yes," I said.

No word of love had been spoken, not even liking, but at the time it didn't strike me as odd. I had nothing to compare this proposal with except the romantic stories I had read; and these I knew at bottom were but fragments of the authors' imagination, nice figments, but nevertheless, figments. So when he said, "Well, my dear, what do you say?" I said politely, "Thank you, Howard. I would like to, I mean, become engaged. Yes, thank you very much."

At this he leant towards me and slowly put his lips on mine. I didn't see what his face looked like because I closed my eyes. But his lips were moist and soft and sent a shiver down my spine.

"That's settled then." He rose from the couch and buttoning his waistcoat — he was always buttoning his waistcoat; odd, but I never saw him unbutton it, yet he was always buttoning it — he said, "I must now go and tell the happy news to May. She'll be delighted. She's very fond of you is May."

I made no answer to this. Even if I wanted to I couldn't because there he was, that great black shining beast with the white tail, the two front hoofs and a spot of white between his eyes, galloping round the room like mad. He was kicking things right and left and as I walked towards the door with Howard he galloped between us and I stepped quickly to the side and Howard put his arm out, saying playfully, "Oh dear, you're tipsy. It's all the drink you haven't had."

I managed to laugh.

I opened the door and he stood on the step for a moment looking out into the night, saying nothing; then abruptly he patted my arm, said, "Good-night, Maisie," and was gone up the street.

When I turned into the hall, there was Hamilton sitting on his haunches, his front legs well apart, his head thrust forward, a wild angry expression on his face. As I passed him he said, Don't kid yourself he's in love with you or . . . And I snapped back, "I'm not kidding myself. As he said, it's for companionship. In a way he seems as lonely as I am."

Lonely, me foot. You know what he's after. George knew what they were both after. You must have been blind if you haven't seen May's envious eyes round the house. And they don't own their property either. And they know you've got a bit of money.

"Shut up!" I thrust open the study door, went to the desk and started to write.

I wrote to Hamilton rather than talked to him because I always seemed to come off second best when I talked to him, and at the moment I was upset. I was engaged to be married, I told him; I knew that no word of love or affection had been spoken, but that I didn't expect it, I was lucky to get a proposal. All right, all right, May might have encouraged her brother along the line he had taken with her eye on this house, but I wasn't marrying May, I was marrying Howard. May would have her house, Howard and I would live here. I would clear out the end room and he could bring his collection of bottles with him. He'd like that. And I must really learn to cook. I could never hope to serve him meals like May, but I would improve on what I was turning out now. So Hamilton, there it is, I wrote, it's as much as I can expect from life, more, because you know I never thought any man would ask me, or would want to live with me. I have no brilliant conversation, I've talked too long to you to be at ease with people, but he seems to understand me, and . . . and I shall try to make him happy. So there, this chapter is closed, Hamilton. Once I am married, I . . . I'm not likely to want you any more and you can go back to . . . well, wherever you came from in me. But I'll never forget you, never, because you have given me moments of glee that I would never have known otherwise.

I took the pages, went up into the attic, raised the floorboard and put them among their companions, thinking, That episode of my life is finished.

Some hope. The voice sounded like Gran Carter's, but as I turned round there he was, jumping out of the attic, down on to the landing. As I myself reached the landing I saw him galloping through the window in the end wall, then right across the playing fields, across the park, on, on, that beautiful, shining, magnificent friend that my mind had given me for comfort during all the lonely trying years.

CHAPTER 6

"Aw, lass. What have y'been and gone and done? Promised to marry that fellow!" The look on her face made me squirm and I turned my head away and walked to the fire and held out my hands towards it. And when she said, not intending to cause me any pain but nevertheless doing so, "Lass, if he's proposed to you he's after something, and it isn't far to look. It's your house and all the fine bits that's in it, and your nest-egg. I'm sorry to say this but he's the type, that man, and his sister an' all, who don't do things without a motive like. Aw, don't be upset, lass, I mean it kindly. I . . . I think too much of you. You're like me own and I don't want to see you makin' a mistake."

I turned to her, blinking the tears from my eyes as I said, "I won't get the chance to make many mistakes, Gran, not me. All right, it might be a mistake, but I've got to take it."

I watched her sit down on the couch with a plop, then bend forward and lift up the bottom of her skirt, turn the hem towards her and start picking at it as if she were pulling at the threads, and as she did so she muttered, "Eeh! I wish our Georgie was here. He'd know what to do."

"Gran" — I sat down beside her and took her hand — "I'm going to marry Howard. I know you won't be the only one who'll think he had ulterior motives in asking me, but over the past months I've got to know him and I think he'll make a good companion."

"Oh, to hell with that, lass!" She threw my hands off her. "Bugger companions! That's not what you want out of marriage

113

at your time of life. That's all right for the old 'uns. Even me, you wouldn't get me at this stage taking anybody just for a companion. Don't you know what it's all about?"

"Yes," I said, "I know what it's all about."

"Well then, all I can say is if you do, you're a bloody fool to go on with it. Companionship!" she snorted, then rose from the couch and went into the kitchen.

I'd said I knew what it was all about. But what did I know all about? Quite candidly I knew nothing about marriage except what I'd read in the romantic books. There had been no whispered conversations in corners with other girls for me; there had been no innuendoes; no hints that I could pick up and dissect. Katie hadn't been like that. And she was married and she would know all about it now. But she must have been unhappy for she had left her husband. If we had still been friends, we might have talked . . . I hadn't understood Katie's changed attitude towards me, nor her mother's, not at that time anyway. It was her father who explained it to me. I met him in the street one day when he was very drunk. He had doted on Katie and so he was very bitter about this, and he said to me, "Life's funny, Maisie. Aye, it's funny. The wife was against you and my lass being pally because she thought it would spoil Katie's chances, you being as you were then. She thought Katie wouldn't be able to meet any suitable fellow if you were along, and who did she meet? That rotter. I never liked him, not from the word go. But here's you now, comfortably settled in your own house. And you've filled out a lot, you've changed. And what is our Katie's life? Two bairns, and separated from her husband. Life's a puzzle, Maisie, life's a puzzle."

I remember at that time I too thought it was a puzzle and how wrong he had been in thinking I was changed.

But here I was at Gran's, and she was dead set against my marrying Howard. Yet I knew firmly in my own mind that I would go through with it; Katie and her unsuccessful marriage were far removed from my mind.

Perhaps it was she who sent Father Mackin to the house, thinking that if I was set on going through with it then it should be done properly. Anyway, there he was one day when I answered the door bell, cheery and chatty, but both these facets of his character hiding a deep purpose. As he once said to me, there were different ways of driving a cuddy besides kicking it. And on that day and for weeks following he did his best to use these ways to drive this particular cuddy into the Catholic Church. And he might have succeeded if it hadn't been for Howard.

"Now this is a nice house," Father Mackin said. "Oh dear me, what a surprise." And he looked round the hall and through the open door into the kitchen. The ceiling had imitation rafters and the units were all scrubbed oak. My mother had had them specially fitted. Then laying his hat down on the hallstand and rubbing his hands together, he said, " 'Tis nippy outside. It is that, very nippy."

"Would you like a cup of tea, Father?"

"Now whoever said no to a question like that? Yes, I would indeed, I would love a cup of tea. What is your first name again?"

"Maisie."

"Oh . . . Maisie. It's a very friendly name that, Maisie. Yes, Maisie, I would love a cup of tea. May I go and sit down?" he said, already walking towards the sitting-room door. This was half open and I pushed it wide and he entered, exclaiming loudly, "Well, whoever did this had taste: grey walls and a blue carpet, and those dull pink curtains. Now who would ever think about those colours combining into such harmony.

'Tis a lovely house. Have you been here long?"

"I was born here, and my mother too. My grandparents came into it when it was first built, but since then there's been a lot of alteration done."

"Well now" — he sank on to the couch — "if I lived in a place like this the church would get the go-by, I'd promise you that."

I went out laughing and hurriedly made a tray of tea. And when I returned to the room he was examining some pieces of china in the cabinet that stood between the windows.

"You don't mind me being nosey, do you?"

"No, Father, not at all."

"These are nice pieces. I know something about porcelain and I can say these are nice pieces."

"I understand my grandfather brought them from abroad."

"Yes, he would do, he would do."

He sat down on the couch once more, and I poured out the tea and handed him a plate on which there were some scones, and after biting into one he exclaimed loudly on its merits. But I had to tell him that I hadn't baked them, that a friend of mine along the

117

terrace was a very good cook, she had done them.

"Now then, if she can bake scones like this, I bet she's not single."

"There you're wrong, Father, she is. And she is soon to be my sister-in-law."

"Oh, yes. Yes —" he put his cup down on the side table, wiped his mouth with a coloured handkerchief then said, "I heard that you're to be married. And really, to tell the truth, because I must do that sometime, mustn't I?" — he grinned at me — "that's partly why I've come, to see what arrangements you are going to make for the wedding."

"Oh, Father." I made to rise from the couch but his hand stopped me, and he said, "Now it's all right. It's all right. Don't take off in a balloon, I know that you're not in the church yet, but I've got a strong feeling that you would like to be. I understand you used to come to mass with your stepfather at one time, so as I see it, just a little push and you'd be over the step."

"I'm sorry, Father, but my fiancé is not that way inclined at all."

"What do you mean? He's an atheist, he doesn't believe in either God or man?"

"No. Well, I think, if he's anything, he's Church of England."

"But at present he's nothing?"

"I'm not really sure. We haven't discussed it."

"Well then, if you haven't discussed it, perhaps he and I can get down to a little natter, eh?"

"No, Father, please. He has already suggested we get married in the registry office."

"Oh, now, now." The smile went from his face. "Registry office." For a moment I thought he was going to spit. Then someone did spit. Sitting behind him, just to the right, there was Hamilton. I gasped because I hadn't seen him for some long time now. His head was turned and he was looking towards the floor, and then he brought his big lips into a pout and he spat. And I heard myself say, "Oh dear me."

"Now, now, there's no need for you to get worried. But I maintain that a registry office marriage is no marriage, not in the eyes of the Headmaster."

"The Headmaster?"

Father Mackin now turned his eyes upward until little but the whites of them could be seen, and, his voice lowered, he added, "Aye, the Headmaster, the Headmaster of men."

He was referring to God as the Headmaster of men, and I heard myself saying almost skittishly now, "And what about women, Father?"

"Oh" — he put his head back and laughed — "that's good, that is, that's good. Well, it's a mixed school. A . . . ha!" He was leaning towards me now, his head bobbing, and he repeated, "A mixed school. And there's coloureds in it too, yes coloureds: blacks and browns and yellows and a few Red Indians if I'm not mistaken."

We were both laughing now and I wasn't looking at him, I was looking towards Hamilton, and he was mimicking me. His big mouth wide open, his lips baring his teeth, he was doing a horse ha! ha! ha! bit. I could see that he didn't dislike the priest but that at the same time he had taken his measure: the iron hand in the velvet glove so to speak with a dusting of laughing gas inside it.

I don't know what made me think of that bit except that up in the attic I had come across a glove tree. It was in its own box with a canister of dusting powder; it must have been used by my grandparents at some stage.

He had three cups of tea and four scones and when he took his leave he put his hand on my shoulder and, his face and voice devoid of all laughter now, he said, "Think seriously on this, Maisie. It's a big step and it's for life. Never take marriage lightly. It's for life."

How often I was to think of those words in the years to come, it's for life.

Chapter 7

I was married on the second Saturday in February 1969, and before the day was out I was to experience humiliation as I had never really known it before, although I'd been acquainted with it; but terror, with which I had had no acquaintance, was almost to paralyse me.

It was ten days later when I ventured to Gran's. She was out, and the woman next door said she had gone along to the Community Hall. The Community Hall was only two streets away, and so I went to the door and asked the volunteer porter if he would ask Mrs Carter if I could see her a minute. "Why don't you come in, lass," he said, "an' see her yourself? They're having a sing-song."

"I'd rather not," I said.

"Is it important?" he said, and when I nodded he left me.

A minute later Gran was standing on the

pavement looking at me, saying, "Aw, pet. Aw, pet."

"Can you come home, Gran?"

"Yes, like a shot, lass. What is it? Aw, don't tell me. Let's get inside first."

Inside the house, the first thing I did was to burst out crying and she held me in her arms, saying, "There now. There now. Oh, my God! What's happened to you? Your face is like a sheet of lint. You never had much colour, but you never looked like this. Sit yourself down till I make a pot of tea, and keep talking. Aye, keep talking."

I sat on the couch, but I didn't start to talk, I didn't know how. It wasn't until I gulped at the hot tea that I looked at her and said bitterly, "Why didn't you tell me, Gran?"

"Tell you what, hinny?"

I turned my head away, only to have it pulled sharply round towards her again, and with her hand on my face she said, "I asked you, and you said you knew all about it. Is it that? That's upset you?"

"Oh, Gran." I bent my head deep on to my chest as I muttered, "I never dreamed. It . . . it was awful. It still is."

When she said no word I lifted my head and looked at her, and after a moment, her voice low, she murmured, "That's marriage, lass. That's marriage. Was he rough?"

I gulped in my throat and turned my whole body away from her. My head almost in my shoulder, I stared wide-eyed down the room. "Was he rough?" she had said. Was a hungry lion rough? Was an insane man rough? Because that's what he had been like. The only thing I was thankful for on my wedding night was that it took place in my own house and not in an hotel, for my screaming protests would surely have caused a disturbance. I wondered now if Mrs McVitie hadn't heard me, but then the bedroom was to the front of the house and both hers and Mrs Nelson's bedrooms faced the back. Anyway my screams had been smothered by his hand over my mouth and, his face contorted out of all recognition, he had hissed at me, "You are my wife."

The following morning was, in a way, as big an astonishment to me as the events of the night before, for his manner had reverted to the ordinary; it was as if nothing had happened between us, that dreadful struggle before the exhaustion overcame me had never been.

I dreaded the second night coming, and when it did he spoke quite calmly to me before he got into bed. Standing by the bedside he looked down on me and said again those words, "You are my wife. I am only taking what is my due." I remembered stupidly reminding him what he had said about companionship. And his lip had curled as he reacted, "Don't be so stupid, woman." It was the first time I had been called "woman". I was eighteen and hadn't felt up till then that I was a woman; however the previous night seemed to have made me into one. I begged him, "Please, please, don't." And again he said, "Don't be so stupid. You surely knew what to expect: being associated with a woman like George Carter's mother you couldn't have remained all that innocent."

Being acquainted with George Carter's mother, I *had* remained innocent, not only innocent, but ignorant, blind. Not only was I afraid of the savagery of the intimacy, but I knew now that I didn't even like the perpetrator. As for companionship, how could you make a companion of someone during the daytime who tore at your body like a savage repeatedly in the night?

"Was he rough?"

I didn't turn round as I muttered, "Terrible."

"I would have put you wise, lass, but you seemed to know. And you know, hinny. Look. Look at me." I looked at her. "It can

124

become a sort of beautiful thing like. Yes, yes, it can."

I almost bounced up from the couch and began walking up and down the room, my hands gripping each other. Talking rapidly now, I said, "Gran, you don't know. He acted like a wild beast. No words, nothing. Just a sort of an attack."

"He didn't love you? I mean, fondle you like, lead up to it?"

"No, no, nothing like that."

"He's a swine then. Aw, pet." She too got up now and stopped my pacing, and holding me tight she said, "I knew from the beginnin' it was wrong. But you were for it. You thought nobody else would want you. You silly lass."

"Can I come and stay with you?"

"No, lass, no! You can't." Her tone was emphatic. "This is something you've got to work out; you can't run away from it. And anyway, what would happen if you left that house? He wouldn't leave it, nor his sister. They would be planted there for good. But that's what they were after from the start; it's the best house in the terrace. I've heard a lot about him since. He was engaged to a woman in the office of the shop and when he broke it off she left. Nobody seemed to know what had happened atween them. I

understand from Florrie Ridley, whose lad's an apprentice there, that the lass's mother was for setting about him 'cos the lass got a lot of bits and pieces together. Now I ask you, why should he break that off and turn to you if he hadn't a deeper motive? To my mind that big lump of a sister of his arranged everything. So . . . well lass, as much as I'd like you to come here, an' I'd welcome you, but if you did, it would be just playing into their hands, and you'd have a job to get that property back, I'm tellin' you. And a house like that is worth thousands. You'd have to get a solicitor an' likely go to court, and that'd cost something, and in the end he'd get his share. Men are for men when it comes to the push and, if I'm not mistaken, there's some law about it. At one time the husband could claim the lot. I don't think it's the same now, but they've still got some rights along that way. I'll look into it. In the meantime, make a stand against him. If he starts any more hanky-panky, rough like, take a hatpin into bed with you. It's been done afore. Oh aye." She nodded at me, her face solemn now. "I'm not jokin' . . . What has big May to say about it?"

"Oh, I couldn't say anything to her."

"Do you see much of her?"

"Too much. She's always in and out. Yet

at the same time I'm sometimes glad of her company, especially at night when he's in."

"Look, pet" — her brows knitted and her eyes narrowed — "are you really frightened of him?"

I hesitated before answering, and then it was only half an answer, "In a way I am," I said. "Yes, in a way I am."

"What do you mean by that?"

"Well, looking at him in the daytime he doesn't seem to be a frightening person. It's . . . it's just at night. He . . . he seems to change entirely once we're alone upstairs. It's strange, odd."

"Oh, hinny" — she turned away from me — "I wish I could do something for you, explain things to you. But I can't; you only come to this kind of knowledge through experience. Everybody's different. Every man's different. An' you never know how different until they get you in that bedroom. Yet I've had nothin' to grumble about. No, indeed, no. Georgie's father was what you call a gentle man." She turned to me again. "You know it's a pity you hadn't come across somebody like our Georgie. He doesn't know B from bull's foot education like, but about livin' and lovin', well, there isn't much he doesn't know. He's like his da. A man like that would have suited you down to the ground. If you only had waited. Aw!" She shook her head violently. "But what's the use? It's done. But you go back now an' brace yourself an' make a stand, because that's your home and I know you love the house. You were happy in it from your ma died, you could see it in your face, and you kept it nice, as nice as she did. And I know one thing for sure, pet, you couldn't put up with this kind of life for long," and with outspread arm and hand she indicated the room; "you cannot swing a cat here. And there's no privacy around these quarters. Why, you can hear when Mrs Pratt, two doors down, has been to the lav. No, lass, this kind of habitation isn't for you. So go on home and stand up to him. You've got a lot in your napper that hasn't come out, I know that. Our Georgie used to say that an' all about you."

I picked up my hat and coat and as I put them on I said, "Have you any idea when he's coming back?"

"No, lass. He seems to have settled in Falmouth these last few weeks. He's likely found a dame down there. One thing's certain, he won't show his face here till Wicklow gets hooked up with somebody. I don't go back to her for me hair. She came round here and raised the house on me after he went, as if it was my fault. You should have heard the names she called me. But she learned a few new ones afore she left, I can tell you that." She smiled her old smile; then putting her arms around me, she kissed me and said, "Look, I'm in most days atween one and half past two. If you need me slip round then. Or atween five and six round tea-time. But I suppose that's his time for coming in."

"No," I said, "he doesn't get in most nights until half past six." And as she led me to the door she said, "What does he do nights?"

"He mostly goes upstairs and arranges his bottles."

"Arranges his bottles! What bottles?"

"Oh" — I hesitated — "well, I didn't tell you but he collects bottles."

"Beer bottles?"

"No; all kinds of bottles."

"Bottles?" Her lips remained wide apart when she finished the word.

"Yes, sauce bottles, ginger beer bottles, vinegar bottles. Any kind of bottle that's ever had anything in it. He's got hundreds of them upstairs."

"Oh . . . my . . . God!" The words were spaced. "Have you married a nut?"

"I . . . I understand lots of people collect

bottles."

"Well, that's the first I've heard of it, except beer bottles. But they don't collect them, they take the empties back, if there's anything on them. And he's got them all up in the bedroom?"

"No; I've given him a separate room. It takes a full room."

"Eeh!" — she looked upwards — "Gordon Highlanders! Go on, lass." She pushed me towards the door. "I'll be lookin' forward to seein' you the morrow. And do what I told you, mind, make a stand."

I went out down the street and walked across the town, then through the park, and for the first time since I'd been at school, I sat down on one of the seats opposite the pond and looked at the ducks. It was very cold. The world seemed empty. The future seemed empty. What was I going to do? Were all my days going to be like this? Gran had said, make a stand, but how could I do that? . . . Oh Hamilton what have I done?

I'd continued to keep Hamilton at a distance for some time now, but there he was standing at the end of the park seat. His coat didn't look so bright and shiny. He looked as if he had been galloping through bad weather; his mane looked wet, his tail drooped. His eyes were sad. I spoke to him, first apologizing, saying, "I wouldn't listen to you; you were right."

What's done's done, he said. The question is, how are you going to go on from now? Would you consider following Gran's hatpin suggestion? His upper lip moved slightly from his teeth, but I couldn't raise the slightest smile in return. "I could never do that kind of thing," I said. "You know I couldn't."

Then what do you propose to do?

"I don't know. Can't you tell me?"

Use your elbow, he said.

"My elbow?" I looked down at my arm, the foreshortened forearm resting as usual across my waist. This part of my arm had very little flesh on it compared to my right one. The doctor had referred to it as withered. The elbow was very bony. I had once playfully jabbed Katie with it and she had cried, and I was so contrite I swore I would never use it again in that fashion.

I looked at Hamilton. He was standing straighter now, and looking not so shaggy. I said to him, "But what am I going to do in all the days ahead?" And his answer was, Take one thing at a time. What you could do is take up your writing again, about me or anything.

"Oh, I don't know about that," I said. "I

131

get all flustered when he's in the house, even when he's up among his bottles, and I haven't attempted to do any of my kind of writing in case I say something about him or May, for as sure as I did he would come and say, as he did the other evening, "What's that you are writing?" And when I said, "The grocery list," he retorted, "Do you never find anything better to do! May will see to that."

May was taking over. With a greasy smile on her face and a soft tone, her progress into the house was insidious. The little liking I'd had for May had evaporated.

When Hamilton came and stood by my side, his legs astride the park seat, I turned my head and looked at him as I said, "I feel trapped, Hamilton, and I . . . I feel I've been tricked."

You can say that again. Well — he brought his thick lips together and his head bobbed up and down — you've got to play them at their own game. He hasn't given you any money for housekeeping, has he?

"No."

And you paid the bills last week?

"Yes."

Well, stop paying them. He's got a decent wage; he's taken on the title of husband and head of the house, let him see to them.

"But he knows I've got money."

Well, use your napper, as Gran would say; think about it. If you hadn't any money what would he do then?

I turned my head and looked over the lake. The ducks were quacking loudly. One was skimming across the surface leaving a white arrow of froth behind it.

Go to a solicitor, put your money in Gran's care.

My head jerked round towards him again. "Could I do that?"

Go to a solicitor and find out. He seemed a nice enough man, the one who made the will out for your mother. You could pass the lot over to Gran with certain provisos, such as, she would hold the money in care for you, and that if you should die, it had to be split between her and George, or all of it go to the one who survived.

I smiled for the first time in days. "You think of the cleverest things, Hamilton. What would I do without you?"

I don't know, he said. I only know that life is very dull at the moment and it's a long time since we had a laugh together. I've never kicked anyone in the back of the front for some time now, although it isn't that I haven't wanted to. But you weren't about. Or you were but you had shut the door on me, and it's no good a horse acting the goat on its own; anybody who's capable of acting the goat needs an audience.

I rose from the bench feeling somewhat better. I would beat them at their own game as far as the money was concerned and I would see to that as soon as possible. And as for my weapon, well, I might even put that into use before tomorrow.

I did.

At half past six when Howard came in, May was there. She had brought a shepherd's pie down, saying, "I know you give him his dinner but he also likes a warm snack at night, and he needs to be fed. He was very delicate as a child," which made me almost snap back, "He has the strength of a bull now;" but that certainly would have led to questioning.

When he came in his face was bright as if with excitement. Even before he had taken his hat and coat off he called through the hall to May, "What do you think I've heard today?" And she, passing me, went to the kitchen door and said, "What, dear?"

"They're making tennis courts in Brampton Hill Park."

"No."

"Yes."

"How lovely!" May turned to me.

"They're making tennis courts in Brampton Hill Park. Isn't that exciting?"

When he came into the kitchen he actually put his hand on my head in passing as one would on a dog's. Yet the gesture was so unexpected that it made me smarmy and I could have kicked myself for saying, "You'll enjoy that, being able to take it up again." He smiled at me as he said, "Oh, yes, yes indeed," and looking at May, added, "We were very good at it one time, weren't we, May?"

"First-rate." She jerked her chin upwards and repeated, "First-rate. We were always picked to represent the club. When will they be ready?"

"A couple of months' time, I think. And oh, by the way, I'll have to be off again in half an hour." And noticing that the table was set for the high tea, his eyes resting on the casserole dish, he said, "Shepherd's pie. Oh! May; I'm sorry I won't be able to do justice to it because —" He paused and his glance took me in now as he said, "I've been invited to supper at Mr Hempies'. What do you think about that?" His eyes did a flicking movement from one side to the other of us; then to me he said, "Put me a clean shirt out and my brown shoes. See they're polished, will you?"

I paused a long moment before leaving the room, and I was at the foot of the stairs when I wondered what brown shoes he wanted. He had four pairs. I returned towards the kitchen door again but stopped to hear him say, "He seems impressed at my being married. I think it's the house; and he seemed to know about her mother and that she was quite well off. It can't be anything else; eleven years I've been there and this is the first invitation."

"Didn't he ask to see her?" This came from May. And my breath stuck in my throat as I waited for his answer. "Yes, he did," he said, "but I made excuses, saying that she wasn't at all well. And that's how she's going to remain, if I've got anything to do with it."

I took three silent steps backwards before turning, and I slowly crossed the hall to the stairs, and there I stopped and looked upwards to see Hamilton. His head was lashing from one side to the other, his mane falling over his face. I went up and into the bedroom — he had preceded me — and I spoke aloud now, really aloud: "Tomorrow the solicitor." And he nodded his head twice, saying, Yes, tomorrow the solicitor . . .

Howard was late coming in. I had fallen

asleep, and he woke me up to tell me all that had taken place at Mr Hempies'. "And you know something," he said; "his is a semi-detached in Durham but it isn't half as substantial as this. Nor is his furniture anything like ours."

Ours. My dulled mind repeated, ours.

I couldn't bear to watch him undress and I turned on my side and buried my face in the pillow but couldn't shut out his chatter. Then I stiffened as he said, "If you made yourself a bit more presentable we could have him here. That would show him. You want to go and have your hair properly done and get something done about your face. There's places. They can alter noses to any shape; and mouths an' all. And if you put make-up on . . ."

I swung round in the bed and glared at him now as I cried, "I am as you married me and like this I stay. I'm not changing for you or God Almighty."

That he was surprised by my retaliation was evident, but he was more surprised a few minutes later when, on my side once more, his arm came on me in a grabbing movement, for it was at this point I took my elbow, and *wham!* I stuck it into his ribs. The squeal that he let out was comparable with those he had wrenched from me on the night of our marriage. And now gasping and holding his side, he said, "What do you think you're up to? You . . . you could injure me. You have. You have."

He screwed round and sat on the edge of the bed. The bedside light was still on. That was another thing: he never put the lights out until he was about to sleep; he seemed to enjoy watching my torment. I watched him now pull his pyjama coat open and look at his ribs, and pathetically he repeated, "You could have injured me." And then his tone suddenly changed: he glared at me and growled, "Don't think you'll get the better of me by using that stump."

When I said, "Well, it's either that or a hatpin," his face seemed to stretch to twice its length.

"You're mad!"

"I shouldn't be a bit surprised; I must have been to fall into this trap."

"What do you mean?"

"You know what I mean. Would you like me to put it into words for you?"

He bent over me now, one hand still holding his side: "You've found your tongue all of a sudden, haven't you? May said you were out all afternoon. Where were you? Along at the old hag's again? Did she put you up to this?"

"My gran's not . . ."

"She's not your gran. She's your stepfather's mother, and she's an old hag, a common old cow."

Hamilton was rearing at the foot of the bed, standing right on his hind legs as I yelled, "Don't you dare put that name to Gran!"

"I'll put what name I like to . . . . Gran! She's an old . . . ." And he came out with a mouthful of short four-letter words that up till now I hadn't heard anyone voice — I'd seen them written on the walls of toilets and the subway that led to the station — and nothing he could have done could have affected me more, this tall, thin, well-dressed, gentlemanly looking individual who had the appearance at times of an ascetic monk as portrayed in the films, using the foulest of language.

I felt immediately it was a mistake to let him see how it affected me; but I couldn't have known then that I had given him a weapon which was to be his main line of attack down the years. If I had told anyone that Mr Howard Stickle was a foul-mouthed individual, not only would I not have been believed, but I would have surely been accused of slandering a gentleman; indeed one of nature's gentlemen. I'm sure that even

139

May wasn't aware of this trait in him.

It was some long time before I went to sleep somewhere in the middle of the night. And when, across the breakfast table the next morning, he looked at me and said, "You look tired, you should get more sleep," and he laughed, I thought, I can't stand it. I won't be able to stand this. He can have the house and all that's in it.

Yet once he was gone and I was alone, I walked from room to room. Hamilton went with me, and as I stood in the sitting-room he said, Don't do it. Don't make it easy for them. Do as you said yesterday, go and see the solicitor.

"Oh," I said, "I've got to start that woman's story."

You can work late tonight. That'll keep you out of bed. Go on, go now, else you won't go at all.

They called the solicitor Mr Pearson. He was middle-aged and very nice. He said yes, such a thing as I proposed could be arranged but could I tell him why I was taking this step.

Could I tell him? Could I say that although I knew deep within me my husband had married me for my house and for what money I had, I wouldn't have minded except that he had turned out to be a horrible individual. How horrible was only known to myself. What I answered him was, "I have good reason for doing what I'm doing, Mr Pearson." He stared at me for some seconds before saying with a slight smile on his face, "I'm sure you have;" then adding, "I've always thought of you as a very sensible girl, not at all like your mother, if I may say so, who was more erratic in her dealings. What you must do in this case is to take your grandmother to see your bank manager." He stopped here and pulled a slight face as he said, "Aren't you afraid of her spending your money?"

"No, not at all. She wouldn't do that. But if she did it wouldn't matter; there's nobody I'd like to have it more than her or my stepfather."

"Well" — he stood up — "you seem to like your relations better than most and it's a very nice attitude to come across. Although at the same time" — his face now took on a solemn look — "I am sorry that you feel obliged to do this."

"I am too, Mr Pearson."

We parted with a handshake after I had asked him not to send the document concerning the matter to my home but to Gran's address.

"You must be up the pole, lass. God in heaven! you can't do a thing like that."

"I have done it, Gran."

"Look, lass, all that money. What did you say? Nearly three thousand pounds worth of bonds an' all that money in the bank an' building society. Eeh! lass." She backed from me and leant against the little kitchen table. Then rubbing her hands across her mouth, she said, "What if our Georgie gets his hands on it?"

"He would act the same as you do, Gran. Anyway, you are just sort of being guardian to it."

"But you say it's in my name an' I have to go and see the bank manager?"

"Yes. And if I want any money I've got to come and ask you."

"Eeh, bugger me eyes! I've heard everything now. But what's made you do this, lass?"

I could tell her what had made me do this, even about his vile language, and she surprised me by saying, "Oh, that's not uncommon that. I know that at first hand, 'cos you see I went into service when I was fourteen. It was over Morpeth way. Gentry they were; not the top drawer but the riding, shooting, fishing kind. They had six bairns and the master was a warden in the church, an' all

142

the servants knew about his language. Butter wouldn't melt in his mouth during the day, but at night-time he went for the mistress as if he was talking to a whore from the streets. His drink was port and brandy mixed. Men are queer cattle, lass, but yours is a dirty-minded bugger to take that line with you. One thing you mustn't do, pet, is to let him see it upsets you. That would give him satisfaction. An' if he gets too bad you go and tell your doctor."

I couldn't see myself going to Doctor Kane and saying, "Will you speak to my husband, please, because he uses bad language?" I could hear him over the distance exclaiming, "Who doesn't, woman! Who doesn't!"

But there was a difference in bad language and swearing. Gran swore. George swore. All the people in this district seemed to swear — as I walked down the street you could hear them, and the children too — but in a way it was clean swearing compared to the words that Howard used, and it was not only the words but the way he had of saying them.

The fact that I was penniless was not brought to Howard's and May's notice until almost six weeks later, when a final demand was sent for the electricity bill. I had left the previous bill together with the coalman's bill, the butcher's bill and a bill for wood that Howard had ordered to make more shelves for his bottles, and when on this Friday night, as once again I had received no housekeeping money, I quietly placed the bills in front of his plate, he looked down on them, then at me, and said, "What's this?"

"What does it look like? They're bills."

He turned now and glanced at May who had given herself a permanent invitation to our evening meal, which I must admit she herself provided very often. And it was May who, smiling smarmily, said, "But you see to the bills, dear."

"No, I don't." I hadn't sat down at the table; I was standing to the side of it and I shook my head like a little girl might as I repeated, "No, I don't."

"What do you mean, no, you don't?" His voice had taken on the bedroom tone.

"Well" — I looked at him — "how do you expect me to pay bills when you never give me any housekeeping money, you give it to May."

I saw him grind his teeth; then with his hand he swept the bills towards me, saying, "Don't you take that tack, madam, with me!

You pay those bills like you've always done."

"I can't. I haven't any money."

Now they both screwed up their faces at me before turning and looking at each other, then back to me again.

"You haven't any money?" His words were slow. "Yesterday you had more than three thousand pounds and today you haven't any money. Have you gone really mad?"

"That's what I used to have, but I haven't anything now." I watched him slowly rise up, and even from the other side of the table he towered above me, his thin length seeming to stretch with each second of the silence that followed, until I broke it, saying, "I gave it away . . . legally."

Again the brother and sister exchanged glances; and now May was on her feet. *You what?"* They both spoke together, and I repeated, "I gave it away legally. It's all been signed and sealed by my solicitor."

Slowly he came round the table now until he was my short arm's length from me, and I saw his jaw working backwards and forwards. His pale skin had turned almost purple, and for a moment I thought he was going to choke before he brought out the words, "Who did you give it to?"

"Well, you would know who I would give it to, wouldn't you? There was nobody but

Gran, and failing her it goes to George." He turned slowly from me, only I think to prevent himself from striking me to the floor, and then he took his hand and swept it across the table, and in its passage my plate of fish pie, my cup and saucer, the sugar basin and the milk jug, all went flying; and then he let me have it from his mouth. "You bastard! You deformed stinking little bastard." And there followed a spate of words that not only shocked May, but surprised her into protest, and she cried at the top of her voice, "Howard! Howard! Stop that! No! no! Stop that, please. Such language."

"Shut up!" He rounded on her now. "You got your way, didn't you? You . . . you got your way and this is the result. Tied to that!" He thrust out his arm and pointed to me as if I was some crawling creature; and he made me feel like that. Yet I felt not the slightest remorse at what I had done. I had paid him back. I had paid them both back in part, even though I knew that wouldn't be the end of it; he being who he was would make me pay.

And he did.

■ ■ ■ ■

PART TWO
THE EMERGING

■ ■ ■ ■

CHAPTER 1

The years that followed I look upon as the doctor and dog period because Doctor Kane became my bulwark and I fell in love with dogs. Hamilton didn't seem to mind, for, as he said, dogs were much more trustworthy than people.

My real association with Doctor Kane began one Wednesday morning. I had felt sick in the morning for some time now and when I told Gran about this she said, "My God! lass, you're pregnant."

Pregnant? Yes, I should have realized that; I was stupid. So I was going to have a baby. How wonderful! How marvellous! Yet, no, because it would be a part of Howard, if not all of him. People turned out like that, all of one or all of the other. But then equally it might turn out to be like me. Oh, no, not physically anyway. Oh, please. I found I was praying, until Gran said, "Now don't get upset. It's just normal, I suppose, only I would have wished for a better father for it. Still, you'll be its mother and it can't go far wrong with that. You'd better go and see the doctor."

"Well, well; so you think you're pregnant. How far have you gone?"

"I don't know."

"You don't know? Well, you should; if you don't know, nobody else does. Get your clothes off." He pointed to the screen.

A few minutes later he said, "Put your clothes on again." And when I was once more sitting before him he looked at me in silence for a moment, his hands joined on the desk in front of him, and he asked quietly, "How do you feel?"

"About what?"

"Oh, my God!" He turned his head to the side; then looked back at me again, saying, "About everything: the fact that you're going to have a baby; how you are finding marriage; about life in general. How do you feel?"

I smiled weakly at him as I replied, "Taking it in a lump, awful, except I think I'm pleased about the baby."

"Taking it in a lump." The hairs on his face moved in different directions as he twisted his mouth from one side to the other. Then he asked abruptly, "Why did you have to do it, marry that man?"

I answered truthfully, "Because I thought it would be my only chance."

"And now you've found out your mistake?"

"Yes."

"I'm surprised at you, you know. Behind that quiet exterior, I always thought you had a lot of horse sense."

There, he had said it again, and as before Hamilton appeared, standing behind the doctor's chair, his forefeet on the back of it, nodding at me.

"Don't look over my head when I'm talking to you; I'm not wearing a halo, not yet anyway." The doctor grinned at me now and, leaning forward, he said quietly, "You want to get out of the habit, you know, when people are speaking to you. You're always either looking up or down or sideways but never to the front. It gives folks the wrong impression of you. As I said, I always give you credit for some horse sense at least, and you should have known a fellow like that who looks as if he'd been let out of a bandbox wasn't marrying you for your looks. Oh, yes, yes, I know. I'm being blunt, but then you've faced up to it long before this. That's why I could never understand why you did

151

it. Now if your mother had done it, and she might well have at that, I could have seen a reason for it, a good reason for it . . . Anyway, how do you find life with him?"

"Awful."

He sat back in the chair as he said, "Really?"

"Yes; yes, really. He's two different people."

"What do you mean by that?"

"Well, he appears to be a sort of gentleman to all outsiders but" — I now forced myself to look him straight in the face "savage would be the kinder word I'd use with regard to his attitude towards me, my . . . my person, I mean."

He said nothing, but continued to stare at me.

"And . . . and there is something else."

He waited, and now I did look to the side and above his head and down to the floor before I said, "He talks at me in vile language, every night, just sits up in bed and talks at me."

"What do you mean by vile language? He swears?"

"No, not just swearing. I don't mind swearing. It's vile, filthy."

He leant forward and started to scribble on the blotting-pad as if he was doodling and there was silence between us for a moment; then lifting his head abruptly he almost bawled, "You brought this on —" only to realize he might be heard in the waiting-room for he lowered his voice as he ended, "yourself, girl." Then his head to one side, he said, "Have you refused him? You know what I mean?"

I knew what he meant and I said, "Yes; at least, when I can."

"Well, that's not going to help you. If you could try."

I moved in my chair as if my body was shrinking down into the seat as I repeated, "I can't. I can't. He's so cruel; no thought, nothing."

"What are you going to do about it?"

"I . . . I don't know. I thought about leaving the house but I think that's what they want, him and his sister. I know now that she pushed him into marrying me. She liked the house . . . and the fact that I had a bit of money. But" — I pulled a slight face — "I potched them there."

"Potched them? What did you do?"

I told him. And when I was finished he sat back in the chair gazing at me; then, his big hairy head flopping back on his shoulders, he let out a great laugh. I don't know what the people in the waiting-room thought because it went on for quite a while. And then he had to take his handkerchief out to wipe his eyes, and as he did so he said, "I was right. I was right about your horse sense. Well, if you had the courage to do that, girl, you will have the courage to work things out for yourself. Go on now. I'm not going to worry about you any more. Oh no." He got up. "Pop in again next week. Eat plenty, and take exercise. What do you do with your days?"

"Well, I'm running a little business, typing manuscripts and such."

"Oh, well now, you've got something there. That's good, good. But still, that's sitting; so get yourself out and march round the town at least once a day."

At this I saw Hamilton walking through the door into the waiting-room. His knees were almost coming up to his shoulders; his tail was flashing from side to side in rhythm as a soldier's arm does when marching. He stamped out into the street and I followed him, smiling to myself. I liked Doctor Kane, I did.

I didn't tell Howard my news; I told May. If it had been conveyed to her before they had known I was virtually penniless, she would have clasped her hands together at her breast and exclaimed, "Oh, how beautiful! How delightful! Howard will be pleased." What she said was, "I hope you make enough money at your typing to engage a nurse when the time comes;" then she added, "I don't think Howard will be overjoyed."

Howard wasn't overjoyed. He was now having his midday meal out and she must have either gone to the shop or waylaid him on his way home. He came in as usual, took off his hat and coat in the hall, hung them up in the cloakroom and washed his hands, then came into the kitchen. I was frying some fish that May had brought in earlier; she still did the housekeeping.

He paused in the doorway and looked at me. I turned my head from the stove and looked back at him. He didn't speak until he was seated at the table; nor did I make any remark but as I placed the meal before him he gripped my wrist and, looking at me, he said, "So we are going to have an addition to the family, are we?"

To this I replied, "As May says, we are going to have an addition."

"It would have been nice, don't you think, if there had been a little extra money to provide it with the essentials of life."

"Most husbands I know of provide for their children," I replied; at which, he threw my hand from him. It hit the side of the table, causing me pain, and he said, "Most husbands have women they can call wives."

"And most wives have husbands who don't act like savage illiterate brutes," I snapped back. I don't know why I put the illiterate in, and I think this upset him as much as the other adjective, for he sprang up, his arm raised, his fist doubled; but at the same time my right hand shot out and gripped the frying pan. It was still hot and had the fish fat in it, and, holding it in mid-air, I screamed at him, "Don't you start that! Just don't start that, because if you do, you'll get as much as you send. I cannot retaliate by uttering filth for filth, but I can physically, and every time you hit me you'll get double in return with anything I can lay my hands on. I promise you that. Now, let's come to an understanding: you leave me alone and we can live in this house together, but you attempt any physical force on me and, you know, this house will go where the money went. I promise you that." I now lifted up my short arm, and my forefinger wagged to the side of my face, emphasising what I'd said. And I repeated it: "I'll sell this house. You can't stop me, nobody can. I've gone into all that an' all. So you have your choice. Your main purpose was to live here. All right, you may, and if I have a child I would like it brought up here, but not at any price." When he jumped back from me, I realized that I was waving the frying pan and the hot fat was spilling on to the tiled floor. Slowly, I replaced the pan on the stove; then, skirting the table, I walked just as slowly out of the room, leaving him purple with rage. And I knew he was utterly dumbfounded.

I had won another battle. Even so, I felt that the war had just begun.

Looking back down the years, I wonder how I could have tolerated this state. Could the loss of the house and its possessions have been such a force as to tie me to that man? Yes, I suppose it could. Well, it did. But there were other factors. Where would I have gone had I left there? To Gran's? Gran was wise. She knew I couldn't have stood living in that house in that quarter, as much as I loved her. The surroundings would have stifled me. I myself would have become like a caged animal in that one room, and perhaps become tired of Gran's mode of expression. It was amusing, taken in small doses, but with no variation, would I not become tired of listening to it?

Yet, I ask myself, what variation had I in my own home? Only the sound of my own voice talking to Hamilton most of the day. But then, that was the point, in my own home I could talk to Hamilton, but in Gran's I would have been unable to do that, for there was no privacy from the neighbours and the whole council estate would have soon known of the daft lass in Gran Carter's who talked to herself. She should be put away, they would have said. And they were not the only ones who would have been of that opinion, had I tried to explain about Hamilton.

So I stayed on in my house, and six months of my pregnancy passed.

Towards the end of this period I had joined a writers' circle. Oh dear me! it was a surprise. I had expected to be enthralled listening to literary geniuses; I had expected to be overawed by the possessors of literary merit. What I met with was a conglomeration of people who really looked as dowdy as myself. They were mostly women, and half of them wrote about kittens, dear little kittens and dear little cats. They wrote short stories about them, and poems about them. There wasn't so much said about dogs; it was always kittens or cats.

Howard never gave me one penny, but I was making enough now from my typing to buy odds and ends I felt I would need when the baby came. Life in the daytime was tolerable. Life when I entered the bedroom until the lights went out was almost unbearable. The nights when I wasn't being obscenely talked at, he handled me, and my elbow wasn't always a deterrent.

I was just on six months gone when I said to him, "I'm going to sleep across the landing."

"Like hell you are!" he said.

"Like hell I am!" I repeated.

"I'll make it worse for you if you do," he said.

"I don't think it's in your power to make it any worse."

"You know nothing yet."

I looked him straight in the face, and I said quietly, "Howard, if you start any new tactics with me I shall go to Doctor Kane and tell him exactly what happens." This seemed to deter him; as also did my manner of speaking; yet he came back with, "And what can he do?"

"He will know that I have registered a complaint against you, and it will help me when I tell you to get out of this house or I decide to sell it. Now I'm going to sleep across the landing. It's up to you to decide what the future holds for you."

What he said to me now was, "You ugly,

pig-eyed, little snipe, you! If you think you're going to get me out of this house, you're mistaken. And I'm going to tell you something else. I'm bringing May in here to live; I don't see the reason to pay rent when there's rooms going empty. And anyway, she looks after me now as she's always done, because you damn well don't."

"I won't have May here permanently."

"You'll have her whether you like it or not."

"I mean what I say, Howard. You force my hand, and I'll sell this house. As much as I love it, I'll sell it. I will not have May here permanently."

I could feel his hand coming up again and the effort it took him to refrain from hitting me. . . .

It was a Saturday night when I began to feel ill. It couldn't be the baby, I told myself; I had felt it kicking vigorously only a short while before. I couldn't quite put a name to my feeling of illness, but in the middle of the night, sleeping alone now in a single bed and the door locked, I became worried; more so when the feeling of illness was still with me on the Sunday morning.

How I struggled to Gran's on the Sunday afternoon, I don't know. As soon as she saw my face she said, "My God! lass, I think you're for it. How much are you gone?"

"Six and a half months," I managed to say before collapsing onto the couch.

I came to myself sometime later, with the bushy face of Doctor Kane hanging over me. "It's all right," he was saying gently. "It's all right. You're going to be all right. Now listen carefully, Maisie. You're going into hospital; your baby's on the way. It's a little early, but you're going to be all right. You're going to be all right." . . .

I lay in hospital a week, and they were so kind to me, but I seemed to know from the beginning that I was going to lose the baby. When they eventually took him away from me, he had been dead for some little time. . . .

After I returned home, Gran came every day to see to me. But she left the house before Howard came in. May hadn't visited me in the hospital, nor did she come and see me at the house. I understood she wasn't well. And this was true, she wasn't well; she was so unwell that Howard spent most of his evenings with her.

For weeks after returning home, I couldn't pull myself together; my body seemed depleted and my mind in a very low state. If I saw Hamilton at all he was bedraggled, his tail between his legs, his head drooping, no shine to his coat. He was no help to me. And what was worrying me now was that my lip was jerking like it used to.

It was some time later when I went to see Doctor Kane. He had come to see me on several occasions, but the last time he visited me he said, "A walk won't do you any harm. Pop in next week." Poor Doctor Kane, I was to pop in every week for months on end, until he was to become sick of the sight of me and, candidly, I of him. . . .

On this particular visit, he said to me, "Now what I've got to tell you is going to be disappointing: you're made in such a way that you can't carry babies."

"Why not?" I said. "My body seems all right to me."

"Oh, your body's all right. It isn't your body really, at least it's a part of it, it's your blood."

"What?"

"I said, it's your blood."

"What's wrong with my blood?"

"You're what is called Rhesus negative."

"What?"

He took a long breath and said, "I said you are what is called Rhesus negative."

"I know what you said, but what does it mean?"

"Well, it's to do with monkeys."

"Wh . . . at?" As if I were imitating the creature, I rose up from the chair as if about to climb the wall. My whole body was stretched with indignation, until he said, "Get off your high horse —" It was odd how he always connected me up with a horse. "It's an experiment they did during the war with monkeys."

"And I've got the same type of blood?"

"No. Most women have an antigen in their blood which is also in the blood of a Rhesus monkey. You haven't such an antigen. I don't know a lot about it, but it does happen in such cases as yours that the blood of the mother and that of the child are not compatible, and so she is unable to carry the baby. Some women have had six, seven, eight miscarriages, trying to carry through, and failed."

"Monkeys?"

"Don't take on like that, girl. It's just a name. I've explained to you you've got no monkey blood in you. But still" — he gave a short laugh — "the fact of the presence of these antigens does open up a big question of evolution via the apes. Was there a Garden of Eden? Hell no; I plump for the monkey blood coming down through the ages."

163

"I . . . I won't be able to have children then?"

"As far as I can see now, my dear" — his voice was soft — "you would be able to conceive again, but it's the carrying of them. But you have one consolation, you're just one of thousands who are in the same boat. Under other circumstances I would suggest adoption, but not in yours, not the way you're placed."

Oh no, he was right. Certainly, there wouldn't be any adoption the way I was placed.

"How are things, any improvement?"

"I have a room to myself. I don't know how long it will last."

"I could have a talk with him. I think I should. You're in a very poor state of health at present, very low. Tell him I want to see him."

"I don't know whether he would come."

"Well you can tell him and we'll see." . . .

I told him. Surprisingly, he made no comment, and he went to the surgery. But when he returned later that night he came into the study where I was typing. He stood just within the doorway and there was a sneer on his face as he said in that flat toneless way he had when spewing obscenities at me,

164

"Monkeys. That explains it. My God, yes, that explains a lot. I always thought you should be in a zoo."

When he closed the door, not banging it, just drawing it slowly and softly into its place, I laid my head down in the crook of my arm on top of the machine, and the swelling in my chest burst up through my throat and the tears poured out of my eyes, nose and saliva out of my mouth, and from that great unfathomed depth of me there emerged a new pain that made me cry out to God and ask Him why He had put me into this world to make me the victim of such people as, first, my mother, and now this man. Wasn't it enough that He had made me plain to the point of ugliness, besides having deformed me. Why hadn't He gone the whole hog and made me mental, then I wouldn't have been aware of my state?

When I raised my head Hamilton was gazing at me. He didn't look like himself somehow: he was a horse and yet he wasn't; the white of his tail seemed to have spread all over him. He said quietly, You'll get your answer; just work at it.

I dried my eyes and, strangely, for the next few days I felt calm inside.

Then I met Bill.

I had been to a printer's on the outskirts of Bog's End. I found I could get a good quality typing paper cheaper there than I could from an ordinary stationer's. To get to the building I had to pass along the waterfront. I liked this walk. Before you got to the high dock wall you could glimpse the ships along the quayside, and, too, everything around this quarter seemed to be full of bustle.

I had bought three reams of paper and was making my way back along by the wall now when I heard the screeching of brakes and above that a pitiful cry of a wounded animal. I swung round and saw, some way behind me along the road, a small lorry had stopped. For a time, nobody got out of it. From where I stood I could see this dark bundle lying in the gutter writhing and whimpering. After I reached it, the man got down from his cab and, looking at me, he said, "The damn thing ran right under the wheel. It's a wonder it wasn't knocked flat." I had put my parcel down on the edge of the pavement and was now bending over the dog, yet afraid to touch it. I liked dogs, although I'd never had one of my own, and, remembering my mother's warning, never to stroke a stray dog, I stayed my hand. The animal tried to raise itself from the ground, then flopped back again, and from there turned its head and looked at me. It wasn't a nice looking dog; it had a sharp pointed face and a blunt head, and its dark coat had white patches on it.

Another voice now joined the driver's, saying, "Oh, it's that bloody animal, is it? He's been runnin' round here for the last three weeks. It's a wonder he hasn't caught it afore now. Somebody gettin' on one of the boats must have dumped it. A bull-terrier he is, isn't he?"

A bull-terrier. The name sounded ominous. Yet, as the animal continued to look at me I put my hand down and touched its head, and for a moment it stopped its whimpering.

"What are you going to do with it?" The voice was from above my head again, and another answered, "Knock it on the head. It would be a bloody kindness to knock it on the head, because nobody's been looking for a lost dog around here. And anyway, they don't go in for bull-terriers. Whippets more like."

"You can't do that." I turned to look up at the men. "It's only his foot. It could be attended to."

"Aye, but who's going to attend to it?"

I turned my head and saw that the animal

was still looking at me. What would Howard say if I took a beast like this home? Anyway, I couldn't take it home; it would have to go to a vet first.

"Is there a vet near?"

The second man answered, "Yes, there's one in Roland Street."

I looked at the driver and asked him, "Will you take him there?"

"What! Me? Look, I've got a job to do."

"I'm only asking you to carry him for me, or let me ride in your lorry with you. I'll . . . I'll have him on my knee."

The two men looked at each other; then the other man said, "Well, if you don't you'll have to report it, won't you? It doesn't matter when it's a cat, but when it's a dog I think you've got to report it. But if she wants to take over . . . well, let her."

This seemed sense to the lorry driver and so without further words, he stooped down and quite gently lifted the animal from the ground. Then looking at me, he said, "I do run into them. By God! I do run into them."

I knew he wasn't meaning running into dogs, but running into misfortunes.

The other man gave me a hoist up on to the seat, and when the driver put the dog on my knee I was amazed at the weight of him. I also thought it very strange that although he was lying at an angle, he turned his head and kept looking at me. It was as if there and then he had decided that he wasn't going to let me go.

When we reached the vet's the lorry driver helped me down from the cab, placed the dog in my arms again, then drove off without a word.

When eventually we met the vet, his approach to the problem was that stray dogs were a nuisance; they should be sent to the pound. Did I realize what I was taking on?

"What exactly do you mean?" I asked, and the reply I got was, "This is a stray dog, you say. Are you intending to keep him? If you want his foot seen to, and this will need an operation because the bones are shattered and the ligaments torn and he will be in plaster for some weeks and then need further attention, it is going to cost you money."

"I'm aware of that," I said.

"That's all right then," he said.

"Well, that's all you can do for now. Just leave your name and address with Miss Fennell, and then come back tomorrow and take him home."

I looked at the animal lying on the table. He was quiet now. I said, "Is he an old dog?"

"No, no. He's little more than a pup, I

should say. Not quite a year old."

"Really . . . that's nice."

He looked at me narrowly, and I, embarrassed, now said, "Well, what I mean is, he's not going to die shortly after the operation then? I . . . thought he might have been thrown out because he was so old."

"No, he's not old; but he's the runt of the litter I should say." My eyes questioned him, and he went on, "Legs too short for a bull-terrier and the body much too heavy. There's been a slip up somewhere, I think. Anyway, there's one thing certain, miss, he'll never win any prizes for you."

"That won't matter to me. I've never won any prizes myself. Good-afternoon."

Why on earth had I said that?

As I gave his secretary my name and address, I saw him looking through the top half of the glass door at me. I was in two minds about him: I didn't know whether I liked him or not. But it didn't seem to matter. Yet at the same time it did: if he was a nice man, he'd be careful in his treatment of that poor animal; if he wasn't, and knowing the dog was a stray, he might hash the whole business. . . .

Mr Biggs turned out to be a nice man, a very nice man. We were to become well acquainted over the coming years.

It wasn't until I reached home that I discovered I had left the new packet of typing paper on the kerb.

I wasn't going to mention the dog to Howard. It was to be a *fait accompli*: I'd install him in the house and that would be that. . . . Or would it? But he happened to be at home when I arrived at four o'clock, which was most surprising. I didn't ask why he was there because, looking at my blood-stained light grey coat, he said, "And what's happened to you?" in a tone that indicated that he wasn't interested but would just like to know out of curiosity.

"A dog got run over. I took it to the vet's."

"Huh! If you concerned yourself with humans it would be more to the point. May's ill. But do you care? Oh, no. You go to the rescue of stray dogs. Or sit talking to that moron of a council house woman." Then, turning swiftly from me, he said, "I'm bringing May here," only to turn swiftly towards me again, and, his arm out-stretched, his finger almost touching my face, say, "And don't you put any obstacle in the way. May's ill. She could die. She's coming here."

I hadn't seen May for a fortnight; the last occasion only for a few minutes. She had been very quiet, not her usual self. And so I

171

said now, with some concern in my voice, "What is the matter with her?"

I saw him swallow deeply. It was also obvious that he was very worried, and it was a moment before he brought out, "Leukemia. She's got leukemia."

"Oh no."

I had a very guilty feeling as I hurried from the room. I hadn't realized she had been so ill. I had thought that since the business of the money, she had been putting it on as an excuse for not cooking the meals any more, sort of letting me get on with it, and making a hash of it, as Gran had once said. . . .

I was shocked at the sight of her when he brought her into the hall. I went up to her and said softly, "I . . . I have your room ready, May." And she said, "Thank you." Her voice was quiet; all her boisterousness seemed to have disappeared.

Up in the bedroom, when I went to help her undress, he pressed me aside, not roughly, but firmly, saying, "I'll see to her." I hesitated and he turned and looked at me and repeated slowly, "I'll see to her." And on this I walked out. I thought it was odd.

But during the next four weeks, which was all she had before she died, I learned that if he loved anybody, it was her. Not once during that time did he go near the bottle room. From the time he came in, he fetched and carried and saw to her till he went to bed. During the day my own hands were more than full, for I also had Bill to see to.

So changed did I find May that, the day after her arrival, I felt I could tell her about Bill, because that's what I had christened him in my mind, and I asked her if she would mind if I slipped out and brought him home. And she answered quietly, "No, of course not. I'm perfectly all right."

I was confronted by Bill standing on three legs and what looked like a thick white stick. The plaster cast, the vet said, would have to remain on for some time, but I had to bring him back next week.

Bill could walk in a dot-and-carry-three fashion. The funny part about it was, he kept stopping and looking back at his leg, then looking up at me, as much to say, what are you going to do about it?

When I got him home I made a bed in the clothes-basket for him, and gently pressed him into it and told him to stay. I had taken two steps away from it when he got up. The "stay" business went on for about five minutes before he got the message.

I then ran up to May to see how she was.

She seemed to be sitting in bed exactly how I had left her, her hands on top of the cover, her head propped up against the pillow. She said, "Did you get him?" And I said, "Yes. But he won't cause any trouble."

Surprisingly, she now said, "I've always wanted a dog, but never got round to having one. Perhaps you'll bring him up sometime?"

"Oh yes." I smiled broadly at her and again said, "Oh, yes." That she should like Bill would surely give him an entry ticket to get past Howard.

That evening, Howard came in the back way hurriedly, then stopped dead on the sight of the anything but beautiful three-legged-and-one-white-stumped dog. I'd heard the back door open as I came downstairs, and I raced to the kitchen, there to see him and Bill surveying each other, mutual dislike evident in both their faces. And Bill was giving voice to his in a low growl. As I bent and patted him I looked up at Howard and said, "I had to bring him home."

"Well, he's not staying here, not that thing."

"He is."

"I said, no."

"You can say what you like, Howard, he's staying. And May wants to see him. She tells me she's always wanted a dog, and . . . and she wants to see him."

"May said she wanted to see him?"

"Yes. Ask her yourself."

For the evening meal I had cooked some lamb chops, potatoes, and vegetables, and I had May's tray ready to take up when Howard entered the kitchen. Looking down on it, he said, "Where's the gravy?" And I said, "Well, I didn't think you would need gravy with chops; I've . . . I've put some butter on the potatoes."

"Don't need gravy with chops! . . . Stupid!" He drew in a quick sharp breath, then grabbed the tray from me and went out.

And I stood and repeated, "Stupid!"

The following morning I took Bill up to see May. I had a job to get him up the stairs. It was evident he had never had to manipulate stairs before and we were only half-way up them when I sat down and laughed; and he licked my face and gave one whoof of a bark as if he was enjoying the joke. But I silenced him, saying, "Shh! Shh! No barking in the house."

When May saw him, she smiled and, looking at me, she said, "You do pick them, don't you, Maisie?"

"I couldn't do anything else," I said; "I was so sorry for him." And then I added, "It isn't so much me picking them, as they picking me." She stared at me for a long time, and then, her head drooping, she said, "Yes, you're right, they picking you. I've done a lot of thinking lately, Maisie. . . . You know I'm dying?"

"Oh no! Oh no!"

"Don't be silly." Her voice sounded as of old; but she paused before saying, "I've faced up to a lot of things, and one of them is, I know I did wrong by you."

I stared at her silently. Then she went on, "I liked your house . . . this house. I never expected to die in it though. The main thing was, I wanted security for Howard; I felt he hadn't had his rightful chance in life. I was wrong. But there, the excuse I have is that so many mothers are wrong, and in a way I've always looked upon myself as Howard's mother, because I've mothered him from the day he was born. I think it's because I knew early on that he'd be the only man in my life. You see" — she moved her head slowly now — "I've . . . I've never been able to like men, except . . . except Howard. But I'm not blind to his faults. And Maisie —" She put her big bony hand out towards me, and I lifted mine from where it was resting on Bill's head and let her clasp it, and now, her words halting and her eyes cast down, she said, "I . . . I know you've had a hard time with Howard. I didn't imagine he would be like that. You are a girl who would have responded to kindness, been grateful for it. I recognize that, and I thought that, once you were married, he would see the other side of you, the kindness, and . . . and would therefore come to . . . well, care for you in a way. But from what I understand now, I fear that can never be. And . . . and I feel full of remorse for saddling you . . . for saddling you both with each other, when you are so unsuited."

I could not look at her. I turned my gaze down on Bill. His eyes were on me. And now she said, "We made a mistake about you. I . . . I imagined you were very amenable. We didn't realize that behind your sort of inoffensive manner there is a strong character."

I now raised my eyes to her, my mouth was slightly agape. I didn't know I had a strong character: I had looked upon myself as weak, easily led, rather inane. Her head drooped back on the pillows now as if she was tired, and I rose slowly from the bed and was about to release her hand when her grip tightened slightly and she turned and looked at me again as she said, "I shouldn't say this, but I must: stand up to Howard. He'll respect you more for it. If . . . if you let him get the better of you, he will treat you like . . . like . . ." She closed her eyes and swallowed deeply, and I heard myself murmur, "It's all right. It's all right, May. Don't worry. But . . . but thank you." She opened her eyes and looked at me, and I repeated, "Thank you, for talking to me as you have. And . . . and if I can help it, you'll not die; I'll look after you." I bent towards her, smiling slightly now as I ended, "I'll even cook you a tasty meal." She gave me an answering smile and said, "That'll be the day."

I laughed outright now. "Just you wait," I said. "Just you wait. I'll make a hash that I won't make a hash of."

I found I had to get out of the room quickly. There was no need to call Bill; he followed at my heels. And out on the landing, I stood with my hand pressed tightly against my cheek, the tears were blocking my throat, and I muttered aloud, "Please, God, don't let her die. We could be friends now. I could see that, we could be friends. She understands the situation. Please, please, don't let her die. . . ."

During the following days that were left to her I learned to make junket, egg custard, and light pastry, and I served her these appetisingly. But as time went on she ate less and less.

The atmosphere of the house had changed completely. Different people from the terrace came in to see her. And Doctor Kane visited her every day. It was during the middle of the fourth week that, after coming downstairs, he put his hand on my elbow and led me into the sitting-room, and there he said, "I don't think it will be long now."

I couldn't speak for a moment; then I said, "Shouldn't she be in hospital getting special treatment? Couldn't they do something there?"

"No, they couldn't do anything for her now that isn't being done here. I would have had her in weeks ago, but she refused. There's only one good thing that has come out of this sad business; she speaks very well of you now. Strange that, isn't it?"

"Yes, yes, it is," I said.

"It was she who pushed you into this marriage. I know that and she knows it. But in her own way she's been trying to make amends, although if that'll have any effect on her dear brother, I don't know. We'll have to see what happens when she goes, won't we?"

I made no answer to this, just stood looking into his face. I seemed to know every hair on it. I had seen it every week for months now across his desk, mostly on a Monday morning. It was something I had come to look forward to. I knew all the regulars who visited the surgery. I had very little to say to them, but I listened a lot, and the snatches that came to me made me want to laugh, even when I didn't feel like it. There was one woman in particular who, when she sat beside me, would say, "You here again?" Hamilton laughed his head off about that. He would sit on his haunches in the middle of the round table where the out of date magazines were and rock with laughter. You here again? he would mimic. She would then give me a running commentary on her ailments: " 'Tis the neck of me bladder. He says it wants seeing to. Me water's like nobody's business, 'cos I've had it all taken away, you know. Hysterectomy, you know; yours is only nerves. By! you're lucky. But you're always here. Men don't understand. He said to me, me husband,

'Well, what about it, are you or aren't you? Come on, make up your mind; it's either that or I go to the club.' So I said, 'All right,' and we got down to it and papered the front room. But I didn't feel like it."

On that occasion the women on the other side of her spluttered and choked. They had evidently placed the wrong construction on her words.

I don't think it had dawned upon the woman that she was as frequent a visitor as I was or else she wouldn't have known I had been there so often.

As I now stood looking at him, there came a scratching at the door, and when I went hurriedly and opened it and Bill marched in, the doctor turned his gaze down on him. "Who's he?" he said. "Where did he spring from?"

"It's Bill," I said; "he's a bull-terrier. I've had him for some weeks. I keep him in the kitchen. He must have got out."

He stared down at Bill. Then looking at me, he said, "You could have picked a better looking one. Where did you find him?" When I told him, he smiled and said, "Maisie, you're a funny girl."

"Funny ha-ha, funny peculiar, or just funny?"

"A bit of all three, I should say."

Yes, he would.

At that moment Hamilton appeared. He was standing in the corner of the room, and I thought, Yes, if I were to tell him about you, it would be the middle one that would head my certificate. At times I longed to tell someone about Hamilton, just to see what effect it would have on them. Would they think I was barmy?

Definitely, they would. Well, I didn't feel barmy, and I wasn't barmy. Then why did I talk to Hamilton?

I didn't know, not really. But talk to him I did. I felt I always would. I saw him now walk slowly across the room and stand by my side, facing the doctor. I say, stand by my side, he seemed enormous, my head only came to his shoulder.

"What's the matter?"

I blinked at him, "Nothing."

"You worried about something besides . . . ?" He jerked his head backwards.

"Not really."

"Not really? What do you mean? Has he been at his games again?"

"Oh, no, no. He spends all his time, every evening, with May until very late. I . . . I think he cares deeply for her."

He turned now and walked up the sitting room towards the door, saying, "A man like that cares for just one person, Maisie, and the quicker you realize it the better. That person is number one."

I wanted to say, you're wrong there, he cares for May, but I remained silent. At the door, he said, "If you see any definite change, give me a ring, straightaway."

"I will. Thank you."

I wasn't in the room with her when she died. It happened suddenly one evening. I went upstairs with a tray on which there was a glass of hot milk. I opened the door, and there I saw Howard sitting on a chair, his body bent forward, his face buried in the coverlet near her limp hand.

I didn't speak; there was nothing I could say. Her face looked white and thin; the flesh had dropped off her of late; her cheek-bones stretched the skin. I went quietly out, taking the tray with me, and down in the kitchen I sat on the chair, my elbow on the table. I put my hand over my eyes, and found myself muttering, "Good-bye, May. Good-bye, May. I'm sorry we didn't get to know each other better earlier on. But you're all right now. You're safe now. Good-bye, May. Good-bye, May."

I had to make an effort to stop myself talking. It was as if she was in the room. As I made to get up I had to push Bill aside. His muzzle had been against my knee, and I looked down at him and said, "She liked you. Yes, she liked you. That was something, wasn't it?"

I went to the phone and told the doctor. He came almost directly, and when half an hour later he left, he stood on the doorstep and looked at me and said, "He's all yours now, Maisie. He's all yours now. It's up to you how you deal with him. The only thing is, don't let him trample on you, or you'll be finished for good."

I stood in the hall and looked up the stairs. May's presence seemed to have gone from the house. There was only his in it now, and in this moment I asked myself how I was going to prevent him trampling on me, because I didn't think that anything May might have said to him before she died would make any difference in our association.

CHAPTER 2

It seemed that I was wrong, because for the first few weeks after May's funeral he treated me almost like a human being. During this time I did my best to make the meals attractive. Usually before, whenever

184

we had eaten together no word had passed between us; now, he began to talk, but it was all about May. I didn't mind that in the least, as long as he talked, and normally, without that dreadful sneer in his voice. May, he told me, had been everything to him, mother, sister, friend. He didn't know what he was going to do without her. When I said, "You will have to go back to your collecting and take up tennis again," he nodded at me, saying, "Yes, yes, that's what I must do."

When this situation had gone on for about four weeks I began to think he was right, regarding companionship, as he had suggested before we were married. Perhaps, I thought, if he continued in this way I could forget what had happened and life would be tolerable, more than tolerable, perhaps enjoyable. He would have his pastimes and I would have mine.

I was trying to catch up on the orders for typing, and I was also beginning to write myself, not just scribbles, not just about Hamilton, but little pieces about different things that had happened to me. Like the day I took Bill to the vet's to get his plaster off.

Only one unusual thing happened on our way there: we passed some buskers, and Bill stopped and, putting his head back, howled to the accompaniment of a man playing a fiddle and another a mouth-organ. A third was going round with a cap. Try as I might, I couldn't get Bill away from them as long as they continued to play, and a lot of people stopped, and the man who was playing the mouth-organ shook with laughter and his mouth became so full of spittle he couldn't go on playing.

As soon as they stopped playing, Bill allowed me to lead him on. But the man who had played the mouth-organ called after me, "Will you loan him to us, miss?" which caused the crowd to laugh.

I was always addressed as Miss, no one ever took me for Missis.

As I led him along in his dot-and-carry-three step I thought, Oh, my goodness! If he starts that every time he hears music, we are in for something. Yet I'd had the radio on and there had been music and he hadn't reacted in this way. I was to learn that he was only affected by reed or wind music such as the flute, the mouth-organ, and yes, brass instruments; the piano and the violin didn't seem to take his fancy.

I was brought to another halt at a butcher's shop. Bill tried to tug me into the shop, and I kept saying, "No, no, Bill." The customers in the shop turned round and laughed, and the butcher, leaning over his block, shouted to me, "If you want him cut up, bring him in." And, of course, this caused more laughter.

When I eventually got him into the surgery after a slight contretemps in the waiting-room when Bill took a strong dislike to an Alsatian and then showed his preference for a cat whose head was poking out of a basket. The owner of the cat laughed when Bill wanted to lick her charge. She said she had never seen anything like it. Nor had the owner of the Alsatian. Her dog never fought, she said, he was as quiet as a lamb. I nearly asked her why he was baring his teeth at Bill. Of course. Bill wasn't only baring his teeth at the moment, every stiff hair on his body seemed erect. I was to learn that Bill loved people, but didn't like any of his own kind. And, too, being contrary, he tolerated cats. Once he brought a young kitten home in his mouth while the mother was trying to tear him to bits. I think Bill was a male who should never have been a male. There are a lot of poor souls like him kicking about. Anyway, once the plaster was off his leg, Bill turned round and looked at his new paw as if it was something that didn't belong to him. The vet told me I must massage the limb every day. I promised to do so, then I paid his bill, which staggered me somewhat and made me realize that it was as expensive for a dog to be ill as it was for a human being.

Outside, Bill continued to walk as he had been doing with his dot-and-carry-three step until, stopping abruptly, he looked round at his back leg and slowly stretched himself; then his leg went out, his head went up, his body stiffened, and he was off.

It happened so quickly I didn't know what had hit me. I was hanging on to the end of the lead and he was racing ahead like a greyhound after a rabbit. When we came to the open quay, men stopped working to watch our progress. We had passed the turning that I usually took for home. Then as quickly as he had started he stopped, and at a lamp post. Like a top spinning, I wound round it before I, too, stopped; then I leant against it, gasping, and all I could say was, "Oh, you bad dog. Oh, you bad dog."

A man approached us from along the quay. He had jumped up from a small boat, and I could see that he was shaking with laughter. And when he stood in front of me, he said, "Enjoy your trip, miss?" Then looking down at Bill, his grin spreading from ear to ear, he said, "I shouldn't be surprised to see you in the greyhound stadium shortly, lad." But then, his glee subsiding a little, he asked with some concern, "You all right, miss?"

"Yes; a little out of puff."

"I'd say. I thought you were going to take off. I've never seen anything so funny afore. You pay to go to the pictures, but what you see for free on this waterfront is nobody's business. If —" he started to shake again and spluttered, "If you could have seen yourself, lass, you would have died."

"I felt I was going to."

This seemed to add to his amusement. Bill, in the meantime, had been examining the lamp post from all angles, twisting his body back and forward in order to get the right position to leave his mark. I now pulled hard on his lead, saying, "Come on. Come on, Bill." And as the man repeated, "Bill? You call him, Bill? Well, he's well named," what seemed to be the last straw happened: I gave one sharp tug, and off came his collar.

If the man hadn't been there and eager to help, everything would have gone smoothly. I would have said, "Stay! Bill," and Bill would have stayed. But the man made a grab at him and Bill, likely remembering other men who had made grabs at him before he had come under my protection, took to his heels, crossed the road and scooted back in the direction from which we had just come.

I didn't stop to say anything to the man, but took to my heels. Did I hear him laughing? It didn't matter. I ran, yelling, "Bill! Bill! Come back! Bill!" When I saw him turn the corner into the road we should have taken on our way home, I thought, Good. Good. He's making for home. But when I got to the corner, there was no sign of him. The road was a long one, and I was sure he couldn't have reached the end of it. Then I remembered the butcher's shop.

When I arrived gasping at the door, there he was, sitting on the sawdust, looking up at the butcher. There were three customers in the shop and they were keeping well away from him. The butcher looked at me and said, "He's determined to be chopped up, this one."

As I grabbed him and thrust the collar over his head, he didn't even bother to rise to his feet; he just sat looking up at the butcher.

"What do you feed him on?" said the butcher.

"Dog food, tinned dog food."

"Huh! That dog's got sense; he knows

what's best. Do you want a pound of scraps?"

"Oh, yes. Yes, please."

I got the pound of scraps, then handed the butcher the sixpence he had asked for, and now, tugging at Bill, I said, "Come on. Come on." But Bill just looked at me and turned his gaze once more on the butcher.

Without a smile on his face now, the butcher said, "He doesn't want meat, he wants chopping up. He's suicide bent, that dog." There was a deep chuckle in his throat and the three women, still keeping their distance, gave nervous sniggers.

"I wonder if a bone will do it?" He now turned to the bench behind him and, taking up a marrow bone about a foot long, he came round the block and said, "This what you want?" Whereupon Bill stood up and took one quick step towards the butcher who, taking two quick steps back, thrust the bone at me, saying, "It's all yours."

When I handed Bill the bone he took it quite gently from me; then turned his thick stumpy body about and led me from the shop. At the door, I pulled him to a temporary halt, saying over my shoulder, "Thank you. Thank you." And the butcher called after me, "You're welcome, but don't bring him back."

I wish I could remember all the remarks that were passed about us as we walked across the market place, Bill carrying that huge marrow bone and still doing his dot-and-carry-three walk and I almost slinking by his side.

At home, I tied him up in the yard on a long piece of rope and there he sat for the next two hours gnawing happily at that bone, after he had licked the marrow out of it as far as his tongue would reach.

After making myself a cup of tea, I sat down and reviewed the events of the past hour. I wished I had somebody to relate them to. It was too late in the afternoon to go to Gran's; and anyway, I'd wasted enough time today. I must get on with the typing. But wouldn't it be nice, I thought, if there was a man coming in for his tea and I could tell him what had happened. Yes, yes, it would have been very nice . . .

A man did come in for his tea and I didn't tell him what had happened, but the dog became the topic of our conversation and, in a way, the beginning of the bribery. Or would you call it blackmail? Whatever it was, it meant if I wanted to keep Bill and, too, something of my personal privacy, I had to part with money.

As soon as he sat down to his tea I knew

there was something in the wind. Since May had gone, at least up till now, he hadn't grumbled at his meals, but, looking at the sausage, egg and chips I had cooked, he said, "Doesn't your mind go beyond fries?"

"I thought you liked sausage and eggs?"

To this he answered, "You can get too much even of a good thing if you have a repeat pattern every week: sausage and egg, bacon and egg, egg and chips, scrambled eggs, boiled eggs. And when I'm on, there's another thing I'm going to tell you: this kitchen smells of that dog. The whole house smells of him. Get rid of him."

The fork almost sprang out of my hand as my whole body jerked in the chair, and I said, "No, I'll not! I'll not get rid of Bill."

"Well, if you won't I will, by the simple process of leaving the back door open and letting him go. And he'll go straight back to where he came from, the dock front. Dogs, like people, always revert to their beginnings."

From between tight lips I said, "That's a pity."

"What do you mean?"

"I was just agreeing with you about people reverting."

His face reddened. The implication of my words seemed to have struck home. I knew nothing about his real early beginnings, only May's reference to the nice life they had led in Gosforth, which I surmised now must have been only a brief interlude.

Following the meal, he went upstairs and changed, and when he came down again he was ready for outdoors in a new suit, and over his arm was what looked like a new light overcoat. Well, he was in the trade, it wouldn't cost him all that much, I thought. Grudgingly, I had to admit that he looked very smart, and he surprised me when, going out of the door, he turned and looked at me saying, quietly, "Why do we always have to get off on the wrong foot?"

It was the nearest to an apology he had ever come. He didn't wait for an answer and went out.

I was surprised still further when, two hours later, he returned home. He came straight into the study where I was working, another unusual procedure, and, sitting down in the big leather chair that I understood had been my grandfather's favourite seat, he looked at me for a moment before he said, hesitantly, "I've got to talk to you."

I waited, not knowing what was coming. Here was a different man, likely the one May had known.

He said, still hesitantly, "I've been offered

the chance of something big. You know, ours is a very good class shop and Mr Hempies has the idea of opening a branch in Durham or somewhere near, and . . . and if he does, that will mean he will go and manage that one most of the time as he lives out that way, and the management here will be going . . . Paul Richardson, he's been there longer than me and he's mostly over the cutters and the stitchers, but he's dying for the job. Well, I might as well come to the point, it means buying oneself in, sort of partnership like."

Oh, so this was it.

"You see with the money I got for the furniture and the bit I'd saved, all I can raise is two hundred and fifty five pounds. And from what I understand, well . . ." He uncrossed his knees, and then crossed them again the other way before ending. "I'd need a thousand." There was a long pause before he said, "What about it, Maisie?"

"I'm sorry," I replied. "You know what I did with my money; I haven't got it. All I've got is the bit I earn from my typing." And, I nearly added, the measly bit you give me for housekeeping, which was three pounds a week.

His face was straight and tight now as he said, "You can get it if you want to. She'll give it back to you."

"I . . . I couldn't ask her."

"Look." He suddenly sprang to his feet and was leaning forward now, his hands gripping the ends of the desk, his face close to mine. "It'll make all the difference to . . . to everything, to my way of life and to your way of life. Yes, to your way of life." And he nodded his head at me now. "Just think it over.

"I've got till the end of the month to make the decision." He straightened up and turned about, but took only one step before he stopped and looked down on Bill who was sitting by my side. And he held this position for some seconds and it spoke louder than any words he might have uttered concerning Bill's future if I didn't comply with his demands.

Two hours later I was on the point of sleep when the light flashed on, and he came to the bed and said, "Move over."

"No . . . please."

"Move over!"

When I didn't, he gripped my short arm and almost lifted me out of the bed . . .

Fifteen minutes later I was alone with my head buried in the pillow.

The following day I was sitting on Gran's

couch and she was putting into words my thoughts of Howard.

"The bloody blackmailing swine. That's all it is, blackmail. Now what'll happen, lass, if you give in to him this time? There'll come another and another until he has the whole damn lot out of you."

"He won't. He won't."

"How can you say he won't when you're breakin' under it now? Seven hundred and fifty pounds! Eeh, my God! . . . Well, it's your money, and you seem determined to let him have it, but, lass, I would have some agreement in writing, mind, that he leaves you alone, an' the dog an' all."

That was an idea. But how could I do it? Ask him to sign a paper saying that he wasn't to come near my person for such and such a time, nor molest my dog? Yes, yes, I could do that. Yes, I could. I could type out a statement and get him to sign it. Why shouldn't I? And stipulate a year . . . no, two . . . Or three? No, I'd better just leave it at two. Two years is a long time; something could have happened by then. Yes, that's what I would do. I said to Gran, "You've given me an idea, Gran. I'll write out a statement and get him to sign it."

"Aye, and you can add that you'll expose him and take him to court if he doesn't keep his word to whatever you demand. My! I'm glad our Georgie isn't here, 'cos if he was Mr Howard Stickle would have to pick out his teeth from his guernsey. But, by the way, I forgot to tell you, he says he's comin' this way with a load a week come Tuesday. Eeh! I can't wait, lass. It's months since I clapped eyes on him."

"I haven't heard from him for ages. Did you get a letter?"

"No, you know he's hardly any hand at writing letters. He made an effort at first like, but that soon stopped. You know yourself the kind of thing he writes: 'I hope it leaves you as it finds me at present.' And what I know about our George, I've thought to meself when I've read that, oh, lad, those days are past for me."

She put her head back and let out a laugh, and I laughed with her. It was so seldom I got the opportunity to laugh with anyone these days. I used to laugh inside a lot when Hamilton got up to his antics, but Hamilton's antics these past weeks had been anything but funny. Most times, when I encountered him, he was lying down and looked very shaggy and had little to say, except as a sort of recrimination: Why can't you stand on your own feet? Or throw the dinner at him, right in his face?

Well, things like that weren't very helpful and wouldn't solve any problems, and I told him so. My salvation was: I had to become strong inside, self-reliant; I had to become somebody that could ride above people like Howard and Mrs McVitie next door who was always complaining about Bill, not that he barked, but that he howled.

I had told Howard he could have the money on one condition, and when he enquired what that was, I said, that he had to sign a note to the effect that he had received the money and on my terms.

"Well, let's have a look at your terms," he had said. And when he had read the sheet of paper I passed to him, his mouth fell into a gape. Then he used a common phrase, as common as Gran Carter ever used: "You're not so green as you're cabbage-looking," he said; and then added, "But you must have sense enough to know that this doesn't hold water; you are my wife."

"It'll hold water," I said quietly.

My tone caused his eyes to narrow, and he said, "That old witch put you up to this, didn't she? But anyway, what's her word?"

"It doesn't only rest with that old witch, as you call her, there's another who is aware of the transaction."

His face now took on a tight look as he said, "Which other? Who?"

"That's my business. I just want to impress upon you that this will hold, even though" — I paused — "it should come to the push and is taken to court."

"My God! As our May said to me, you hadn't been hoodwinked so much by us as us by you. But don't get too clever, because there's . . ."

"You were going to say ways and means, weren't you? You haven't got the cheque yet, Howard."

He drooped his head now as he muttered, "I can never understand why we go for each other like we do."

Instantly, I saw Hamilton: he looked huge and sleek and his lips were well back from his teeth as he said, The slimy bugger!

Eeh! dear, dear. I was getting as bad as Gran. I must stop myself using swear-words in my mind. I had never used one verbally in my life, not even a weak damn. It was very disturbing when I swore inside.

I said now, "Are you going to sign it?" And for an answer he took up a pen and wrote his name, in an almost illegible form, across the bottom of the page, and as I looked at it I said, "That's no good, Howard. That name could be anybody's. Sign it legibly."

I saw his whole body rear; but he snatched up the pen again and signed the paper clearly this time.

When he stood up, he held out his hand and said, "The cheque."

"I'll give it to you tomorrow," I said, "after I've lodged this in a safe place."

The following day, when I handed him the cheque, signed by Gran, he stood looking down at it as if slightly amazed. He did not say thank you, not even in a sarcastic tone, but turned round and went out.

Three days later he said to me, "I've got it; I'm manager. And Mr Hempies has asked me over for the week-end to . . . his place. He's a widower, you know, and getting on. You don't know what it might lead to."

Some days later, as I was walking down the street, Mrs Nelson came to her door and remarked on the weather; then she added, "I hear your husband's been made manager of Hempies'. It's a good position that. You're very lucky, you know. You're a very lucky girl to have a man like that."

I had Bill on the lead, and I let him tug me away without answering. . . . Lucky to have a man like that! Did anybody know what went on behind the closed doors in this terrace? Or, for that matter, behind all the doors in Fellburn and Newcastle and

Sunderland, on and on down the river and over the whole country, over the whole world? Did anyone really know how people reacted to each other in their own homes? Everybody seemed to have a face that they put on for other people. Who would think, watching Mr Howard Stickle go out every morning in his smart tailored suit, carrying his brief-case — oh yes, he carried a brief-case now, as also he left home a quarter of an hour earlier and got a different bus into the middle of the town — who would have thought that he was a coarse, dirty, cruel individual, and that small mouth of his could utter words that were so vile they made you sick to listen to them. Very definitely, no one in this terrace.

Then Bill took ill; well, not exactly ill, but there appeared great wet patches on his coat. The hair disappeared and the skin became mattery. I washed these parts in disinfectant and put salve on. But to no avail; they spread. So I took him to the P.D.S.A., because, there, sixpence on the plate would cover the advice I needed, whereas the fee from the vet's could run into shillings, and my shillings were very scarce these days. I couldn't stretch the three pounds Howard threw on the kitchen table every week to cover the groceries and the window cleaner and such like, let alone the bills, and so I had more often than not to supplement it with my earnings from the typing.

The P.D.S.A. attendant gave me a bottle of liquid and told me to apply it to the dog's coat.

If he had seen the result of the application he would never, I'm sure, have handed out another bottle of whatever it was, because the first dab of it on Bill's bare flesh nearly sent him berserk. He raced round the kitchen and tried to get out of the door; but, as I told him, it was for his own good, and so I clutched him tightly to me as I aimed to dab the stuff onto his writhing body. I didn't find out till long afterwards that I was applying a strong carbolic.

The patches got so large as to become evident to passers-by when we went out walking, and they shook their heads at this poor dog; in fact, a couple, strolling in the park, one day remarked, "You should have that animal put down. He must be in pain."

I couldn't bear the idea of putting Bill down. I'd do anything rather than put him down. He was my only contact, the only thing I could touch, hold, cuddle. And he liked being cuddled. With his head tucked into my shoulder, I would hold him and talk to him like I would to a child.

Then I had myself to cope with. I started to come out in spots; well, not quite spots, it was more like a rash. It started on my hands, covered my fingers, and there were bits on my forehead.

I visited the doctor again.

He looked at my hair, then said, "It's dandruff."

"Dandruff?" I was indignant. "It can't be dandruff, I wash my hair every week."

"All right, it isn't dandruff. If you know what it is, or isn't, why come seeking my advice? I've got a roomful of numskulls out there who *don't* know what's wrong with them, so you're wasting my time . . . I'll write you a prescription for ointment," he ended tartly.

I applied the ointment for a fortnight, but it only seemed to aggravate my rash and soon my whole body became unbearable; and when my face became covered and I could hardly see out of my eyes, there I was in the surgery again.

"God in heaven! What's happened to you?" he said.

"I don't know. It's all over me," I said.

"Been mixing with foreigners?" He peered at me.

"Mixing with foreigners?" My voice went high. I'd never mixed with anybody, never mind foreigners. "Why should you think I've been mixing with foreigners?" I said.

"Well," he barked at me, "for the simple reason I haven't seen a rash like this before." He tentatively turned my head to the side, then said again, "My God! You can't put a pin between them. Painful?"

"Yes, and very irritating. I want to scratch."

"You haven't been abroad? No, no, of course you haven't. Let me look at your arms. Take your clothes off."

I took my clothes off.

"In the name of goodness!" he said. "Well, well, what have we here? What have we here? Put your clothes on."

I put my clothes on; then I sat down and watched him pick out one book after another from his bookshelf. When he took out a very thick tome, he put it on the table to the side of me and as he flicked the pages I could see diagrams of people in all poses, and he kept talking at me: "You haven't been handling any foreign substance, or eating foreign foods like these package things?"

"No."

"And sure you haven't been in contact with anybody . . . well, I mean with somebody who's been abroad? There are carriers, you know."

"No, I've hardly been out of the house these last three weeks. Just to take Bill to the P.D.S.A. He's got mange, and his hair's dropped out and . . ."

His hand remained poised over a page. He turned his head very slowly towards me and stared at me for quite a long time; and then his fingers began flicking the pages over at a great rate. When he found what he apparently wanted, he stopped and began to read. After a moment he straightened up, ran his hands through his thick hair that seemed all a part of his face, and, his voice awe filled, he said, "You've got mange. Trust you. You've got mange, woman. There's only one in a million humans contract mange, but you would have to be that one. You've got mange."

"What!"

"I said, you've got mange."

"Mange?" I stood up. *"I've got mange?"*

I was feeling my face now, my fingers patting it.

"Well, you've just said you've been nursing your dog with mange, and his hair's dropped out. It's lucky for you that yours hasn't." He closed his eyes tightly, screwed them up, put his head back and held his brow for a moment before, his face returning to normal, he said, "Oh, Maisie, Maisie, what next?"

Yes, what next. "Well, there's one good thing," I said, "you can't put this down to wind, can you?"

I saw a flicker pass over his face, and, his thick hairy lips moving one over the other, he went back behind his desk and sat down, saying, "You don't believe about the wind, do you? That you can give yourself indigestion and all kind of stomach pains by swallowing wind."

"I'll believe anything after this . . . mange!"

He was now writing on a pad; then he said, "Sheep-dip."

"What?"

He straightened up, sighed, then drew the air back quickly into his lungs. "Maisie," he said, "you've got the unfortunate habit of using that word, 'what', and in such a way that must be irritating to anyone who's got to listen to it all the time. It's irritating to me, and I only hear it now and again, at least on a Monday morning."

"Well!" I was bridling now. *"Well!"* I found myself almost glaring at him. And there was Hamilton in his usual position when in the surgery, with his feet on the back of the doctor's chair, nodding at me and encourag-

ing me; and so I went on, "Wouldn't you say *what* if somebody was writing out a prescription for you to put on your face and your body and they said, 'Sheep-dip,' just like that. *Sheep-dip.*"

"Maisie," he said, "I suppose I'll have to explain to you. The book doesn't say sheep-dip, but this prescription does a similar job; mange is caused by a mite, and sheep-dip is used to cleanse sheep of vermin, and like them you should be dipped in it. I'm giving you a big bottle of it, at least the chemist will. Now, take it home and cover yourself from head to foot with it, and I mean exactly that. And don't wear any clothes for three days. And you'd better buy a distemper brush to put it on with."

"Wh . . . at!"

"*What!* You heard what I said, buy a distemper brush, a three inch one would do. And I repeat don't wear any clothes for three days, just a loose kimono or something like that. Then have a bath. And if you've done the job properly you'll be rid of your mange. If not, you'll have to start all over again. Now, do as I say and don't leave any parts bare." He paused. "And remember that. It's important."

"You're not joking? You expect me to do that?"

"Joking? woman. Have I time to joke" — he pointed to the door — "with that menagerie out there waiting to invade? Joking? Good gracious! girl, have some sense. I never joke."

As we stared at each other, there appeared on the screen of my mind a scene: I saw a farmyard, and in it a trough full of sheep-dip, and there I was, starkers, being prodded through it by grinning yokels. I took up the prescription from the desk, turned without another word and went out. I made for Gran's; she was looking after Bill.

"Mange?" Gran squealed. "Never! lass. God Almighty! What'll happen to you next? *Mange.* And all through that bloody beast. I'd get rid of him. I would, I'd get rid of him. You've never known a minute's peace since you got him."

"Gran," I said slowly, "I never knew what companionship was before I got him. And I can tell you this, if he was to get smallpox and leprosy I still wouldn't do away with him."

She looked at me for some seconds; then she said quietly, "I'm sorry, lass. I know what it must be like for you, loneliness, I mean. Here's me gets out and about, yet when I come back in the evenin' and I know our Georgie isn't comin' in half-bottled, or so bottled that he's popping his cork, I sit down here and I can tell you, lass, I feel very sorry for meself. So what in the name of God you must feel like, I don't know. Aw" — she went to pat Bill but her hand stayed some inches from him; then she laughed nervously as she laid it on his head, saying, "What am I frightened of, anyway? I've been sticking zinc ointment all over him since you left the house. My God, just fancy . . . if I got mange. Eeh! that would be a scream. It would that. It would cause a sensation at the club, and I bet I'd get lots of cheeky offers for them to come'n paint the stuff over me. But it makes me think, can you manage it by yourself? Will I do it for you?"

"And go home with my face plastered white?"

"Yes, there is that, I suppose. Well, get yourself off. And take your bloodhound with you. Eeh! just look at him. Isn't he a sight? Poor bugger. That stuff they gave you isn't doing him much good, is it?"

"No; and he's terrified of it: he's only got to see the bottle and he goes berserk."

"Well, lass, if the stuff the doctor's ordered you cures you, then it should cure him."

I smiled at her, saying, "You're right,

Gran. You're right. I never thought about that."

"I've got a head on me shoulders, lass. I've got a head on me shoulders."

I left Gran laughing as usual, and when I got home I thought it best that I wait to apply the lotion until after I told Howard . . .

If I'd actually said leprosy, or smallpox, his reaction couldn't have been worse, for he backed from me; his mouth opened wider than I'd ever seen it, and he looked at me with his face screwed up as if there was emanating from me the most foul smell. And when he brought out the word *"Mange?"* it sounded unclean.

"Yes, mange," I answered brightly. "And I don't think it will be wise for me to cook for you for the next three or four days as I've got to apply an obnoxious liquid. I understand it's what they dip sheep in to rid them of vermin and such. Ticks, I think they call them." As I walked out of the kitchen he shouted after me, "And don't you make my bed."

I turned and, the grin still on my face, I said, "Oh, I don't mind making your bed, Howard. I can do that even with the stuff on me."

"I've told you. Keep out of my room."

"Just as you wish."

"And out of the sitting-room."

Now the grin disappeared from my face as I turned and confronted him squarely, saying, "It is my sitting-room, Howard. Your bedroom, you may consider you own, as you may the bottle room, but I'll go where I like in the rest of the house, mange or no mange; and as you are very rarely in the sitting-room nowadays I don't think there's any fear of your catching anything from where I might sit."

"And I'll be in it less in the future."

"That suits me perfectly." I turned on my heel and made for the stairs, but stopped abruptly when I heard a yelp coming from the kitchen.

I was back; in that room as if I'd been shot from a gun. He was just about to leave by the back door, and Bill was standing holding one of his front paws up; and now, my voice almost a scream, I yelled at him, "You do that just once again, just once, and I'll go into the street and I'll yell out what kind of man you really are. Do you hear me? I mean it, mind."

He came back into the room and closed the door and, his voice low now, he said, "Sometimes I think you're not right in the head. Nobody's touched him."

"Look at him!" I pointed. "A dog can't

lie, he's standing holding his paw up. I heard him yelp from the contact with your boot." And then I added, "No. No, I won't do what I've just said, go out in the street, but I'll sell this house over your head."

When I saw him smile, I felt a shiver go through me, and all my bravery seeped away at his next words: "There's only thirteen months to go," he said, and on that he turned and went out . . .

Three days later, I took a bath, and, like a miracle, my mange was gone. I was back in the surgery the following morning, and I started even before he could get a word in, saying, "I haven't come about myself. Look! I'm clear." I tapped my face. "It was as you said, it cleared the mange. But I want another prescription. I mean, will you give me another prescription because I'd like to wash Bill in it, to see if it'll do the same for him."

"Certainly. Certainly. My, my; I've never seen you so bright and breezy for years. I think it would be a good idea if you contract mange every month."

"Don't be silly . . . I'm sorry." I lowered my head, and when I looked up at him again he was grinning, and as he handed me the prescription he said, "Life going all right for you now, Maisie?"

My ephemeral happiness vanished and I answered, "If you're referring to what I think you're referring, no, just the same, but in a different way. I . . . I must tell you about it sometime."

"Do. Do. But wait till I'm on my holidays."

"I thought you were going to Spain for your holidays?"

"I am."

I saw what he meant and pulled my lips tight together while my eyes laughed at him. Then thanking him for the prescription, I made to go out, but I turned at the door and said quietly, "I've made up my mind I'm not going to have anything to do with you for a long time."

"Good. Good. Thank God for that." His voice could have been heard all over the surgery, and when I passed the receptionist she looked at me curiously and I returned her look with a dignified inclination of my head . . .

I duly washed Bill in the lotion, and to save him washing it off himself on the carpets I put his collar back on, fastened on the lead, and took him into the park, where I ran him in and out of the trees until the stuff dried into his coat.

Most of the regulars in the park took no notice. I knew I was known to them as

"That young lass with the bull-terrier", and their opinions were, I felt, that both of us weren't representative of the standards of our particular breeds.

I left the stuff on Bill for five days for good measure; then I bathed him, and behold, his skin was clear. And in no time the hair started to grow on it again.

We had both come through a crisis, which had been funny in its way.

CHAPTER 3

Hamilton, I was finding, came and went on my horizon. There were days at a time when I wouldn't see hilt nor hair of him, and other days when he was jumping about me all over the place. On one of these days the front door bell rang and I opened it to see George standing there.

"George! George!"

"Hallo, hinny."

I threw my arms about him, and he pressed me to him, then held me away from him, saying now, "What's happened to you? There's not a pick on your bones."

"Come in. Come in. How long are you home for? Oh, it's good to see you." I hung on to his arm as we went into the sitting-room, and there he stood in the middle of

215

the room and looked about him. Such was the expression on his face that I didn't speak for a moment or so.

"It's just the same," I said.

"Aye, pet, aye, it's just the same. But it seems a thousand years ago since I lived in it. In fact, I can't believe I ever lived here. I suppose it's the dumps I've been in since." He punched me gently on the shoulder; then, pulling me towards the couch, he said, "Come on, sit down and tell me the story of your life."

"I want the story of *your* life."

"Oh" — he pulled a face — "you'll hear it from me ma soon enough. She's up in arms."

"Why?"

He turned his head to the side. "I'm a naughty lad."

"I never knew you to be anything else." But my banter died away as I added seriously, "You're not in trouble, I mean, police or . . . ?"

"Oh, no." He tossed his head from side to side. "Anyway, that's a small trouble, nothin' to worry about compared to other troubles I get into." He now leant his face close to mine and whispered, "Women. Playing the field."

"Oh, you are a bad lad. But why should

Gran be upset? She knows you."

"Oh, it's a long story. Can I have a sup tea?"

"I'll have to think about it. Come on." I caught at his hand. "Come on into the kitchen and tell me all about it."

I looked at him sitting at the kitchen table, and the years fell away. I was a girl again and he was there, a bulwark: coarse, loving and kind . . . common, beautifully common.

He said, "I met a lass down in Devon. She was a part-time barmaid, a really canny lass in her twenties. I got into the habit of callin' into the pub on me trips, and, like it is, we got to know each other and I got fond of her. Aye; aye, I did." He stretched his neck out of his collar, his chin knobbled and his lower lip pushed itself out as if in defence of his statement, and he went on, "Then . . . well, I must admit I got a bit of a shock, she had four bairns. Her man had walked out and left her a year earlier afore her last bairn was born, and she hadn't heard a thing from him except she heard tell in a roundabout way he had joined a ship and jumped it in Australia. Well, I thought, bugger me, four bairns. No, thank you, Georgie. You've been in an' out of women-trouble all your life, but this is a bit too much of a good thing. So I stopped callin' in. And some months went past; then be-damned if I didn't run into her and the four youngsters in the supermarket. You see, I'd taken a room in this town and was feedin' meself. Well, what could I do? I walked along with her an' the bairns an' she asked me into her house. House, I said; it was a flat . . . It still is a flat." His head bobbed up and down now. "Three rooms you couldn't swing a cat in, a six foot square they called a kitchen, and a similar place for the bath-room. But what impressed me right away was, it was clean, everything was spankin' clean and tidy. And the bairns were clean. The youngest about sixteen months old, and the oldest on five. Two boys and two girls, and what they were starved for more than anything was a father, and they picked on me right away." He now grinned at me. "And anyway, there I am, stepfather again. An' have been for the past six months, and if we could find out where her bloody man is and she could sue for divorce we'd be married. Aye, yes, you can raise your eye-brows. That's what me ma did; and she opened her mouth at the same time, and you can imagine what came out of it."

After I'd placed the cup of tea in front of him, I bent and kissed him on the side of the brow, and as I did so I whispered,

"Lucky bairns."

"Aw" — he put his arm around me — "there'll never be another like you. You were always an understanding lass. I loved you, you know. I still do. Oh aye, I still do. Nobody'll take your place."

I knew a moment of deep jealousy: four other bairns had taken my place. How strange I thought, this man who was made to be a father of a large family without a child of his own, yet giving out love in abundance to any child that came under his care.

"You'd like her, Maisie." He pulled a face at me now. "She's not loud or brassy. I don't know why it is that people think that anybody who serves in a bar is bound to be loud and brassy. Anyway, she's just the opposite, she's quiet, even timid. She had a hell of a job gettin' used to bar life, but it was the only thing she could do, to help keep them. You know, she put me in mind of you when I first met her."

"Oh" — I turned my head away from him — "don't stretch it, George."

"I'm tellin' you the truth." He brought his lips tight together for a moment, then added, "Aye, I am. There's something quite akin to you about her."

"Then all I can say is, God help her."

"Don't be so bloody soft." Then leaning towards me, he said, "How's he treating you now?"

I could answer honestly, "At present, things are quiet;" the two years weren't up yet.

"Do you get on better with him?"

"We don't see much of each other. He's manager now, you know, and he's in with the boss and goes to his place most weekends."

"Oh, rising in the world. Doesn't he take you with him?"

"Now would he?"

"Look" — he half rose from his chair, then sat down again — "don't keep knockin' yourself, woman; you've got what lots of the lookers haven't got, personality and a sense of humour. Put you in a taproom of a pub and you'd go down like a bomb."

"Yes" — I nodded at him — "and the explosion would take everybody down with me. Don't be silly . . . put me in a pub! George, it's no good; you don't have to keep anything up with me. I know exactly what I am. I accepted it years ago. People around here think I'm lucky to be married. I don't agree with them on that point, but I know that's the local opinion, and would be a general opinion too, so stop waffling about me and making believe I'm the ugly duckling looking down in the water and imagining she sees a swan, only to find when she lifts her head she's in the middle of a nervous breakdown."

At this point we both started to laugh, and he came round the table and caught hold of me and we rocked together; and as I felt the strong nearness of him and smelt the mixture of sweat and tobacco and maleness, my tears almost stopped being tears of laughter.

Oh, if I could have only married someone like George. All right, he might have gone after other women, seeking a little excitement, but one thing I felt sure of, if he had been mine he would have come back to me; his heart was too kind to leave anybody lonely for long. I gazed up at him now and said softly, "I wish I was one of those four children."

"Aw, Maisie, fancy saying a thing like that." I saw his Adam's apple jerk up and down; then he turned away from me, saying, "How's the business going? Ma tells me you're doin' fine."

"Oh, I get plenty of bits and pieces, but I get bored typing them. I've had nothing interesting since I typed a novel for a woman, but that's nearly a year ago."

When he walked into the hall, I knew he

was going, and I said, "How long are you here for?"

"Just overnight. I'll be away early in the mornin'. But I promised Ma to come back at least once a month."

"That's good. She misses you; she gets very lonely."

"Aye," he nodded, "so she told me. She didn't half rub it in. But as I said, I'm a big lad now." He put his hands out and laid them on my shoulders and he said softly, "Life's funny, Maisie, crazy, barmy, bloody hell one minute, bloody heaven the next, but all the time, barmy. Have you ever asked yourself why we're here? I have. Lately I have. It never used to trouble me at one time, but I woke up the other night and I thought, Georgie lad. Here you are lying aside somebody else's missis an' workin' for his four bairns an' who's to know that he doesn't come back through that door some day and try to knock your bloody head off."

Once again we were leaning against each other. Then all of a sudden, he pushed me away and with an abrupt, "Be seeing you, lass," he went hurriedly out, leaving me staring through the open door at him. He didn't even turn at the gate and wave. When I closed the front door, I stood with my back to it and my head bowed, and I cried for there went the man I loved. Always had, and always would.

CHAPTER 4

It was 1973 and, strangely, I look back to that year as a time I realized I took very little interest in outside affairs; the state of the country, the state of the world passed me by. I didn't get a daily newspaper, but I listened to the radio. Yet, good, bad, or indifferent, it made very little impression on me. My life seemed to be taken up with looking after Bill, doing the typing and cleaning the house, yet I know now that, threading all this and the thing that blotted out the concerns of the outside world, was my fear of Howard. At times I might stand up to him, but most of the time I avoided him so that there would be no conflict. Yet, I saw very little of him. I cooked his breakfast in the morning, but left him to eat it alone while I got on with other things. I found I couldn't sit at the table with him. Now that he had his main meal out at dinner-time, there was only the evening one to see to, and this I left ready for him and had my own on a tray in the study.

Week-ends were the best because he often now left home on a Friday night. Sometimes he returned on a Sunday evening, but very often I didn't see him until the Monday evening. Even when he went to stay with Mr Hempies, he must have spent some time with his bottle hunting, because often he would bring a bagful back and they would be all clean and ready for the shelves; at least I presumed so because he would take them straight upstairs; those bottles the children gathered for him he cleaned thoroughly in the kitchen sink.

As time went on I blessed Mr Hempies, at the same time wondering what kind of a man he must be to take such a liking for Howard. He must be old and very lonely I imagined. And also what idea he had of Howard's wife, the woman that never went anywhere with her husband.

If the neighbours knew that he was never at home at the week-ends, I'm sure they weren't surprised, because when he had lived with May, he spent most of Saturday and Sunday bottle hunting; in fact, the children called him "the bottle man".

The two years' grace I had demanded in payment for the money I had given him had passed, and he had made no move towards me. Just in case, I kept my bedroom door locked.

Then one night I knew the time had come

again. It started in the kitchen. I had left his tea ready. I had mashed the tea and was about to leave the kitchen when he came in and stood behind his chair, looking down at the table. I thought he was about to find fault with the meal, but he said, "Sit down. I want to talk to you."

I didn't sit down, I just stood and looked at him; then he said, "Well, please yourself," and he sat down.

"We've been getting on pretty well together lately, haven't we, not treading on each other's toes?" he said.

I made no response, and he went on, "And that's the way it should be, and could be. Well, I'll come to the point; it's no good beating around the bush with you, I know that. It's just this. I don't think it's fitting that a man in my position should take the bus to work every morning, nor have to go by bus and train to . . . to Durham and Mr Hempies. Everybody else who goes there has a car."

I put my head on one side and said, "Everybody? I thought he was a lonely old man and that you were his sole companion."

"I don't know where you got that idea. Of course, he's an old man, and he hasn't got any family. I mean . . . well, any close family, except a nephew. But he has lots of call-

225

ers at times, and friends . . . well, they come and stay, like me. He looks upon me, I can say, more like a son. So what I need at the moment is about two hundred pounds. I've seen a car. It's second-hand, and I'd like to have it. I've been taking driving lessons."

When I still didn't make any response, he said, "Well?"

Then I spoke. "If Mr Hempies looks upon you as a son, then why doesn't he buy you a car?"

As he got to his feet the fear cork-screwed within me, then seemed to lodge in my throat as he glared at me, his face working.

"I'm trying to keep things on an even keel, but you don't want it, do you? Now, you've got that money stacked away and you don't spend it on yourself. What do you think you're going to do with it?"

"*I* could buy a car and *I* could take lessons."

Why did I say such things? Why couldn't I keep my mouth shut? I was making things worse.

"Yes, you could; then we would both have cars."

"I can't ask Gran for any more."

"You're not asking Gran for anything. Don't try to hoodwink me. Anyway, think about it, but don't waste too much time over it."

I turned from him and made for the door, and when I reached it his words stopped me as he said, "And as for locking your door, if I wanted to get in I could, I've had extra keys made. I think ahead, you see. I said, if I wanted to get in, but I don't, at least not unless you force my hand. As I've said before, there's more ways of killing a cat than drowning it. And there's always Bill, isn't there? Bill."

Bill was standing at my side now waiting for the door to be opened to leave with me, and as if the animal knew what Howard meant it turned its head and gave a low growl. And I think this rather staggered Howard for he stared at Bill somewhat in surprise. As I opened the door I said, "I've told you before and I'm telling you again, if you touch that dog it will be the last thing you'll ever do." And now, what frightened me more than anything else was, I knew that I meant what I said, and the consequences made me feel so sick that I could have vomited there and then.

In the study, Bill lay close to my feet and when I put my hand down on his bony head and stroked it, he turned and licked my arm, and his small round eyes seemed to send a message of love to me. The next minute, I found myself on the floor, my arms about him, rocking him as if he really were a child. And in a way he was, he was my child . . .

It was difficult to see Gran these days unless I went in the morning. But I seemed to be able to get through the typing better in the mornings. In the afternoons, she was either playing bingo or she was at one of the numerous clubs round about. It was the same in the evening. As she said to me, and so often, "Lass, I can't abide in the house, not since our Georgie went, 'cos there's nothin' to stay in for."

But on this occasion, accompanied by Bill, I went to her the next morning early, although I knew what she would say, before I got there.

"Lass, you're mad. You give into him like this an' he'll have every penny off you. Look, go to that solicitor's and tell him what's happenin'."

"I can't, Gran."

"Why not?"

"Well, I just can't. I'd have to tell him everything, and there's some things I can't talk about. How could I, to a strange man? And anyway, being a man, he would likely say, he's your husband."

"What about the doctor?"

"Oh, him! I'm always telling him one thing or another. He must be sick of the sight of me. And I can't say that I look forward to seeing him either."

Gran now went into the kitchen to make the inevitable cup of tea, and from there she shouted, "Something should be done with that fellow. And it worries me at times, 'cos I don't know what's gona be the end of it."

When she came back with the tea, she said, "Stall. Aye, that's what to do, stall. Tell him I'm away on me holidays and, of course, I've got the cheque book. An' that's that."

I smiled at her. "That's an idea," I said. "But he'll have it in the end."

"Well, stop him, you silly little bitch, an' go and blow the lot. Go on a world cruise, or something like that."

"What! By myself?" I laughed.

"No, I'll come along wi' you."

"I believe you would an' all."

Gran threw back her head now and laughed; then on a more serious note she said, "You never spend anything on yourself, do you? Just look at you. When is the last time you had a new rag? Or your hair done properly? Or went to one of them beauty parlours?"

"Oh, Gran." I felt sharply annoyed now,

and she came back at me, yelling at the top of her voice, "Yes, you can say, oh Gran, like that, but needs must when the devil drives, they say. And you could do somethin' with your face. I know I'm speaking with me mouth wide open and there's not a kind word coming out of it, but it's the truth: you needn't look as plain-faced as you do. You never wear a bit of lipstick or a bit of colour. There's a place round Brampton Hill way that transforms people. Why, even old 'uns like me do up. There's a Mrs Maddison comes to the club every now an' then an' shows us how." And at this, she kissed me.

I sighed deeply; then said slowly, "Gran, I've got no desire to change. I know myself as I am and I live with myself."

"Aw, lass." She dropped down on the couch beside me, and, taking my hand, she said, "I wish I could do something for you. You've had a rotten deal all along."

I said, "You do do something for me, just being you, Gran."

At teatime that evening I spoke first. I said, "With regard to the money, I'm sorry, even if I would consent to give it to you, I can't, Gran's gone on holiday. She's gone down to George's in Devon. I don't know when

230

she'll be back."

He stared at me for a long moment, then said, "Is that so?" And I said, "Yes, that's so," before walking out with my knees almost knocking together.

About half an hour later he came downstairs ready to play tennis. He was wearing white shorts, a white shirt, and a light grey coat.

I saw him go into the kitchen. He usually left by the front door. I went into the sitting-room and waited to hear him leave. But after ten minutes or so had elapsed and there had been no sound of the door closing, I imagined he had left by the back door.

Remembering that Bill was in the kitchen and that Howard could have left the back door and the back gate open, accidentally on purpose, I hurried out of the sitting-room, across the hall, and pushed open the kitchen door; then I let out a high-powered scream of pain as the tennis racket swished to both sides of me. As I staggered back against the dresser, Bill sprang from his basket, his teeth bared, and stood in front of me, growling at Howard who appeared greatly contrite, saying, "I'm sorry. I . . . I was just practising my strokes. I . . . I didn't expect the door to open."

I knew he was standing some distance

from me, not daring to move because of the dog. I had my hands cupping my breasts; the double swish of the racket had caught both of them. I felt I was going to faint as everything swam round me. Then his voice penetrated my shaken senses, saying, "Call him off. I want to get out. Maisie, do you hear? Call him off!" As I opened my eyes, he said, "It was an accident. I didn't expect you to come barging in like that. Call him off, the dog."

I followed his nodding head and looked down on Bill, who was braced as if ready to spring. Slowly, I leant over and caught him by the collar, and the very fact of bending nearly brought me tumbling to the floor. Holding Bill with one hand, I groped with my short arm for a chair and sat down, while Howard, now opening the kitchen door into the hall, repeated, "It was an accident. How was I to know you were coming in."

Like hell it was! I heard Hamilton's voice as if from a far distance.

I felt sick. My breasts were never big, but they were shapely. Strangely, my body had grown very shapely: I had a thirty-two bust and a twenty-six waist and a thirty-six hip measurement. Now my breasts were paining as if they'd been punched, which indeed they had. He had caught one with the inside of the racket and the other with the outside as if he were changing from forward drive to backhand. Practising!

Practising. He had been waiting for me. He had likely been aiming for my face, but I'd put my arms up swiftly to protect myself, and my breasts had caught the blows. What kind of a man was he, anyway? A dangerous one. Oh yes, a mean dangerous one. A weakness in me said now, Let him have it all, every penny, and then he'll no more need to get at you.

Bill was at my side, his head pressed tight against my knees. And Hamilton was standing by the end of the table, his long face drooped towards me. That money is your only protection, he was saying. Without it, it could be your life next, with a man like that. Oh yes, you can shake your head, but after he's got all you've got money-wise, he'll start on the house and what's in it. And you'll be lucky if you escape. Stranger things have happened, and to stronger people than you.

After a while, I went upstairs and took a hot bath, and the pain eased somewhat. Then later, when I went to bed, I not only locked the door but stuck the back of a strong chair beneath the handle . . .

I put up with the pain for three days; then I went to Gran's to leave Bill with her while I went to the doctor's again. And all she could say on my relating the story of the tennis practice was, "My God, lass, what next? What next?"

Reaching the waiting-room I found myself sitting next to the "You here again?" woman; and that's what she said immediately to me, "You here again . . . nerves?" She nodded. "Your eyelid's at it. Well, you're lucky, in a way, because you can get over nerves, if you pull yourself together."

When my turn came to go into the surgery, he said, "What now?" It had become his usual form of address.

"It's my breasts," I said; "they're swollen and they're all lumps."

"Your breasts, swollen and all lumps?"

"Yes."

"What have you done to make them like that?"

"I . . . I had an accident."

"To both of them at once?"

"Yes."

He looked at me steadily for a moment, then said, "Mmm. Well, let's have a look-see. Take your blouse off."

I went behind the screen and took my blouse off.

He examined me without uttering a word; then said, "Put your things on."

As I was getting dressed I heard him washing his hands at the sink; and now his voice came to me, saying, "You've got mastitis."

"What?"

"I said, you've got mastitis."

"Ma . . . stit . . . is?"

"Yes, mastitis. Cows get it in their udders."

"Cows?"

"Yes, that's what I said. They get it in their udders and they can't give milk. But you needn't worry on that score."

I came slowly out from behind the screen and, looking at him, I repeated, *"Cows?"*

"That's what I said, cows. They are females too, you know."

He now sat down at his desk and began to write. Presently, looking up at me, he said, "Anyway, you're luckier than the cows, you can wear a camp brassière."

"What?" I watched him now close his eyes and droop his head, and his voice seemed to come from way beneath the floor as he said, "Maisie. Maisie, I've told you before, will you please stop *what-ing* me!"

"Well, a thing like mastitis. You tell me cows get it, and now I've got to wear a . . . a what?"

He put his hand to his head and pressed his lips tight together, and I turned my head away, only to see Hamilton crouched in the corner of the room with his forelegs crossed, his head leaning against the wall, looking as if he was having cramp from laughing so much.

The doctor lifted his bearded face now and there was a touch of merriment in the back of his eyes as he said, "A what is a stiffish brassière, Maisie. It's for conditions such as you've got, mastitis. If you wear it, it will keep your breasts firm and stop them . . ." He didn't say wagging from side to side, but he moved his hand descriptively, and almost immediately I had a mental picture of a herd of cows, and me on all fours in the middle of them. We were all wearing camp brassières, and the only difference between us was that their udders were swinging one way and mine the other.

Why did I see the funny side of things even when I was in pain. There was a very odd side to me, I had to admit.

I leant my elbow on the table and covered my face with my hand, and he said to me, "Well now, what's funny?"

"Just that I've seen myself amidst a herd of cows all wearing camp brassières, and their udders were . . ." I moved my hand as he had done; then added, "but mine wouldn't work like that."

When he let out his rare roar of laughter I knew I'd be in for another funny look from the receptionist when later I passed through the waiting-room.

After a moment, his face became straight and he rose and came round the desk and, looking at me full in the face, he said, "How did you come by this business anyway?"

"I was hit with a tennis racket."

I saw small globules of moisture on the end of his moustache as he leant towards me, his eyes screwed up. "Come again," he said.

"I was hit with a tennis racket."

"On both breasts?"

"On both breasts."

"How come?"

"He was supposed to be practising, when I went into the kitchen."

"Supposed to be practising?"

"Yes. He did a back and forward drive. Bang! Bang!" I demonstrated. "I think he was aiming for my face, but missed."

He now turned his head to the side and pulled at his ear, as if he was thinking; then he said, "If somebody doesn't talk to him, the police certainly will one day. You're a fool of a girl for staying. You know that,

Maisie. The house just isn't worth it."

"It's all I've got."

"Yes" — he nodded — "I can understand that. But still I feel something should be done. I've tried. I couldn't get through to him; he's too smooth, too crafty. You're sure it was no accident?"

"If he had just hit one side, yes, but not both. It was too neatly done."

He sighed now and said, "Well, go along, but take care. Come and see me next week." Bending towards me now, he added, "And I won't grumble at the sight of you."

"Very considerate of you." I nodded at him.

"Go on with you."

He opened the door for me, and I walked through the waiting-room as if I was a privileged person, and felt it, because I'm sure it wasn't very often, in fact, never to my knowledge, that he had opened the door for a patient.

No matter how rough and brusque his manner, I felt, underneath it, I had a friend and that he had been there for a long time.

■ ■ ■ ■

PART THREE
FULL BLOOM

■ ■ ■ ■

CHAPTER 1

How did the years pass? How does any year pass? By months, weeks, days, minutes. And the days sometimes seem as long as the years. Yet looking back, I seemed to have kept myself busy. I must have, looking at the mass of writing I'd turned out, and apparently to no avail. Until one day, the one day that lies buried deep in the heart of everyone who has ever taken up a pen to tell a story.

I was now thirty years old and I had been married for twelve years. Had there been a time when I had never been married? Had there been a time when I hadn't shared this house with a man called Howard Stickle? A forty-year-old man who didn't seem to have aged at all in the last twelve years. He was still tall and fair; nothing about him seemed to have altered except perhaps his manner towards me, which at times made me imagine that I didn't exist, because he seemed to look beyond me; at times he would bump into me, almost knocking me off my feet, and never once with a word of apology. The last occasion he apologized was when he hit me with the tennis racket.

He had by now had all my money with the exception of a few pounds that I had saved from my typing. He had got his second-hand car; but that hadn't satisfied him. A year later, he'd had a better second-hand car; eighteen months later he had a new car. At one period he said he had been invited to go abroad with Mr Hempies for a fortnight and would need two hundred pounds to cover his expenses. I had stuck out at that, until I accidentally fell down-stairs; the clips that held the brass rod had become loose. I became really frightened after that. My arms and legs were black and blue with the tumble and Doctor Kane had said, "Now you've got to do something. Nobody else can do it; it's up to you." And I knew it was up to me. But what proof had I? Because as Howard had made great play of knocking the clips back into the stairs, he had pointed out to me that there was wood-worm in the treads.

It was three months ago he got the last of the money that was in Gran's care. She had given up offering me advice. However, once she surprised me by saying, "Do you care for the fellow?"

Care for him? The idea sounded preposterous, but she came back with, "Well, there's no other thing I can think of that'll make you stick with a man like that."

"It's my home," I had said.

"Well," she answered, "he'll have you out of it, in a box. You mark my words. And nobody'll be able to say a word against him, because, like a damn fool, you've kept your mouth shut all these years, and because you've kept yourself to yourself too much. You've got a funny name among the neighbours. Do you know that?"

Oh yes, I knew that. I also knew that Howard's standing with the neighbours was high.

It was also about three years ago that I started dropping into the church, the Catholic church, not for the services, but just going in and sitting quietly and looking at the side altar. It was very peaceful. Sometimes I had a word with Father Mackin. He was always jocular and very nice to me. It had been in my mind for some time to talk to him, in a form of confession, and tell him about my life, what I was going through, what I was afraid of. And I did just that. The result was rather surprising.

On this particular day I was very down. I hadn't seen Gran for over a week. By the way, George had now married his lady with the four children. There was Betty, now fourteen, John thirteen, Kitty twelve, and Gordon nearly eleven. They were nice children. I had met them a number of times and liked them. But George was no longer my George. He was the children's George and Dad, and his wife's George and husband. That was another pain I couldn't get rid of. Anyway, there I was this day sitting in the pew when the priest came out of the vestry, accompanied by a fat young woman and a young man who seemed little more than a boy. They stood in front of the main altar, the priest talking to them. It was when she turned round that I saw she was very pregnant. A few minutes later, after he had seen them out of the church, he came to my side and, after genuflecting, he sat down in a pew beside me, saying, "Well, now. Well, now, here we are again. Did you see that couple? They are going to be married."

It was jealousy of her condition that prompted the thought, not before time, and I had voiced the first two words when I stopped myself, and he put in, "Oh yes, yes, condemn. Not before time, you were going to say. Well, better late than never, I say."

As I said, I'd been feeling very low this day, but of a sudden my depression lifted when I saw Hamilton galloping up the aisle, dressed all in white, and on his hoofs four big navvy's boots. I lowered my head and made a slight choking sound. And now the priest's voice came to me, saying, "Some of us are luckier than others, and they get through life without making mistakes."

I lifted my head quickly, my face straight now. "Oh, Father," I said; "I . . . I wasn't laughing at them. You see, it's . . ." I turned my head to the side. "Well, how can I put it? It's a quirk I have."

"A quirk?" He leant towards me and repeated. "A quirk?"

"Well, that's the only way I can describe it. You see, even today when I'm feeling very down, sort of low and depressed, even at times like this I sometimes think of very funny things. Well, you see, it's like this, Father." I began to look from side to side before I went on, "I suppose I could tell you in a sort of confession like." There I was using the word like, the same as Gran did. "I suppose it's because I've always been rather alone. At one time I just used to natter to myself. You know, like people do."

He nodded at me now, a smile on his face as he said, "Yes, yes, I understand. We all natter to ourselves. But go on. Go on, my dear."

So I went on, and by the look on his face the next moment I think he wished I hadn't, because I could see his opinion of me taking rapid strides towards the asylum.

"Well, you see, Father, I talk to this horse."

His eyes became round.

"I . . . I call him Hamilton."

His mouth fell open.

"He appears quite real to me."

His eyebrows took on points.

"For instance, what made me laugh a moment ago was that the young lady changed into him and he galloped up the aisle all in white, with boots on."

His head moved slightly downward, his lips formed a kind of rosebud.

I became a little apprehensive and I said, "I'm . . . I'm not daft, or . . . well, anything like that, Father."

His head moved slowly from side to side.

"I suppose he's just a figment of my imagination, but it's very strange. When I want the truth about anything he gives me the right answers. I don't always pay heed to them. But on looking back, I wish I had."

His chin seemed to draw his face to the side now and his pointed eyebrows and round eyes, his puckered mouth, were joined by his nose, which was twitching, and the dreadful thing about it all was that there was Hamilton standing to the side, looking at him and shaking his head slowly as if he was sorry for the poor man and the position I'd put him in. But surely priests, I thought, were used to listening to all kinds of things, murders and such, but what I had just said seemed to be affecting him more than if I had confessed to something terrible.

His dog collar now jerked so quickly that it caught him under the chin and it seemed to affect the way he spoke. "Have you talked, well . . ." his voice went falsetto, "about this to anyone else . . . your doctor?"

"No . . . not my doctor."

He now joined his hands between his knees and bent over them and surveyed them for a time before he said, "Have you had a breakdown of any kind?"

"No, Father, no; but I've been troubled with nerves."

"Yes, yes, I can understand. Yes, troubled with nerves."

"Father" — I leaned towards him trying to look into his face — "I'm not bats."

He straightened up quickly, and now his voice quite loud, he said, "No, no, of course

247

you're not. Who said you were? There's no suggestion of it, no, no. But about this horse. What did you say his name . . . you called him?"

"Hamilton."

"Hamilton. It's a very nice name, very nice name for a horse. And . . . and you say he acts the goat a bit?"

"He does a bit, and all at the wrong moments." I'd say he did at the wrong moments. "That's what I mean by this quirk in me seeing . . . well, I suppose the funny side of things. It's sort of like the bishop and the banana skin."

"Ho! Ho!" His head went back now and he laughed. "Yes, yes, the bishop and the banana skin . . . dignity defiled."

"Yes, yes" — I agreed with him — "it's always funnier with people like that who are . . . well, up to the eyebrows in God, so to speak."

Oh dear me, dear me, that had nothing to do with Hamilton. Now, why had I said that?

The priest's face was working again, but without the contortions of astonishment on it. Then I noticed the front of his tunic starting to bob, and I knew he was laughing inside. Presently, he said, "You are a funny girl, you know. I've heard a lot of descriptions about us but that's a new one on me, up to the eyebrows in God. By the way, do you go out to work? I mean, do you do anything other than . . . well, housework?"

"I do typing in my home: people's stories, you know, and articles; anything they want doing."

"You do? Well now, I should have thought you would have seen an opening in that line for yourself. Have you ever thought about writing? All these funny little things you think about, this horse business?"

"Oh yes, I've written lots about Hamilton. For years and years I've done bits on him."

"You have?" His voice was now high with surprise, and he went on, "Well now, well now, you should put all those bits together into a book. I could see it as a bestseller."

I smiled at him now in a patient sort of way. I must have typed dozens of stories for the members of the Writers' Circle and others over the past years, and the percentage of publications had been painfully small.

But it was at that moment that the priest's suggestion set something moving in my mind. I remember he set me to the church door and, looking down on me, he said, "You're not so troubled now, are you?"

"No, Father," I answered, "if you can talk things out with someone it's half the battle."

It was then he said, "Can't you talk to your husband about it . . . I mean, what troubles you?"

Looking at him fully in the face and because he was a priest and, I understood, had to keep things to himself, I said, simply, "He's my trouble, Father, if I had a good husband I wouldn't need Hamilton . . ."

I've seen him at intervals since that time and we've always had a laugh together. But, I remember, I went straight home that day and up into the attic and sat on the floor reading through the pile of bits and pieces I had written since the very first day I'd given Hamilton a name. And I found myself laughing out aloud at some of the things, and at others hardly being able to suppress my tears, such as, the page I had written the night George had left, and then again, my lacerated feelings after the first few days of my marriage. And the fears seemed to leap freshly from the scribbled lines as I read.

It was from then that my mind got to work on how to go about putting all these pieces into book form. I'd learned a great deal from the mistakes of others over the years and, up till now, without any thought of putting what I had learned to my own use in a big way. So it came about that I set out the plan of a story.

It didn't have any plot, so to speak. They were always going on about plots at the Writers' Circle. I had never been able to see why plots were so important. To my mind, if you got a couple of good characters they made the story themselves; the environment you set them in created all the incidents. Hadn't I proof of that in myself? The fact that I was made as I was and had the good or bad fortune, however you looked at it now, to own this house, had attracted May and her brother to me, and in that setting, because of our diverse characters, the incidents had seemingly happened naturally; they hadn't been plotted. Yet, hadn't they? What about Howard?

But I found the arranging of all these bits and pieces much harder to do in actual fact than it had appeared in my mind, and as I could only type for myself at odd times, and then each day see what I'd done was safely deposited underneath the floor boards once again, it was nearly two years before I had completed the story of Hamilton.

When at last, I reread it through, to my surprise I realized I had been telling the story of my own life up to that time, and I also realized that the story hadn't turned out the way I had intended. What I had imagined to be screamingly funny parts had resulted in a sort of pathos. What I'd written as straight serious parts turned out to be amusing when read. There were times when I wrote about myself being deeply worried, but in some strange way they read as the funny bits.

But it was completed. Now, I asked myself, what to do with it? And up came the question of markets. The members of the Writers' Circle were always yammering on about markets. I suppose they were right up to a point, markets meant publishers. So I went to the reference library and got out the *Writers' & Artists' Yearbook,* and there they were in their hundreds. Which one was going to have the honour of reading this daft story? Because that's what it would be called, a daft story about a nondescript woman and a talking, laughing, sad at times, merry at others, mad galloping horse.

Needless to say, Hamilton came along with me that day, and after I had been pondering for some time which publisher to choose he put his left front hoof on the page. It looked very dainty at this moment, and didn't obliterate any of the print, and I saw it was pointing to Houseman and Rington, Ltd., 42 Chapman's Yard, London, WC2B 3AR.

"So that's it," I said to him.

That's the one, he answered.

Well, Houseman and Rington, get yourself fortified, because here we come.

The next day I took my manuscript, all neatly parcelled up together with an enclosed very short note, to Gran's.

It was half past nine in the morning and she said, "You're up afore your clothes are on, lass. What is it now?"

I showed her the parcel, saying, "It's a kind of book I've written. I'm sending it off, and it will likely come back. I've given this address, so I'm just telling you like" — there I went again; I was getting as bad as her — "that when it comes back you'll know what it is. Oh yes, and I'm calling myself Miriam Carter."

"Does he know about it?" She laughingly pointed to Bill, and I said, "Yes, he knows all about it, every word, even as much as Hamilton."

The name had slipped out, and she screwed up her face at me and said, "Hamilton? Who's he, Hamilton?"

I knew my face was red, and I said, "I must tell you about him some day."

"A fellow you know?" Her expression became bright, and I said, "No, no." And at this she said, "Oh, it's all right, you needn't blush; I wouldn't blame you if you had three fellows on the side every night."

"Oh, Gran."

"Yes, oh Gran. So his name's Hamilton?"

"Yes, Gran." I said slowly. "But please don't get your hopes up; he's not that kind of a man."

"Well, what do you write about, lass . . . I mean, to make a book?"

"Oh —" I turned my head away from her and thought for a moment for a way to describe what I wrote. Then looking at her again, I smiled at her as I said, "You won't believe it, but I write funny bits."

"Funny bits?"

"Yes, funny bits. Anything that tickles my fancy, mostly about . . . Oh, I can't really explain. You can't explain humour, Gran, because people's tastes differ. What we laugh at, other people would think silly."

"Well, make me laugh. Go on, make me laugh."

"Oh, Gran."

"Don't say, oh, Gran. Make me laugh."

"I can't, not like that, not to order; it's got to come sort of offhand, spontaneous."

"Aye, well, you want to tell that to some of the comics we get in the club. Eeh! if I couldn't do better than them, I'd walk on water just to see if God was on my side."

At this Hamilton did a gallop round and round the kitchen. His mane was flying, his white tail was stuck up in the air, and I was flapping Gran on the shoulder with my good arm while my short one was tight around my waist to ease the pain of my laughter. Gran was laughing too, but more at me than what she had said, and I now spluttered, "That's it, you see, Gran, that's it."

"What's it? Just what I said there?"

"Yes, yes."

She wiped her face with her apron, then said, "Well then, lass, if that tickles your fancy, you're easily pleased."

"I'm not easily pleased, not in that way, Gran. You see, it isn't the content of humour but how it's said."

"Aye, an' it's how I say it, I suppose. Me common way."

"Exactly, Mrs Carter." I stood up now and repeated, "Exactly," and we were laughing again.

And once more I said, Oh, thank God for Gran.

Chapter 2

A month had passed and no word.

Like the fool I was, I had expected a reply

within a week; and every morning of the second week, there I was on Gran's doorstep well before ten o'clock. But there was no letter, and no parcel, and I think she got a little tired of seeing me.

She dampened my spirits well and truly one morning by telling me that there had been a programme on the wireless the previous night about people sending manuscripts to publishers and some of them received so many in a week, amounting to hundreds, that they never even looked at them . . . well, not after the first two pages, because they could tell straightaway if it was worth going on reading the stuff. When she had finished, she said, "I'm not trying to put you off, lass, but that's what they said." And I said, "Well, Gran, I hope I'm not in need of being cheered up when you do try to put me off."

I didn't go back for four days, and when I did, she was very sweet to me and apologized for telling me what she had heard on the wireless, and ended by saying, "Come on, lass, buck up and be a rabbit."

Then the third week passed, and the fourth week almost passed.

It was a Friday. I didn't go round to Gran's until nearly dinner-time, and I hardly got in the door when she yelled at me, "Where've you been?"

"What do you mean, where've I been?"

"You've practically got me out of bed durin' the last month, an' look!" She now took a long cream envelope from the mantelpiece and pushed it into my hand; then pointing to the heading on the top, she said, "It's from them people that you sent your story to, Houseman and Rington."

I stared down at the envelope. My stomach gave a leap and seemed to land between my breast bones. I turned the envelope over and fingered its good quality paper, only to give a start as Gran shouted, "Bugger me! lass, open the blasted thing. You've been waitin' for it long enough."

I opened it and read:

Dear Miss Carter,

It is with great interest that we have read the manuscript of *Hamilton*. We find it most unusual and very amusing, and if you would care to call at our office at a time convenient to you we would be very pleased to discuss the possibility of publishing it.

In the hope that we shall come to an amicable agreement.

I am,

Yours faithfully,

There followed a scribbled signature and a typed one underneath that read,

Bernard Houseman.

I sat down with a plop, then handed the letter to Gran. Then she very slowly sank down by my side, and we stared at each other. "Eeh! God, lass," she said, "you're gona have a book published. Eeh! . . . aw, hinny." She fell against me and we put our arms around each other and both of our faces were wet, but not through laughter. When we straightened up again, she said, "What is it about, really, hinny? I know you said it was funny, but is it a love story, or what?"

"It's about a horse, Gran."

"A horse?" Her face puckered.

I nodded at her now, swallowed, and said, "It's about a horse called Hamilton."

"What do you know about horses, lass? You've never been on one, have you?"

I bit on my lip as Hamilton kicked up his back legs and almost knocked the plant-stand near the window flying.

"It isn't that kind of a horse. Well, what I mean is, you see, it's a horse" — and I tapped my forehead — "that . . . well, I just think about; and I talk to him."

258

She turned her chin almost to her shoulder while keeping her eyes on me, and she said, "Did I hear aright, lass?"

"Gran" — I leant forward and took her hand — "it's a long story, but, you know, like children have imaginary playmates . . . well, it's like that."

"And you've got a'maginary horse?"

"Yes."

"At your age?"

I looked downwards because Hamilton was standing to the side of me now. His round eyes I knew were right on me as I admitted, "Yes, at my age."

"Eeh! God help us." Now her voice rose a couple of tones. "You mean to say, that's what the story's about and they're gona print it?"

"Well, it seems so."

"There's some funny people in the world."

"And there's one of them sitting here."

"You're not funny . . . well . . . aye you are. You've never been like other lasses. But then what chance did you have? My! I've just thought, wait till our Georgie hears about this. He'll be over the moon. He always said you had it up top. Aye, he did. He used to say, 'Ma, there's more in that one than meets the eye.' An' he was right. By God! he was right. You a writer an' goin' to London."

She stopped and stared at me, then she said, "*London.* Do you realize that, lass? It isn't like Gateshead or Newcastle. You can't walk round there in your bedroom slippers or lookin' as if you've been pulled through a hedge backwards."

"I don't go round in my bedroom slippers, Gran . . ."

"You know what I mean."

I knew what she meant.

"We'll have to do somethin'. Eeh! yes, we'll have to do somethin'."

"You mean, I'll have to do something with meself."

"Aye, yes, I suppose that's what I mean."

"Well, forget it, Gran. They are not interested in what I look like."

"Don't you believe it. Half the world gets by on appearances. If everybody got credit for what's up in their nappers, things would be topsy-turvy the day. I can tell you that."

She now rose from the couch and took a step backward towards the fire, and, her chin working from side to side, she said, "You'll have to have your hair done properly, and not frizzed this time. And you'll get yourself a new rig-out; I'm sick of the sight of you in that grey thing. You look grey all over. You want something in brown, warm browns. I know what, Mrs Maddison will know what to do with you."

"And who is Mrs Maddison?"

"Well, I mentioned her to you afore, she's a bit of everything. She's got one place in Brampton Hill, and another in Bog's End. She's in the two camps. And she gives some of her time now and again in OAP's clubs, telling us how to make the best of our wrinkles." She laughed now, then added, "She's the right one."

"Gran" — I stood up and again took her hand — "don't try to work any more miracles, will you? You remember the last one you did on me?"

"This is different, lass. And Mrs Maddison is class, not like that other bitch. Now, let me get meself pulled together an' think. I'll go along an' see if she's at her low town one this afternoon an' if she'll see you in the mornin'. I'll tell her it's important . . ."

"Gran." I took hold of both her arms and, my face serious, I said, "I must ask you this, and you must promise me: I want no one to know about this. No one. Do you understand? Just you and me."

"Aw, lass, you're missing a chance of a . . ."

"Gran, if you don't promise me, I can tell you this, I won't go to London. I'll tell them

261

to send it back. I don't want anybody to know. Nobody knows this Miriam Carter, and that's how I want it to be, because if it once got round it would reach Howard. And remember, he had every penny out of me before and he would do it again. He would, Gran."

"But, lass, all the excitement an' that."

"*Gran, promise me.* If it leaks out at all . . . *at all,* do you hear me? I'll stop its publication, that's if they really want to do it, because I've sworn that he gets nothing more out of me."

"What about our Georgie?"

"No, not Georgie. Nobody."

"But if you get rigged up, he's bound to see."

"I can come here and change and get back into me old duds before I go home again."

"Aw" — she bent her head — "you've taken all the stuffing out of me. I could see meself braggin' in the club and sayin' in an offhand way, 'Me granddaughter's a writer, one of them novelists.' " And she now put her hand on my cheek and said softly, "And I've always thought of you as me granddaughter, no step about it, just as our Georgie always thought of you as his. Eeh! he'd be over the moon."

"Gran."

"All right!" she bellowed now. "All right. As you say, 'tween you and me. But for how long?"

"I don't know, just as long as I say. And Gran, I feel so strongly about this that if you let on in any way at all, it will be the finish between us. I mean that."

Her expression became sad now as she said, "I believe you do, lass."

"Yes, I'm sorry, Gran, but I do. You see, I've gone through so much back there." I lifted my head towards the door. "I've had to pay him for every peaceful moment that I've had. I say peaceful, I don't think I've ever known any as long as he's been in the house, and I know if he thought I was getting something for this book, he'd have it. I've still got to pay odds and ends out of my typing money. Twelve years he's been in that house and he's still giving me a mere pittance."

"That's your fault. You should have done something, taken him to court."

"You can't take people to court unless you have proof, and he's too wily to give me that."

"Well, do you intend to go on living like this till the end of your days?"

"I don't know, Gran. I seem to be biding

my time for something. I can't explain it to you."

"Perhaps your horse could."

At this we fell against each other and, as my body shook, I thought yet again, what would I have done all these years without Gran.

I liked Peg Maddison. She was small and dainty and business like . . . very kind. The following morning I sat in a cubby hole that she called her office in her Bog's End dress salon, and she looked me over; then she felt my head and said, "It's a good shape. You don't want a great fuss around it. Your hair wants to be short, taken behind your ears. You've got nice ears." She smiled at me.

"Won't that hair style make my face look smaller?" I said.

"No, just the opposite. It's ridiculous to think that a mass of hair makes the face larger, it doesn't, it acts the other way. Your face is small, but you've got good bone formation. You'll find as you get older your skin won't droop as much as most around the cheeks, because you're high cheek-boned. A little make-up on your eyes to-wards the corners" — her fingers lightly touched my skin — "and they'll be all right. I can do quite a bit for you, but I hope you don't mind me saying this, your best advantage is your figure." She now spread her hands and gripped my waist. "You want a smart rig-out, plain. Is it an evening or day do you're going to?"

"A day do."

"Well, a good suit, sort of semi-fitting. Don't wear anything slack; you want to show off anything you've got."

When I shook my head, she said seriously, "I'm stating facts."

"Yes, I know you are, but I don't feel they belong to me, particularly my figure. And how am I going to get a suit to fit this?" I lifted my short arm.

With a flick of her hand she dismissed this, saying, "Oh, any good class house will fix that. One of their cutters will do it in a few minutes. In fact I know a place where you'll get the very thing to suit you. It mightn't be exactly cheap, but it will be worth it. What do you say?"

What I said was, "Thank you," while thinking, Will I have enough money?

"Your grandmother won't know you when we're finished with you." She smiled now, then said, "Mrs Carter's a character, isn't she?"

"Yes, she is, but a nice one."

"Indeed, indeed. And I love going to the

club and meeting all her cronies." She hunched her smart shoulders and made a face at me, and of a sudden I felt we were compatible. And so it proved, in the time ahead.

On the Monday, I phoned Houseman and Rington and asked if the following Friday would be convenient for my visit — I couldn't see myself getting rigged out and being made new in a shorter time — and the secretary informed me that Mr Houseman would be pleased to see me between twelve o'clock and one on that day. Would that be convenient?

From this distance I didn't think of the times of trains, or how long it would take me, but said, "Yes, yes, thank you."

And so it was arranged . . .

"That'll mean you'll have to get an early train up from Newcastle," said Gran. "And how are you going to explain leaving the house at that time to him?"

I'd thought about this. So I said to her, "We are going down to see Georgie."

"We are?"

"Yes. That's what I'm going to tell him. So I'm sleeping here on Thursday night because we are getting an early train."

"And we're just going down for the day?"

"Yes."

"I hope for your sake he doesn't start working things out because it's a long way to Devon and it would be like, hail and farewell."

"He doesn't know exactly where Georgie lives."

"For your own sake I think you had better tell him we're staying the night, and you can take the couch." She thumbed towards it. " 'Cos Georgie's bed'll be damp. It'll all be the same price."

"Yes, I could do that. Yes . . . that's what I'll do. It will be safest."

"I'm not so sure. What if anybody should see you going off on your own?"

"Well, I hope by the time you and Mrs Maddison are finished with me, nobody will recognize me." . . .

It was on the Thursday evening, as he was going out for his weekly game of tennis, that I spoke to him. Endeavouring to keep my voice level and the excitement out of it, I said, "I'm going away for the day, tomorrow. Gran and I are going to see George. I'm . . . I'm sleeping at her place tonight, and we'll likely stay over at George's tomorrow night an' all. I'm . . . I'm leaving Bill with Gran's neighbour."

He turned and looked at me. Then his

face going into an oily smile, he said, "Good. Good. Coming out, are we? Hair do an' all. But aren't you afraid to leave the house? I mightn't let you in when you come back. Or, just fancy." He poked his head towards me. "What if I had another woman installed when you returned? There's stranger things happen."

My voice deadly flat now, I said, "I wouldn't try it on. What I think you've overlooked for a long time and which it would be wise to consider, is that I have friends and all in influential positions: the medical profession" — I paused — "the legal profession —" I paused again, and then ended, "and in the Church. And they are all aware, in different ways, of the situation."

I thought for a moment he was going to spring on me. His pale skin was suffused with colour; his eyes looked black; then from between his teeth he said, "By God! there'll come a day soon when you'll need all the help you can get. I can tell you that." And on this he went out, closing the door behind him, but, and this again added something deeply sinister to his action, closing it softly: the neighbours could never say that Mr Stickle banged the door in a temper.

CHAPTER 3

I didn't know the person who took a return ticket from Newcastle Central to London the following morning. I had come by taxi from Gran's.

There were lots of people milling about the station but very few on the London train. Never in my life had I been further than Durham in a train, and when it slowly moved out of the station I felt for a moment I would collapse, so churned up with excitement was I.

After a while, being alone in the compartment, I stood up and looked at myself in the mirror. Was that me? Was it really me? I took off my new hat. It was a reddish brown straw with a velvet band around it and a narrow brim, which was turned up at one side making it look perky. My hair was flat on my head; my ears were there for all to see; my large mouth was covered with a dusty pink lipstick, and I had green eyeshadow on my lids and black lines to the corners of them. I had practised this art for days past now. I was wearing a corduroy two-piece suit in a russet brown colour. Underneath was a silk blouse that buttoned decorously to the neck. It was a dusty pink shade. On my feet, I had brown court shoes with a three inch heel. I had never walked on such heels before, but I found them quite comfortable. I was comfortable all over. I couldn't believe it. I wanted to pat myself to make sure I was here, this was me. Although on again looking in the glass I realized it was still my face, it was now a face I could bear to look at, and I refused at this point to admit to myself there was the same old pattern under the make-up.

I now sat looking out of the window and for a moment I wished I had someone to talk to, to tell of my excitement. But there was no one, not even Hamilton. Now that was very strange, but since the reformation had begun on me I hadn't seen him. I'd talked to him a number of times, but he hadn't materialized. I wondered why.

When, sometime later, the door was pulled open, I started and looked at the attendant who smiled and said, "Would you like breakfast, madam?"

Breakfast? Breakfast on a train? I had ten pounds in my pocket. I'd borrowed that from Gran. "Yes, I would like breakfast. Thank you, yes."

"Whenever you're ready, madam."

The door closed. Whenever you're ready, madam. This was a different kind of life. This must happen every morning to somebody. That man would say, Would you like breakfast, madam? Would you like breakfast, sir?

I waited five minutes before I walked along the swaying train and entered the dining-car. Only one other passenger was seated at the tables, and he was at the far end reading a paper. I took the first seat I came to, and almost immediately the nice attendant came and hovered over me. "What would madam like: kippers? bacon, egg and sausages? boiled egg? poached egg?"

"I'll have bacon, egg and sausage, please."

"And to begin with, cereals? orange juice?"

"Yes, yes." I said yes to everything.

I'd never enjoyed a meal like it in my life. At one point, when the train was rocking, I couldn't get the cup of coffee to my lips and I started to shake inside with laughing.

Oh, Hamilton, Hamilton, what a beginning to a day. I looked along the car, expecting him to come galloping towards me and laughing his head off. But there was no sign of him. For a moment, I felt suddenly empty . . .

The train had filled up by now, and I sat in the compartment with five other people, and no one spoke to anyone. But that suited me; I wouldn't have known what to say anyway. Yet, I was bursting inside, shouting inside: I've written a book and it's going to be published; it's about me talking to a horse. At one point, I wondered what would have happened if I had yelled out in my excitement. Somebody would have undoubtedly pulled the communication cord and I would never have reached Houseman and Rington . . .

King's Cross station was a maze, which made me feel dizzy. Just follow the crowd, I told myself, and you'll get out of it. And I did. I'd thought I'd take a bus to the publishers. But where was it? And where would I get a bus?

I next found myself standing in a taxi queue, and when my turn came, and before I got in, I politely said to the taxi driver, "Do you know where 42 Chapman's Yard, is please?" And he answered just as politely but with a streak of something in it that I couldn't put a name to, except perhaps patience, "Miss, if I didn't, I wouldn't be sitting here. Get in." He hadn't sounded nasty.

What had I expected from this address, Chapman's Yard? It didn't sound a very classy place, but here I was now, standing in a sort of courtyard of cobbled stones, and around it were a number of tall houses. They didn't look at all like offices, but each house, I noticed, had a big brass plate outside. I walked towards one. It said, thirty-two. I walked to the next one. It said, forty-two. It had jumped ten. But underneath the forty-two I read the magic name of Houseman and Rington, Publishers. I went through a glass door and into a small hall where, behind a glass panel, a young girl sat typing.

Catching her attention, I said, "I'm Miss Carter. I have an appointment."

"Oh, yes, he is expecting you." She smiled pleasantly. "Just go straight up . . . The top floor, first door. I'll let him know you've arrived."

Inside, the place was like an ordinary house. I went up four flights of stairs and the treads were brass bound and my high heels caught against them, click, click, click, click. On the fourth floor, there was a widish landing and off it went four doors. I made for the first one, knocked, and when a voice said, "Come in," I opened the door, and a man rose from behind a desk and came towards me, his hand outstretched, saying, "Miss Carter. I'm very pleased to meet you."

"How do you do?"

"Have you had a good journey?"

"Yes, very pleasant, thank you."

"Do take a seat. What would you like, a cup of coffee? Or would you rather wait and have a drink before lunch?"

A drink before lunch. They were going to give me lunch. "I'll . . . I'll wait. It isn't long since I had a coffee on the train."

"Well . . . well, now, I am so pleased to meet you at last."

It sounded as if he had been trying to get in contact with me for years. I looked him over. He was tall, well built, rather florid, sixty I would say, very well groomed, and once must have been very good looking.

He went behind the desk again, pressed a button, then spoke down to something on his desk, saying, "Tell Mr Rington and Mr Leviston to come in for a moment, will you, please?"

He turned to me now, saying, "These are the other directors. They would like to meet you; in fact, they must —" he poked his head forward as he added, "for they'll be working with you." There followed a short silence while we surveyed each other; then the door opened and Mr Houseman exclaimed, "Ah! Ah, Tom. Here is Miss Carter."

I saw that Mr Rington appeared a little younger than Mr Houseman and was of quite different stature, being of medium height and plump, with a longish face that bore a serious expression. As we shook hands he bent towards me in a courtly manner, saying, "I am most pleased to meet you, Miss Carter."

"How do you do?"

"Ah, here's Nardy." Mr Houseman turned again towards the door through which was entering a small man. Well, he was small in comparison with the other two. And he was younger; I guessed in his middle forties, because his hair was going grey above his ears. I didn't take much notice of his face at the time, only his eyes. They weren't all that large, but they seemed to cover his face. I suppose it was their kindly expression.

"Miss Carter." He held my hand and shook it up and down as he stared into my face, then said, "I'm delighted to meet you."

When we were all seated, Mr Houseman smiled towards me in a benign way and, indicating Mr Leviston, he said, "You'd better not take a dislike to him, at least not right away, because it's he you'll see the most of, he being your editor."

My editor. All this talk seemed to be floating around me. It wasn't really being addressed to me, but to a sort of dream self. My feet weren't on the ground; in fact the chair I was sitting on wasn't on the floor.

Mr Houseman was speaking again, saying, "It was Nardy. By the way that is short for Leonard; but I don't know how Nardy came about, but Nardy it's always been." The three men were laughing now, and when Mr Rington put in, "It should have been Narky," there was more laughter; and I accompanied it by smiling widely. They seemed to be on very good terms, these three, and they were all so gentlemanly. The whole thing didn't seem real. And he went on, "It was Nardy who discovered you. He happened to glance through your manuscript, and that was that."

"I didn't only glance —" Mr Leviston was nodding at his partners now, and Mr Houseman answered, "No, from what you told us, you took it home and it kept you going till the early hours." He turned to me. "You have a keen sense of humour, Miss Carter. It's very evident in your work. Have you been writing long?"

"I . . . I've been scribbling for years, but nothing big like a book. It's my first effort."

"Really!" They were all nodding at me now, and Mr Houseman said, "Well, it certainly won't be your last. It's going to have a wide appeal, I think. Wouldn't you say so, Tom?"

"Yes, indeed, indeed. I thought it was very

funny." Mr Rington's serious expression moved into a smile. "The part where Rosie gets the mange, well, I've never laughed so much for a long time. And the cows and their udders!"

"Oh, I thought the bit in the church with the priest capped that. Didn't you think so, Nardy?"

We were all looking at Mr Leviston now because he wasn't smiling, and his head was moving slowly from side to side, and after a long pause, he said, "Those bits were funny, in a way, yes, but I . . . I didn't find the book as a whole funny." He was now speaking directly to me. "I . . . I hope you don't mind my saying this, Miss Carter, but I found it a rather sad book, full of pathos."

I said nothing, but continued to look back at him.

"You surprise me, Nardy." There was a stiff note in Mr Houseman's voice now, and Mr Leviston turned to him quickly, saying, "Oh, some people may find it funny, Bernard, but what struck me forcibly was the pathos, the sadness of Rosie's life, so lonely, so isolated that she had to create a horse for companionship and a sort of protection against her husband. But of course —" he turned his eyes on to me again, saying softly now, "In Rosie, you have created a marvellous character. It isn't often one can make a heroine out of a girl who is a bit, shall we say, gormless. Well, she must have been to be taken in by that brute of a man, and then to stay with him all those years. But of course there was the pull of the property, and so many women stick by such men just to keep a roof over their heads." He now glanced towards Mr Houseman as he ended, "You have only to read the daily papers."

"Yes, you're right there, Nardy; and perhaps you're right as you very often are in your summing up."

Gormless! Must have been gormless to take on a man like that. But yes, yes, I had been gormless. I still was in a way. Did these gentlemen realize that I was sitting here with my mouth metaphorically so far open it had swallowed me . . .

"What . . . ? Oh, pardon."

Before Mr Houseman could repeat what he had been saying Mr Leviston put in on a laugh, "That's a habit that Rosie had in your story, saying what. It irritated the doctor. And you know, Miss Carter, it's recognized the author puts quite a bit of himself over in his first novel."

I looked at this kindly man because I recognized that he was a kindly man, and I answered him, "You're quite right, it is a bad habit of mine, saying what."

"Not at all. How many of us go through life saying pardon, or excuse me . . ."

"Or, come again." Mr Rington's face was bright now at his own quip, and once more there was laughter. But it was checked by Mr Houseman saying, "Well, time is going on and if you've got to get to the café, Nardy, you'll soon have to be going. So, Miss Carter" — he inclined his head towards me — "to business. Well now, we are prepared to offer you five hundred pounds advance on account of royalties on your novel, half to be paid on acceptance as now and the other half on publication. How does that appear to you?"

How did it appear to me? Five hundred pounds. I drew in a long breath prior to speaking, but no words came, and he went on, "Of course, there will be royalties. It all depends on how the book sells, and this kind of story, we think, will catch on. It could, if we are all very lucky, start a kind of series about Hamilton, because you make him more of a person than a horse; he is not just a talking animal in a Walt Disney film or a cartoon; I cannot describe exactly how I view Hamilton. So, what do you say, Miss Carter?"

What I said was simply, "Thank you."

"You'll accept that?"

"Yes, thank you."

"Then the royalties. Shall we say ten percent on the first five thousand, twelve and a half percent on the next five thousand, and fifteen thereafter?"

It sounded like double Dutch to me, but I inclined my head in acceptance.

"Well now —" he lay back in his chair and smiled at me, saying, "that's over. We'll draw up a contract and send it to you. Now for the best part of the business, at least I always think it is. Lunch at the café."

Lunch at a café. I was being taken to a café for lunch, not an hotel. Well, well. Mr Leviston now stood up, saying, "I'll be back in a moment," and inclining his head towards me, he left the room.

Now Mr Rington shook me by the hand, saying, "I hope this is the beginning of a long association, Miss Carter." I mumbled something, and he too left the room.

Then Mr Houseman, coming round the desk once more, said, 'We are always very excited when we spot new talent and of your particular type. And you know, Nardy is right, there is a great deal of pathos in your story. But then, the best stories in the world have been a mixture of humour and pathos. And by the way, I like your title. Titles are always very tricky things. We often have to discuss and discuss titles, because they are as important as the jackets. But you'll come to that later on. Yet, I don't think in this case we could have bettered *Hamilton,* just plain *Hamilton.* The only thing that might happen, as was pointed out at the committee meeting, is that it might be taken for Nelson's lady, but as someone else remarked, not with a galloping horse in a bridal gown and wearing boots on the dust jacket."

"Are you going to make that the cover?" My face and voice expressed my surprise.

"Well, we're seriously thinking about it."

I laughed outright now; and at this moment Mr Leviston came back into the room. He was carrying a rolled umbrella and kid gloves. He looked very spruce and for a moment I felt dowdy, until I remembered that I had my new self on, right from my high heels to the top of my flat hair and, of course, my new hat with the cocky side. But that was another thing. Hardly any woman I'd seen in London so far was wearing a hat.

There was more handshaking, and then Mr Leviston led the way downstairs.

A taxi was waiting. "Café Royal, please," said Mr Leviston.

Café Royal! Not just an ordinary café.

"Do you know London at all, Miss Carter?" said Mr Leviston, when he was seated next to me.

"It is my first trip here."

"Really! Oh, then you have lots of surprises in store for you. But you can't hope to see them in an hour or two."

I was stunned into silence by the Café. It was evident that Mr Leviston was well known here. Before going into the dining-room, we sat in a sort of lounge and he asked me what I would like to drink. When I hesitated, he said, "Sherry, or a long drink? Pimms?"

Oh yes, I'd like a long drink, I thought, so I replied, "Yes, thank you, Pimms."

Pimms I found was very nice. It had fruit floating on the top. I'd never seen anything like it or tasted anything like it for a fruit drink. It took me some time to finish it, and when I did I felt warm inside, and for the first time in days, weeks, months, and, oh yes, years before that, I knew what it was to feel relaxed and to experience tenseness leaving my body . . .

In a long room that was all red plush, one of many waiters pulled out a chair for me to sit down. And I sat speechless, and felt even more so when I read the menu. Soup seemed the safest thing to start with. But *no, no,* this was a very, very, special day. *Cocktail de Crevettes?* That was a prawn cocktail. In plays on the television they usually started with prawn cocktails. Yes, I would have prawn cocktail . . . And what else?

Mr Leviston leant across the small table towards me from where he was sitting on what looked like a padded bench that went right along the room. Yet you couldn't call it a bench because everything was so elegant. And he said, "The duck is very nice."

"It is?"

"Yes, I can recommend it."

"Then I'll have the duck." I smiled at him.

He, too, ordered duck, but started with smoked salmon, which I saw to my surprise was a large, pinkish, wafer-thin piece of fish on an equally large plate.

When the wine waiter came, Mr Leviston said to me, "Do you prefer sweet or medium? Ladies don't often like a dry wine."

I felt sophisticated; I said, "Medium, please."

Steady, steady. I wasn't used to drink. What if it got hold of me and I passed out. Don't be silly. Don't be silly. You can have one glass; and it's different when you're eating with it, at least so I understand.

I had two glasses. When, a long time later, which time seemed to have been filled up with laughter, another waiter pushed a table towards us and began cooking pancakes which he then set alight with brandy, I knew that nothing more would surprise me. But something did.

The meal ended, the bill paid, our waiters all smiling, I stood up, and nearly toppled over. Mr Leviston, putting his hand out quickly, said, "It's the chair." And his voice dropped lower. "Ladies' vanity; high heels."

What a nice man he was. What a nice man. But there was something wrong with my legs and my head. Was I drunk? No, no, of course not. On two glasses of wine and a thing called Pimms and some brandy sauce! Could one get drunk on that?

"I will see you in the foyer." He took my arm and led me from the room. And did he point me in the way of the ladies? I'm not sure, but I found myself in that room being attended to by a very nice middle-aged woman. There was no one else there, and I sat on a chair and she bent over me, saying, "It's no good giving you a drink of water, it'll only make things worse."

"I feel dizzy," I told her.

"Well, love" — her face swam before me

— "it appears to me you mightn't have had one over the eight but you've had two up to the seven." She sounded just like Gran, although her voice was different.

I nodded and smiled at her, saying candidly, "I'm not used to it."

"Lucky for you, love; you've got pleasures to come. Look, put your face under the tap; sluice it with cold water." She led me to the basins, and I sluiced my face; then said, regretfully, "All my make-up will be off now."

"Well, here's a bit more." She opened a drawer, full of cosmetics. "Take your pick."

Through slightly blurred vision I made up my lids, dabbed some powder on my cheeks, combed my hair, and put on my hat again; then turning, I thanked the lady of the ladies, as I thought of her afterwards, and after putting fifty pence on the plate, which seemed to me an extraordinary large tip but well worth it, I said good-bye to her and walked out a little steadier but still not right.

Mr Leviston was waiting for me in the foyer. He looked at me closely, took my arm and led me outside; and there I gulped strongly at the air and immediately felt worse. Turning, I looked at him fully and said, "I'm not used to it. I've . . . I've had too much to drink. I'm . . . I'm not used to it."

His soft smile looked to me the sweetest thing I'd ever seen on a face, and he said, "Miss Carter, how refreshing to hear you say that. You know" — his face came closer to mine, but seemed to melt to either side of me — "you are a refreshing person altogether."

"I am?"

"Yes, yes, you are. And now I know why you wrote *Hamilton*."

"No, you don't." My voice sounded just like Gran's, and I saw the surprise on his face. I turned and walked somewhat unsteadily up the street, and he walked by my side, his hand through my arm. "I've got to get the train," I said now.

"What time does it go?"

"There's one something after five."

"Oh. Oh, well, it isn't three yet. We've got the afternoon for sightseeing."

I stopped and looked at him. "We have?"

"We have." He was laughing all over his face, and now I started to laugh. I opened my mouth wide and I laughed and passers-by turned and looked at me and they, too, started to laugh. And while I was laughing Mr Leviston hailed a taxi and we got in. And then we got out, and there was the river with boats on it, and Mr Leviston said, "A walk along the Embankment and a cup of strong tea and you'll be fine."

We walked and walked, and he talked. I cannot really remember all he said, but mostly I know he was describing London. Then he took me to a tea stall and ordered two cups of strong tea. I didn't like strong tea, but having drunk it I felt much steadier. Then we went back the road we had come, that was, through a churchyard, and we sat there.

There was silence between us for a time, and in it I grew ashamed. I had spoilt the day, made an ass of myself, I should have never taken that wine. I said as much. "I'm sorry," I said.

"What on earth for?" He had screwed round on the seat and was looking at me gently. "You're sorry because the wine went to your head? If you only knew how pleasant this outing has been, this lunch has been, for me. I mostly dine with people so pickled in wine that it hasn't touched their heads for years." He laughed now and added, "Oh, Miss Carter, don't be sorry for anything you do or say. It's so nice to meet someone who isn't putting on any literary side."

"Literary side?" I repeated.

"Just that, literary side. You meet all types in this business, and naturally they are all literary, but some . . . I'm going to whisper this —" he leant towards my ear and now he said, "I find some writers unbearable, arrogant, bigheaded, and egotistical. Some think that their first book is the only book that's ever been written, a worthwhile one that is; and God help us if it's successful, because then they imagine themselves little gods . . . and goddesses." He straightened up now and emphasized his last remark again with a deep obeisance of his head as he repeated, "Goddesses? Most of them are fakes."

I looked at him sadly as I said, "I'm a fake."

"You are?"

"Yes, I've . . . I've got to tell you this because it'll be about the cheque."

"The cheque?"

"Yes, the money that is going to be paid to me for the . . . the advanced royalties."

"Well, what about them?"

"Well, it'll be sent to me by cheque, won't it?"

"Yes."

"Well, I thought about this back in the office but I didn't know how to put it to Mr Houseman. I can put it to you though. Do you think I could have it paid in cash?"

"All in cash?" His expression didn't alter, although his tone showed that he was a little surprised by the suggestion.

"Yes, You see, Carter isn't my right name, nor is Miriam. It is my mother's name . . . well, by her second marriage to George Carter, who by the way is Dickie in the book, and his mother who is Mary in the book is my Gran, Hannah Carter. Do you follow?"

He blinked his eyelids rapidly, pursed his lips, then said, "Go on; I'm trying."

"Well, you see, I —" I turned away and looked across the flat headstones for a moment before bending my head and muttering, "I'm Rosie in the book." He was quiet for so long that I turned slowly and looked at him, and I'll always remember the expression that was on his face and what he said. "Oh, my dear," he murmured; "and to think that I said those things about her . . ."

"You were right. I was gullible. I still am, I suppose, but not so much. You see, looking as I did, as I do" — I pointed to my face — "I've just been made up for the occasion today. And . . . and with this" — I touched my short arm which I must say not one of the three men had seemed to notice, which proved them to be gentlemen indeed — "I thought he was my only chance and that nobody else would ever want to marry me. And I was lonely. But as I said in the story, it was the house he was after. He had a sister, but I haven't brought in May, because she died of leukaemia in my house, and towards the end she knew and admitted she had done wrong because it was she who manoeuvred us both into the marriage."

"Is he as nasty as you make him out in the book?"

I looked away over the headstones again before I answered, "Much worse."

"And . . . and you've put up with this for years just because of your house?"

I turned and faced him again, saying now, "It isn't just a house, it's all I've got, and I was born there. And . . . and another thing, I hate the idea of him achieving his aim."

"And you really think it's worth it? He . . . he could have driven you mad. The horse business, was that through him?"

"Not really, no." I gave a small smile now. "I think he began first as a dog, when I was very young, then later on as a little girl friend, at least that's what I like to fancy, because I had the habit of talking to myself. There didn't seem to be anyone else to talk to. Then when I lost George, Dickie in the story, things were bad at home with my mother and I had to have someone . . . something, and so, Hamilton. But he really came into being through the doctor, when he told me I had horse sense. Anyway, now you know. Will you have to tell the others? Will it make any difference?"

"Well, I'll have to tell Bernard . . . Mr Houseman, and Tom too, and perhaps our financial director. But Bernard could explain to him that it was just a fad of yours, not wanting the money to go into the bank. But I think that Bernard, being the chairman of the company, should know. I'm sure we can work out something to meet your wishes. It will not make the slightest difference, though, your going under the name of Miriam Carter. There's one point, however. Would your husband recognize himself if he read it?"

"No, I don't think he would. But the doctor might. Yes, I'm sure he would."

"Anyway, you have set the story in the south country. Do you know that part at all about which you have written?"

"No, not a thing. I looked at a map and altered the names a bit. But I imagine one town is as much like another: there's a high end and a low end and a struggling middle."

He sat looking at me in silence for quite some time, and I had no words with which to break it. Then he said, "You know, I'll remember this day for a very long time as a day on which I met for the first time a remarkable young woman."

I gave an embarrassed laugh. "You know, in some way, Mr Leviston," I said, "you're like George, or Dickie. You're kind."

"Kind? Nonsense. I'm stating a fact, and from now on —" He suddenly leant forward and caught my hand and gripped it tightly as he shook it up and down, saying, "You must look upon yourself as a personality. Forget Rosie, forget Miriam. What is your real name by the way?"

"Mrs Stickle . . . It's an awful name. I was Maisie Rochester."

"Oh, that's a good name, Rochester. Got a ring about it, Maisie Rochester. Well from now on, I shall think of you as Maisie Rochester, a novelist who's going places."

"Oh, Mr Leviston." I was shaking his hand up and down as I said, "You know something? This has been the most wonderful day of my life. No matter what happens in the future, nothing will ever be able to surpass it or dim it. There's only one other desire I want in life and I doubt if I'll ever accomplish it. I have neither the strength nor the courage, but it doesn't matter."

"May I ask what your other desire is?"

For the first time in weeks I saw Hamilton. He came galloping across the headstones to stand right behind Mr Leviston, and I watched him place his right front hoof on his shoulder and rest his chin on the top of his head. I closed my eyes and muttered, "Oh, Hamilton."

"You want to achieve something with Hamilton?"

"No, no." I shook my head. Then, my eyes wide and tears of laughter dimming them now, I said, "Would you believe it if I told you Hamilton was standing right behind you with his right front . . . hoof on your shoulder, signifying to me that he considers you a very worthy man? Would you believe it?"

"Miss Rochester —" He was laughing now, too, his own eyes bright with moisture as he replied, "I'll believe anything you say. If Hamilton is embracing me, then please tell him I am honoured. But now, satisfy my curiosity and tell me of this other thing, this other desire you have to make your life complete."

"I want to hit my husband."

He looked at me. I looked at him. And Hamilton looked from one to the other. And then our laughter joined. We laughed so loudly that the noise seemed to re-echo from one headstone to another. And when two ladies, taking a stroll, stopped in front of us, and one of them admonished us with, "I would have thought you would have found some other place where you could express your hilarity," before walking on, like two children, we slunk up from the bench and Mr Leviston took my arm and, to quote a term, we went on our way rejoicing.

Chapter 4

During the months that followed, my life became so full of concealed excitement that I failed to notice yet another change in Howard's life style. I didn't seem to think it very strange that, having gone out practically every night during the past years, he now seemed to spend more evenings at home in his bottle room. After I had gone to bed I often heard him downstairs, but I was so full of my own affairs that it didn't seem to matter. For instance, I was corresponding regularly with Mr Leviston. He had done some editing on my book which, I understood, meant deleting bits here and there where I had repeated myself and tightening up, as he put it, loose threads.

I was to go up next week for a meeting

with him, as he again so tactfully put it, to discuss whether I was in agreement or not with the alterations he had made. The next step would be the proofs.

They hoped the book would come out in the following spring. It seemed a long time to wait, but I understood that this was the usual procedure: the publishing of a book didn't come about overnight. I was also, at this time, well into another story of Hamilton; but most of this story, I must say, was wishful thinking. In it, Rosie had, on the grounds of cruelty, managed to get a divorce from her husband and was now doing a weekly column all about Hamilton in a national paper. I had found plenty of new escapades to lay at Hamilton's door; I took some of the characters from our terrace and a number from Gran's neighbours. I again brought in the doctor, and the priest, and, too, my kindly solicitor who, in this second edition, was fighting the case against the husband who was claiming damages for libel.

And so it was with some surprise and return of the never far submerged feeling of fear that I viewed Howard as he thrust open the study door and approached my little desk.

There, he stood looking down at me in

silence for a full minute before, leaning over my typewriter, he said, "Carry on, Maisie. Carry on. I've nearly got you where I want you. It's taken time, but everything comes to him who waits." And on this he turned about and walked out, and I found that I was trembling from head to foot and that my good hand was clutching my throat.

When there penetrated my mind the sound of a little whirr to the side of me, I put out my short arm and switched off the small tape recorder I had acquired some time ago. I'd found this instrument very handy, especially when I was along at Gran's and she came out with something that would set me laughing. So that I shouldn't forget exactly what she had said, or the tales she related to me, I had bought this little pocket tape recorder. She didn't know for some long time that I was using it. Of course, when she moved a distance away into the kitchen, the voice on the tape almost disappeared.

When she eventually found out about it and I played her own voice back to her, she wouldn't believe it, and it was sometime after this before I could persuade her to talk naturally, and forget about the machine.

But now I ran the tape back some way, and there his voice came over to me, repeating the words, "I've nearly got you where I want you. It's taken time, but everything comes to him who waits." The words sounded as ominous on the tape as they had done when he voiced them.

But as I sat staring ahead of me, wondering what new scheme he had in his evil mind for me, it gradually came to me that I had a witness. At last I had a witness, a witness that couldn't lie.

I was shaking with excitement when I picked up the little recorder. Yes. Yes, I could put it in my blouse. I could stick it down the bib of my fancy house apron. I grabbed the little instrument and held it to my chest. It could be a life-saver, my life-saver. If this machine could register the things he said to me, and the way he said them, then I too might have the means of divorce in my hands. Oh, wonderful. Wonderful.

Then something happened the following day that seemed to make the use of the tape recorder quite unnecessary.

When I went round to Gran's I found another letter from Mr Leviston. The contents were intriguing. It started:

Dear Miss Carter — he continued to call me Miss Carter — I have great news for you, but unfortunately I may not divulge it. This pleasure, I'm afraid, must be left to Mr Houseman; but I can say, you're on your way.

When I showed it to Gran, she said, "And what does all that mean, d'you think?"

"You've got as much idea as I have."

"He seems a nice man, that Mr Leviston."

"Yes, he is." And now I leant towards her as I said, "You've said that before and I've given you the same answer before: He seems a nice man, that Mr Leviston, and, Yes, he is. And that's that, Gran. He's a publisher. He's on the wrong side of forty, he's going grey, and I don't even know if he's married or not. I don't know anything about him only that he is, as I said, a nice man. What's the matter?"

She had turned from me and gone to the fireplace and, with one foot on the fender and her elbow on the low mantelpiece, she turned her head towards me and said, "I heard something in the club yesterday that I think's very fishy. You know Sarah Talbot? Well, you've heard me talk of her, the one that's had nine and they're all married and scattered round and hardly any of them want to know her now except the one that lives out Durham way. Remember?"

"Yes, yes, I remember."

"She's the one whose husband went to the races when she was in labour with her first bairn. He won a good bit an' he went on the spree, an' she didn't see him for days."

"That's the one?"

"Aye, that's her. Well now, Sarah's youngest lass Maggie was put to the trade in Hempies' down in the sewing-room, and she didn't like it. But anyway, she's married now and that's the one that Sarah visits, an' she tells me, Sarah does, that Bob, that's her son-in-law, took them all out, kids an' all, for a run. Well, apparently the car started to steam up, needed water, so Maggie said. I thought cars ran on petrol." She grinned now, then went on, "Anyway, Bob said to Maggie, 'Go and ask at that cottage for a can of water,' and off Maggie went. And Sarah said she followed her just to stretch her legs, and she reached Maggie just as the door opened, and who should open it in his shirt-sleeves?" She now stared at me, and I waited, and then she said, "Your husband."

"Howard?" I hardly heard my own whisper.

"Aye, Howard. Now our Maggie worked for him, so she wasn't mistaken. And as for Sarah, it was him who she had to see to get Maggie the job. Sarah said he lost his colour for a bit and he seemed unable to speak until Maggie said, 'Hello, Mr Stickle. We . . . we've run out of water, the car's boiling. Do you think you could oblige?' "

"Sarah said he grabbed the can from her, shut the door an' left them standing on the path; but he was back in a minute and he thrust the can at Maggie an' said, 'I'm visitin' a friend.'

" 'Oh,' Maggie said, 'It's nice to get away from the town a bit.' And he said, 'Yes, it is. I always take the opportunity when I can.'

"Sarah said they had just got out of the gate and into the road when round the corner from a narrow side road came two young lads, about nine or ten, she would say. They come pedalling up an', jumpin' off their bikes, they propped them against the railings afore running through the gate, calling, 'Dad. Dad.' Now whether there was another man inside or whether your dear Howard has a family on the side, and has had all these years, I don't know, but it's up to you, lass, to find out."

I sat down on the couch, leant my elbow on the head of it, and rested my head in my hand. All these years, supposedly visiting his boss, Mr Hempies. All the money he had got out of me, all to keep another home going and the woman and children . . . Were they his?

"What are you going to do, lass?"

I lifted my head from my hands and it rocked on my shoulders; it seemed, at this moment, too big for my body. It was expanding, my mind was pushing it in all directions, because I was being filled with a blind anger. *Gullible?* That name didn't fit me; I was *mental.* Yes, that's what I was, and had been for years, *mental.* Why hadn't I gone to the shop? Why hadn't I insisted on being recognized as the wife of Mr Hempies's manager, just for once, just once? Why hadn't I asserted myself in some way, instead of staying in my prison, my privately owned prison, because that's what I had made my house into, a privately owned prison, with a gaoler who was determined to see me die in order to get it . . . and bring his woman there . . . and his children.

My God! I was standing on my feet now and I knew Gran had hold of me by the shoulders, and I was repeating aloud, "Twelve years. Twelve years. I'm insane, Gran. I'm insane. I should have known that no boss, however good, would invite his manager week after week after week, year after year. I'm insane . . ."

"Stop it, lass. Stop it. Now look, listen. Listen to me. You've got a way out. Go and have a look, see for yourself, then go to your solicitor. Now calm yourself. Come on, calm yourself. Sit yourself down again and I'll make a cup of tea and put a drop whisky in it."

"Saturday, Sunday. He won't be there till then, and I've got to go to London on Friday."

"Well, go to London on Friday; there's nothin' to stop you. In the meantime, I'll see Sarah and get her to ask their Maggie to see if their Bob will run you out from Durham next Sunday. Maggie'll fix it, I know, because she can't stand the sight of Stickle."

A minute or so later, when she brought me up a cup of tea that smelt strongly of whisky, I gulped at it; then I said, "I don't think I can go to London on Friday. I wouldn't be able to keep my mind on things."

"You're going to London on Friday. Strikes me things are moving in all directions and you're not going to miss any more chances in life. You're going to London on Friday."

I went to London on Friday, and Mr Houseman told me the good news: not only was a magazine considering the book for serialisation, but a paperback company wanted to do it, too. Wasn't that wonderful, he said.

Indeed, yes, yes, it was wonderful, I said.

There followed more small talk. And then I spent an hour with Mr Leviston in his office going over the alterations he had made on my manuscript.

I was again to be taken out to lunch and Mr Leviston told me that he had chosen a place that specialized in fish dishes. Did I like fish?

Yes, I said, I was very fond of fish.

It wasn't until sometime later, when we were sitting in the fish restaurant, that he suddenly stopped joking about what wine I should drink on this occasion, and, looking intently at me, he said, "Excuse my remarking on this, Miss Carter, but is there anything wrong?"

"No, no."

"You're quite happy with the arrangements Mr Houseman has made?"

"Oh, yes, yes. That's like a fairy tale; I just cannot believe any part of it. And . . . and you're all so kind, it's bewildering. No, it isn't anything to do with the book or . . ."

"But there is something?"

"Yes."

"Oh, well" — he sat back in his chair — "as long as you're satisfied with the business arrangements. I'm sorry if it appears that I'm probing, but your spontaneous gaiety seems lacking today."

My spontaneous gaiety. I never knew I had any gaiety in me. I saw the funny side of things, but . . . spontaneous gaiety. That was putting a fancy name to it. He was very kind, Mr Leviston. Of a sudden, I felt myself choking and I reached out and, picking up the wine glass, gulped at the wine.

From then on Mr Leviston seemed to do all the talking. Would I like to go to the National Gallery, or Madame Tussaud's? Or what about the Tower of London? The whole afternoon stretched before us.

I managed to say, "You're very kind, but I mustn't take up all your time. I really don't expect it, and I can go on my own now."

He put his head on one side and said in what I took to be mock sadness, "You don't want my company?"

"Oh, Mr Leviston." I bowed my head and shook it from side to side, and at this he said, "All right, it's the British Museum."

It was a lovely meal, but somehow I didn't enjoy it, as I had done on the other occasion, for all the time I was comparing this kind of living with what I had to put up with every day. Yet at the same time, I was wise enough to know that the three gentlemen I had met likely lived an ordinary family life away from the office, and that wining and dining clients was just part of the business. But above all, my thoughts were on that man back in Fellburn in the tailor's shop, who had for years treated me worse than a slave. Oh yes, much worse than any slave, for if in the old days they had been tortured it had been physically, but that man had almost maimed me mentally, while all the time he was living with another woman and supporting her on the money he had black-mailed out of me. And . . . a very sore point, those children could be his.

When, later, we were walking along the street, Mr Leviston remained quiet until we came to St. Paul's, Covent Garden, church-yard again, and here he did not say, "Let us sit down," but, stopping in front of me, he said, "Please don't consider it presumption on my part, Miss Carter, but I had so much pleasure from our first meeting and this has continued through your letters. You write a remarkably graphic letter, you know. So I feel that I have known you for quite some time; and then, of course, I have been going over your work and knowing it is partly your life story, so it is with genuine concern that I say to you, would you like to talk about what is troubling you?"

I didn't answer him for perhaps a full minute and then I said, "Yes, yes, I would. But I'm afraid, if I did, I . . . I would start to cry, and make a fool of myself in the open." I glanced from side to side at the people passing to and fro.

He also seemed to take some time in speaking. Then of a sudden, he caught me by the arm and turned me round, saying, "Come on. Come on."

He now led me through Covent Garden, past the Opera House, and into a main thoroughfare. There he hailed a taxi and, pressing me into it, he gave the driver an address. Seated now, I looked at him for enlightenment but he said nothing, simply sat looking straight ahead. It was a good fifteen minutes later when the taxi stopped, in a street of tall houses, each with an iron balcony fronting the upper windows.

After paying the taxi he led me up three broad steps, the top one flanked by urns. He inserted a key in the beautifully polished brown door, then took my arm again and led me into a hall and into a lift, and when it stopped he once more took my arm and led me into a grey-panelled hallway. The floor was covered by a dull rose coloured carpet in which my feet seemed to sink. There was a marble hallstand against one wall and he placed his umbrella on it; then coming behind me, he said, "Let me have your coat. You'll find it warm in here."

Slowly I took off my coat, and as I adjusted the collar of my blouse he said, "And your hat." He was smiling at me now, so I took off my hat; then going before me, he pushed open a door and called loudly, "You there, Janet?"

At the same time he had thrust one arm behind him and caught hold of my hand and so led me into the most beautiful room I'd ever seen. It was large and high, and beyond the big window at the end I could see the iron balcony. I could just take in that the colour of the walls was grey and that the carpet continued from the hallway; but what stood out like sunshine was the drapes at the window and the upholstery of the big couch and easy chairs. The colour was like a citrus yellow and it gave the whole room an air of bright sunshine.

"There you are, Janet. And don't look so surprised to see me. What were you doing, guzzling tea as usual?"

"Oh, Mr Leonard, there's some time in this place to guzzle tea, with all the work to be done." As the woman spoke she was looking at me; and now Mr Leviston said, in a different tone, "This is Janet. And Janet, this is Miss Carter." And he pointed to the elderly woman, adding now, "Janet keeps me and my house in order, and has done for as long as I can remember."

Now clapping his hands together and his tone becoming light once more, he said, "Well, now introductions are over, what about it, Janet, a cup of your best?"

"Well, I'll see what I can do for you." Janet turned away smiling, and Mr Leviston took me up the room towards the window, saying, "It's right what I said, she's been here all my life. You wouldn't think she was sixty-seven, would you?"

"No, no."

"She's been in this house fifty years, except during those periods she was giving birth to one or other of her brood. She's had eight children."

"Never!"

"Yes." He nodded at me. "She came to work for my mother before I was born and as she will tell you, no doubt, before very long, it was later her daily chore to push me in my pram over there." We were now standing at the window, and he pointed to where in the middle of a square was a garden. "It wasn't railed round in those days," he said. "But now, all the residents who support it have keys to it, although you hardly ever see anyone in there except the gardener. But it's nice to look upon."

"It's lovely . . . it's a lovely view. And this room." I turned about. "I've never seen anything so beautiful."

"It is a nice room, isn't it? My mother designed it. It was her hobby, interior decorating. There are six other rooms like it, almost as large. As my father used to say, you could drive round the bed in a coach and pair. These were all bedrooms up here at one time when we owned the whole house."

"You owned the whole house?"

"Yes, but what could I do with a huge place like this? So I had it turned into three flats, although you could hardly call them flats. Now" — he motioned with his hand — "come and sit down. But before you say anything, I want to say my piece, and it's just this: I'm not in the habit of bringing young ladies — not even when they're authors — to my home. I may tell you you're the first author who has ever been here. I'm not" — he laughed now — "inferring that it's an honour, only I want you to know I don't make a habit of pushing young ladies into taxis and landing them in my apartments. In fact, if I told Bernard or Tom . . . Rington you know, that I had abducted you, they wouldn't believe me."

He was talking to put me at ease, and when Janet brought the tea in, he joked with her and she chaffed him back and for a moment I thought, here was another one who sounded like Gran, only more refined.

"Would you like to pour out? Or shall I?"

"You do it, please."

I drank my tea in silence, but my mind was working rapidly. I was bewildered by events and not a little surprised to find myself sitting in this beautiful room drinking tea with this kind man, who was a very surprising individual. Somehow I had imagined him to be married with a family; I never thought of him being a bachelor. Perhaps he was married and was separated from his wife. Perhaps he had been married and she had died. But that wasn't the point, the point was that he had brought me here so that I could tell him what was troubling me, and cry if I must.

I put my cup down and with my right hand I gripped the upper part of my short arm. I only just in time stopped myself from rocking backwards and forwards, but abruptly I started. "I . . . I got a shock," I said, "I learned something about my husband and it upset me. Not that it hurt my feelings in the way it might have done if I cared for him. You understand?"

He said nothing, but inclined his head towards me.

"But, over the years he has —" I closed my eyes tightly and bowed my head now and my throat filled up; then with my head still bowed I said, "Like in the story, my mother left me the house and furniture, but what I didn't mention in the story was that she also left me over four thousand pounds, and after what he had put me through when we were married I determined he wouldn't get it and passed it all over in trust to Gran, my step-grandmother. But over the years he got every penny. It was the only way I could save myself from . . . his physical abuse or keep my dog. The first amount, seven hundred and fifty pounds, supposedly to enter in partnership with the owner of the shop. Anyway —" I gulped again and found difficulty in going on, but he remained silent, and after a moment I said, "And now, I have found out that all the time he must have been living with a woman. And . . . and there are children, so perhaps they are his. All these years he is supposed to have spent the week-ends at his employer's house." I raised my head now and, the tears streaming down my face, I muttered, "What . . . what hurts me is the fact that he has treated me like a brainless idiot, and also that at times I have been so paralysed with fear of him I wanted to fly away. But then I used to ask myself where I could fly to. Only to Gran's and her two little rooms, you see." I dried my eyes now. "I loved my house. It's nothing like this." I spread my hand out, my wet handkerchief dangling from it. "But it is nice and it's all I have. In those early days I couldn't see me ever holding down any kind of a post outside the house. I had this" — I patted my short arm — "and then, I was so painfully plain, still am . . ."

His hand came out now and caught my wrist but he still said nothing, and I went on, "And recently, he has something else hatching. He told me so. What it is I don't know. But this is the kind of thing that attacks one's nerves. Anyway, on Sunday I'm going to see this cottage where I'm told he lives, and I shall take matters from there."

"My dear Miss Carter." The tone of his voice almost caused the tears to flow again, and then he said, "It's incredible that you should have put up with this for so long, yet I understand your feelings about your home; I feel the same about this." He lifted his eyes to the moulded and painted ceiling. "I cannot imagine my feelings if someone tried to take it from me . . . He must be a demon of a man."

"I don't suppose you would think so if you met him, because . . . he appears to have a certain gentleness of manner. It's the salesman in him. And the irony of it is, the people in the terrace think he's quite a gentleman and that I have been more than lucky to have married him; in fact, I know they pitied him for having such a wife."

"Oh, Miss Car. . . No, I'm not going to call you Miss Carter any more, I'm not even going to ask your permission, I'm going to call you Maisie."

I smiled weakly at him as I said, "That's an awful name too."

"Of course, it isn't. Maisie" — he seemed to roll his tongue around it — "sort of indicates jollity, and, you know, there's a lot of jollity in you. Your humour testifies to this."

Yes — I thought for a moment — I suppose my frolics with Hamilton could be put down to jollity, but at the present moment I felt anything but jolly, for I was beginning to feel foolish in having unburdened myself like this to a man who was . . . well, almost a stranger . . . Nonsense! I chided myself, for I don't think I've got to know anybody in my life, with the exception of George and Gran, as much as I have done Mr Leviston.

Now he was repeating his name, saying, "And no more Mr Leviston, everybody calls me Nardy. I'm not quite sure if I like that name or not, but I'm stuck with it. It was given to me by a very charming man. You see, James Houseman, Bernard's brother, started the business, the publishing business, and James *was* a very charming man. But he had a bad stammer, and when I joined the firm at eighteen — I never made university" — he smiled widely now — "I never had that kind of brain — James, who was a friend of my father, said, send the lad to us. And so the lad went to them, and I've been there ever since. But with regard to my name: James had a booming voice and you can imagine, with the stammer, how it sounded, and as my name was Leonard, he seemed to have some difficulty with it and he would shout, Le . . . n . . . nard . . . y, so in the end it sounded more like Nardy, and this stuck."

I was smiling at him now as I said, "It's a friendly name."

"Well, do you think you can be friendly and call me by it?"

Oh dear. I wasn't good at calling people by their Christian name.

"Try; it won't be too hard; you get used

314

to it after a time." But now his tone changed to a serious note, and he went on, "If you confirm your suspicions on Sunday, you must go directly to a solicitor. You have one?"

"Yes, and he knows a little of the situation. I had to go to him to arrange about the money in the first place."

"Good. But about your fear of this man, can't you have someone in the house as a sort of companion for the present time, a friend?"

It took me a moment to admit that I had no friends to speak of. I said, "I know a number of people who go to the Writers' Circle. They are all acquaintances, but somehow . . . well, I suppose it's my fault, I don't seem to be able to make friends all that easily. I had one very close friend in my young days; she lived down the terrace. You know, I mentioned her in the book; I make her mother the High Church lady who didn't think I was a suitable companion for her daughter, rather obstructive in the marriage market. And that's true. I found out, and only in recent years, that that was why Katie's mother stopped our friendship: I would be a drawback to her meeting the right young men."

I watched him rise from the chair and

walk to the window and stand there looking out; and this he did for a good few minutes before he said, "You know, Maisie, I hate to admit it, but there are lots of cruel people in the world. I have such a nature that I want to think everybody is nice, everything is rosy and comfortable. I was brought up in this house in the most happy atmosphere and it didn't serve me to any good purpose when I went out into the world. When I recognized the meanness, the cruelness, and the vindictiveness in human nature, I was for running back into this nest. But my mother was a very wise woman, she pushed me out. She even wouldn't let me live here; she made me set up in a flat on my own. Oh, that was an experience." He half turned, pulled a little face at me, then turning fully towards me, said, "You know, Maisie, I think it's the petty meanness that hurts one the most, the trickery, the chicanery that one meets in business. Not so much, I'm pleased to say, in our line, although it still goes on. Yet none of it seems to have the impact on me as does the small meannesses. I'm afraid that I allow these to grow out of all proportion in my mind. However, at this moment when I'm comparing my life with yours, I'm really ashamed that I allow such trivialities to worry me. But Maisie —" he took a step towards me and caught my hand and, bending his face down to mine, he said earnestly, "you really have the best years of your life before you, you are still so young."

"I'm on thirty-one."

"Thirty-one!" His voice was scornful. "You could start anew from here and really live . . . and I mean really live, a happy successful life, because you've got a talent that you've only recently unearthed, and it will ripen and grow. Come on, now, up and at 'em!" As he pulled me to my feet he said, "Sunday is your turning point; you'll know where you're going from then on."

Sunday didn't turn out to be my turning point. I rode in the car with Mrs Talbot, her daughter Maggie, and Maggie's husband Bob, and we stopped some distance from the cottage and we saw nothing, no movement. When we got in the car again and passed it, two boys were kicking a ball on the grass patch that was edged by the railings. Bob stopped the car some distance away at the other side of the cottage; then he said he would dander back as if he was out for a walk. Nobody would recognize him.

He was away almost fifteen minutes, and when he returned he said he had seen the woman. He reckoned she was about forty, and a blonde, but she had a head scarf on and a coat. He had skirted the back of the cottage by walking along the edge of a field, but he hadn't seen the sight of any man, and when he came back past it, the woman was playing football with the boys.

There was always another time, Bob said. He might be playing clever and sitting tight in the house. What about trying on a Saturday? He'd be pleased to run me out. I thanked him and said, "All right, next Saturday."

The following day, Monday, I wrote to Nardy, as I now thought of him, and told him what had transpired. By return of post he was brief and to the point: to keep trying, he said. His letters were not a bit like his conversation, because that wasn't stilted at all.

Towards the end of the week, I received another letter from him. This said that at a board meeting the previous day they had decided to bring the date of publication of the book forward and were going to do a rush job on it in order that it would be in the shops for Christmas. Wouldn't that be nice? he said.

Yes, it would be . . . or would have been if my mind hadn't been in a turmoil, for I knew Howard was brewing something.

But what?

I kept a close watch on Bill. Bill was aging fast and he hadn't been well of late. I'd had him to the vet's who said he had a little trouble with his kidneys. This had confirmed my suspicions that there was something wrong internally with him, because he didn't visit as many lamp-posts as usual, and when he deigned to stop at one his acquaintance with it was mostly half-hearted. I was so afraid that something might happen to him through Howard's hands or feet that I was now taking his basket up into the bedroom, but whereas at one time he would bound up the stairs after me now he would lumber laboriously, and I often had to assist him from half-way up.

I didn't know what I would do if anything happened to Bill, or when it happened to Bill, for the vet said he was old for a bull-terrier, nearing thirteen, he thought. I had Hamilton. Or did I? Hamilton seemed shy of me these days, standing in faraway corners, even sometimes turning his back on me. This would happen when he didn't seem to agree with my thinking. But Bill was a different matter. Bill was something I could hold . . . no not something, someone, for his love for me was a thing apart from any other feeling I had ever experienced. This ugly lumbersome piece of animal flesh had shown me more affection than anyone else in my life; yes, even than George.

So I was worried about Bill. If it had been possible I would have left him at Gran's, but he was too much of a handful for her. She said so openly. She didn't mind looking after him for a day, but I knew she was always relieved when I took him home . . .

I went with the Talbots to Durham the following Saturday, and the Saturday after that, and the Saturday after that, and the Sunday after that, but not one of us saw anything of Howard, not even of any man. We saw the children and the woman. They were always about the place, but no man was present. I later said to Gran, "Mrs Talbot must have made a mistake."

"Look, lass," she said: "if Sarah made a mistake, Maggie didn't. She spoke to him and called him by his name. He's there but he's lying low. He's playin' a game with you. I'd bet me bottom dollar that he knows you're on to him."

"No, no, I don't think he does . . . And yet."

"What do you mean by, an' yet?" she said.

"Last night I was going upstairs just as he was about to come down, and he stopped and he pushed his face almost into mine and said, 'Ha, ha!' "

"Ha, ha?"

"Just that, ha, ha!"

"Well, if you want any proof, there you have it; he's laughing up his sleeve at you. If I were you, you know what I'd do? I'd take some of your money and put a private detective on to him. I would. I would that." . . .

I thought about this. I thought about it for days. And the days went into a few weeks, and then it was November, and it became bitterly cold and the heavy frosts in the morning lay like snow on the window panes.

It was partly through the frost that the climax came about, and *I did it.* I did what I had wanted to do for the past thirteen years. *I did it . . .*

During the past month my eyelid had begun to flicker and the corner of my mouth to twitch and I had once again been paying my weekly visits to the doctor. And on this Monday morning when I went into the surgery he glanced up from writing something on a pad and his look said, "Oh, you again." At least that's what I thought. I had come to the conclusion that in spite of his telling me I had a lot of horse sense, he thought that I really was stupid at bottom, or I wouldn't put up with the cause of my twitch.

His hands flat on the desk now, he sat back in his chair and said, "Well, what now?"

"I'm feeling awful," I said.

He sighed, dropped his head to the side and began, "Maisie, the cure's in your own hands. I've been telling you that for years. In fact, I'm tired of telling you, tired of seeing you. Do you know that?" He now poked his head across the table towards me, but there was a slight smile behind the whiskers which I noticed had gone grey half-way down the cheeks. It was as if he had put a false beard on, because I hadn't noticed the change in colour before. Likely too concerned about myself, I thought. He now asked quietly, "Any change? . . . I mean, with him?"

"Yes."

"In what way?"

"He's acting oddly, and I didn't tell you before but he threatened me. Some weeks ago he threatened me."

"What did he say?"

"I can't remember the exact words but it was to the effect that it wouldn't be long now, that he had something on me."

"He can get nothing on you, can he? You don't do anything that you shouldn't do?" It was a question.

"No."

"You don't sound so sure."

I longed at this moment to tell him about my book, and I felt if I had he would have been so pleased for me. But I couldn't, so what I said was, "I do a bit of writing."

"What kind of writing?"

"Oh, well —" I looked down at my hands as I muttered, "funny bits. Well, all kinds."

"You write funny bits?"

He was surprised.

"Yes —" I looked up at him now, and, my tone slightly arrogant, I said, "I write funny bits . . . about a horse."

His features became lost in the fuzz of his beard as he repeated, "Funny bits about a horse?"

"Yes." And when I said, "I talk to this horse; I've talked to him for years," he rose from the seat, then sat down again, and after a moment he half muttered, half growled, "Maisie, what are you telling me?"

"I'm telling you, Doctor, that I write funny bits of things about me talking to this horse and the antics he gets up to."

"Maisie, Maisie." He stared at me silently for some seconds, and then he said, "Do you leave these bits lying around?"

"No; I . . . well, I hide them in the attic under the floor boards."

"And you've been doing this for years?"

"Yes. I had to have someone to talk to and . . . and something to make me laugh, or else I would have gone insane."

I knew by his face I'd said the wrong word, and now he said, slowly, "Maisie, if that husband of yours gets his hands on those bits of writing, he'll try to prove just that. He's that kind of man."

"Yes, yes." It was as if a light had come into my mind clearing the fog. Had he discovered all that stuff under the floor boards? It could be, and . . . and that was what he was holding against me, thinking it would — I could hardly think the words myself — certify me insane. But no, no. I shook my head at the very thought. Lots of people talked to animals . . . Yes, but not in the same way as I talked to Hamilton. People talk to real animals. I talked to an imaginary horse, who had become so real to me that at times he wasn't a figment of my imagination at all; and this had definitely come over in my writing. That's why they had taken the book.

I felt sick.

"You're a very odd girl, you know, Maisie."

He was staring at me; I answered him in the same vein: "In my experience I've found that I don't happen to be the only one," I said.

"Oh no, you're right there." He gave a small laugh. "But in this case, your oddness might give that husband of yours a very strong lever. Not that I can see it would be strong enough to do anything drastic, but say for instance he decided . . . or he took it further with the idea that you weren't capable of running the house unless you had treatment or some such. It's been done. Oh, it's been done. He would then have the house to himself, if only for a time . . ."

"And bring a woman in."

"Well, you said it."

"Yes, yes," — I nodded at him — "I said it. And . . . and I can see it now. Yes, I can see it now." I was on my feet and, leaning over the desk towards him, I blurted out, "The business of the cottage and him being recognized there, and his supposed staying with his boss at weekends."

When I finished, he was round the desk, his hands on my shoulders pressing me down into the chair again. "Maisie," he said quietly, "what you've got to do is to go to a solicitor and tell him all this. Oh no, you needn't tell him about your horse, just what you found out about the cottage, and ask his advice. Myself, I know what I would do, but I'm not a legal man; and in this case, it's better that I keep my mouth shut, at least at present. Now, do as I tell you. You get yourself to a solicitor. You have one, haven't you? Do you like him?"

"Yes, he's a very nice man, thoughtful."

"Well, spill the beans to him. Go on, and do it this very morning. You will, won't you?"

"Yes, yes, thank you, Doctor." I stood up feeling a little calmer now and, strangely, for the first time I spoke in an ordinary way to him, not as if he was a doctor, and what I said was, "You know, you've been like a friend to me all these years. And there's something else I would like to be able to tell you, but I can't, not yet awhile. But when I can, you'll be the first to know."

"Something else? Now, come clean. Is it to do with . . . ?"

"No, no; nothing like that. It's one good thing that's happened to me, but because of Howard I'm frightened he'll get to know, and so I can't tell you what it is yet."

"You *are* a strange lass, Maisie."

"You said that before, Doctor. And you know something, some day you'll know just what I think about you."

He screwed up his eyes until they were almost lost in his hair then he shook his head gently while guiding me to the door, and with no further exchange of words I went out.

As he had advised, I went and saw my solicitor. His office was only a bus ride away in Gateshead. I told him not only about Howard's suspected double life, but why I had withdrawn the money bit by bit after putting it in security through Gran, and the fear that I had lived in for years.

"You've been a very foolish young woman," he said; "you should have made a stand right from the first, and I'm sure none of this would have happened." And to this I replied, "Oh yes, it would, Mr Pearson; you don't know my husband."

I arrived back home about half past twelve. It was freezing cold. I had to be careful in mounting the three steps to the front door because they were still slippery with the frost as the wintry sun hadn't got round to the front of the house yet. A cardboard box was lying to the side of the door. It was full of bottles, a dozen or so, I would say, in it and two or three lying across the top. Someone knowing of Howard's interest had left them there. The children very rarely left the bottles, they always knocked on the door and expected a copper for them.

I left the box where it was and went indoors. Bill heard me and set up a weak bark from the kitchen. I hadn't taken him to Gran's this morning as he didn't seem too well, and I'd had a job to get him to do his usual business. But now, after greeting me, he went to the back door, and I opened it and said to him, "Well, just go on round the yard." I had closed the front gate and the back gate was locked, so he couldn't get out. I always left the storehouse door open so that he could go in and take shelter if he wanted to. I had put a hessian bag there with some straw in it and covered it with a blanket, and often he would snuggle down in this.

I next made myself a cup of tea, and while drinking it, I opened two brown envelopes I'd found on the mat. They were articles from members of the Writers' Circle asking for them to be typed. I still had quite a bit of work to catch up on, but seemed disinclined to do it these days as I wanted to get on with my own book. Up to the past week or so, it had been going very well. I'd devised some quite funny pieces concerning Hamilton's reactions to my thinking.

After pouring myself out another cup of

tea, I picked up the manuscripts and went into the study. The room was icy cold and, after switching on the electric fire, I had to hold my fingers over it before I could get them flexed in order to type. But then, with my hands on the keys, I found that my mind wouldn't work, either to do the request for typing or, yet, get on with my book: I was asking myself what would be the outcome of it all, would I ever have sufficient proof to get a divorce from Howard when I heard Bill bark, not ferociously like he used to do when anyone came in the gate, but nevertheless, he was barking.

I rose from the chair and had just reached the study door when I heard the key grating in the lock. That was Howard, and it was just on one o'clock. The shop closed between half past twelve and half past one for lunch, but he never came home for a meal.

Almost with a spring, I was sitting on my chair again in front of the typewriter, and two things happened almost immediately: I saw Hamilton standing near the window rearing upwards on his hind legs; at the same time my hand went out and I switched on the little tape recorder that was lying on the desk by the side of the typewriter. It was half hidden by the remains of a ream of typing paper.

The door opened and there he was. My heart was beating so rapidly that it was vibrating in my throat. I looked towards him as he neared the desk. And then he was leaning on it, his hands sprawled flat and his body bent towards me, and he began, "Well now, little Maisie, so you've been snooping around, eh? And what did you find, eh? Nothing. You just had to take the word of your friends, hadn't you? You've had nice little journeys out there on Saturdays and Sundays, haven't you, Maisie?"

My whole body was trembling. I took my hands off the keys because they were beginning to rattle, and he went on, "You think you've got me where you want me now, don't you? But what proof have you? None whatever. I was visiting a friend the day Maggie Talbot happened to come to the door. My friend's name is Mrs Ribber, and her two boys are called Ribber. No, Maisie, you've got nothing on me, but by God, I've got something on you. Something that, if it doesn't fix you for good, it'll prove you are in need of psychiatric treatment and should be put away for a time."

It was as if his voice was echoing words that I'd heard just a short time ago, and it went on echoing as he said, "And while you're away, I'll have to have someone to look after me, won't I? So I'll bring in a housekeeper, all very proper, and who better than Mrs Ribber and her two boys. And should you ever come out of wherever they send you, you'll have to have someone to carry on looking after you, won't you, Maisie? And Mrs Ribber will see to it, and I will see to it, for as long as you care to stay. Do you understand me, Maisie?"

I found my voice. It sounded cracked and it trembled as I said, "You can't do anything like that, as much as you would like to. I have my doctor and. . . ."

"But has he seen these, Maisie?" He now thrust his hand into an inside pocket of his jacket and pulled out what I recognized to be discarded pieces of typing paper that I'd torn up and put in the waste paper basket. I could see that they had been stuck together. Having learned from all the corrections that had to be done on the manuscript of the book that was shortly to come out, I now endeavoured to cut out all superfluous pieces of writing. One is apt to repeat oneself, often telling the same thing in two different ways, perhaps on the same page. So, with this in mind, I had scrapped numbers of sheets. But I always tore them up and threw them in the wastepaper basket under the desk, then every morning I meticulously emptied it. But I'd forgotten about the period between the time I went to bed and the next morning. And now I knew why he had, over the past months, spent so much time downstairs late at night. He must have selected some pieces and stuck them together, but left enough in the basket so I wouldn't notice anything different. He now waved the sheets in my face, saying, "This is just a sample. I've got dozens of them, telling about a woman who's so barmy she talks to a horse that crawls around this house, and gets on buses with her, and goes into the supermarket and stands on its hind legs in indignation when it sees women shop-lifting. Oh, Maisie, Maisie, what have you put into my hands, eh? Well now, can we come to terms, eh? Will I have to have you exposed and put away, at least for a time in order to bring my wife . . . And yes —" His jocular manner changed, and his hands slid over the table and knocked against the typing paper which pushed the tape recorder almost off the desk. I saved it with the side of my hand as he growled at me, "yes, my wife. And if you hadn't been mental you would have suspected something long ago. What did you think I got the seven hundred and fifty out of you for? To give to old Hempies in order to become manager? Huh! I wouldn't give that old sod the smoke that goes up the chimney. As for him inviting me for the week-ends there . . . Eeh! God, when you swallowed that, I realized you'd swallow anything. No, that money went to buy the cottage. And the rest of your four thousand to get my first car and add a bit on the end of the house. Oh, anybody that wasn't mental would have seen through it years ago. But you are, aren't you? You're bats. You've not got one scrap of brain, except to copy what other people think, and any idiot can do that, any idiot." He now banged the typewriter with his doubled-up fist, then added, "And write down your madness. Well now, am I to expose you, or are you going to sit quiet and let me bring in her and the boys? It's up to you, because, let me tell you this, I'll have this house in the end. May persuaded me to marry you in order to get it and get it I will, because by God, I've bloody well worked for it. Just seeing you day after day has been a heavy mortgage. Now I'll give you till this evening to make up your mind, no longer, then I'm going to the doctor. And, by the way, for sometime now I've taken the precaution to mention your oddities to him. I've also said you've denied me your bed for the past ten years or more. Huh! and by the way, I can tell you this, that you can thank my woman on that score, because without her, by God! I would have taken it out of your limbs. What I did to you in the beginning would have been nothing to what I would have done if I hadn't had her. Anyway, there it is."

He straightened up, stood looking at me with that dreadful expression on his face, then turned and walked out.

The door hadn't closed before I jumped up and followed him.

He was buttoning up his coat as he crossed the hall. I watched him pick up his cap — he was wearing a tweed cap these days — and open the front door. I was behind him now and there, through his legs, I saw Bill. Apparently, he had been wanting to come in and had come round to the front door. He had the clever habit of thudding his head against it; it was a form of knocking.

Howard became aware of me behind him as he looked on the dog who was now attempting to get past his legs and into the house. When his foot came out and he kicked Bill and sent him dithering and yelping across the top of the icy steps, the explosion happened. I think it would have come about in any case, but that was the match to the powder. I heard myself scream as, at the same time, I stooped down towards the box of bottles. The top one happened to be an old-fashioned brown stone ginger beer bottle. I caught it by the neck and in a lightning swing I brought it to the side of Howard's head. Before his scream had time to give itself an echo, I had used his tennis racket technique on him, and brought the bottle to the other side of his face. The blood was spurting in all directions now and the sight of it seemed to elate me, for as he fell backwards down the steps I stooped again for another bottle and threw it at him. It bounced off the back of his head, and he lay still now at the foot of the steps.

As if from a distance I heard a voice yelling as I threw another, then another: "Stop it! Stop it!" When the words, "She's killed him. She's killed him," came to me, some great cry burst soundlessly from me, yelling, "I hope I have. I hope I have."

I looked down into the box. There were no more bottles left; but there was a sea of faces on the pavement, and great narration in the street. People were looking up to me, with their mouths open. I stared back at them until, as if I had two bodies, one of them turned me about and gave me the impetus to dash indoors. Almost tripping over Bill in a headlong rush for the stairs, I made straight up them for the bottle room.

The window of this room faced the front of the house, and I thrust it right up. And then I started my onslaught. I gathered up the bottles in armsful, fat ones, thin ones, three-cornered ones, green ones, blue ones, black ones, red ones, ones with long necks, ones so small they were no bigger than my little finger, and one after the other I pelted them with all the force I was capable of, and so quick was I that it seemed for a time that Hamilton was bringing them to me. As I pelted them down the street I took a delight in seeing the people jumping here and there as if they were on hot bricks.

There were some vehicles in the street now but I couldn't make out exactly what they were because I didn't seem to be able to see clearly, and I was becoming very tired. The shelves were almost empty now. I was grabbing up the last of the bottles from a high shelf when two men appeared in the doorway. I recognized them as policemen. One had his helmet in his hand and his fingers to his brow and there was blood on his hand.

When the other said quietly, "Now missis. Now missis," I saw Hamilton for the first time. He was standing in the corner, his head half buried in an empty shelf, and as I looked at him, the elation seeped out of me. My vision cleared and I realized that the policeman's brow was cut, and a voice within me said, Oh I'm sorry, I didn't mean to hit you, but no words came.

"That's a good lass. Come on, you've done your stuff." It was the same policeman talking. He had a fatherly manner, and I went quietly with him down the stairs. "Have you got a coat, lass?" he said.

The injured policeman spoke for the first time. He had his helmet under his arm now and he pointed with his free hand, saying, "You might find one in there, it looks like a wardrobe."

The kindly policeman still had hold of my arm and he led me towards the hall wardrobe and opened the door, and then he said, "Ah, yes, here's your coat."

He left loose of me and I put my coat on. As I did so Bill came and stood close to me, and the other policeman said, "What about her dog? They say she's here by herself." He spoke as if I couldn't hear him, and at this I stooped down quickly and with an effort lifted Bill up into my arms, which prompted the kindly policeman to say, "Put him down, hinny. Put him down now. He's a heavy beast. Put him down."

For answer I just stared at him, and the

policeman who was again holding one hand to his brow, said, "Take him off her."

"You kiddin'?" The kindly policeman turned his head to the side. "Do you see what it is, it's a bull-terrier?"

"But she can hardly hold him."

The kind policeman's voice was very low now as he said, "The condition she's in, she could hold an elephant, lad. Let's get her to the station. Come on." He didn't take my arm now, but indicated that I should go to the door.

I obeyed him, and on the steps he said, "Mind how you go. Step over your handi-work, lass."

There was a crowd of people at both sides of the gate and they were silent as I passed through them. Then a voice from the back of the crowd came to me, saying, "Has she done him in?" And another voice said, "Had a damned good try by all accounts."

Bill nestled close to me in the car and his weight seemed to press the air and tension out of my body. I was quieter now inside, yet there was still that sense of elation and from somewhere like a voice re-echoing from down the years, the words, "I've done it. I've done it," kept floating around me.

When the policeman helped me out of the car and into the station, my mind seemed very clear. Everything and everyone seemed to stand out in sharp relief about me. Two men in mackintoshes who had got out of another car were now talking to the kind policeman; the other policeman was showing the cut in his forehead to a man who was standing behind a counter. The man listened in silence to the policeman; then he looked at me and, speaking as if I wasn't there, he said, "That little 'un?"

"That little 'un," the hurt policeman said.

"Well, you know what they say." The policeman behind the counter moved along it now to get a better view of me, then muttered, "Well, a stick of dynamite isn't very big after all."

Then my kind escort leant across the counter and said something to him, and he replied, "Aye, yes, I see what you mean. People grow like their dogs, and when that breed get their teeth in they don't let go." Then looking towards me, he said, quietly, "Would you like to sit down, missis?"

I looked round, and then went and sat thankfully on the form that was placed against the wall, and once seated, I let Bill slide from my lap on to the floor.

Now the three policemen and the two men in mackintoshes were joined by a policewoman, and they all talked together for a moment; then my kind policeman, as I thought of him, said, "They say she's got a granny somewhere in Bog's End."

Almost on a bawl now, the man behind the counter seemed to yell, "Well, find her Gran;" only to subside again as he muttered, "Find her, wherever she is. And we'd better get the doctor in here an' all."

There was a general movement around the counter now, and the policewoman approached me. But she came to within only two steps of me, when Bill let out a low growl.

She stopped and looked at him, and then at me, and she said, "Would . . . would you like a cup of tea, dear?"

The voice inside me said, Yes, please, but I couldn't get it past my throat. I was finding this strange. There was a great deal of talking going on in my head but I couldn't give voice to it. I stared at her for some seconds, and she turned away.

One of the men in a mackintosh was now saying to the man behind the counter, "I've never seen so many broken bottles in me life." His voice sounded full of laughter, although his face was straight. "She kept 'em coming. She didn't mean to hit one of your lot, she just aimed for him, her man that was lying on the pathway. By! she must have had it in for him to turn like that. And yet, by the talk around of the neighbours, he was a quiet enough fellow. Very gentlemanly, they said. A bit of a sportsman, played tennis an' that. Manager of Hempies'; had been for years. Well, well, you never know, do you? But by! if it hadn't been so tragic, I would have laughed me head off. I didn't get there till nearly the end, but there they were, coming from that window, all shapes and sizes, the neighbours all under cover and the ambulance men dodging them as they tried to get him into the ambulance. It was as good as a play. As I said, if it hadn't been serious, I would have split me sides . . . And she hasn't said a word since?" They were looking at me now, and one policeman said, "I wonder what Doc will make of her when he comes? One bawl from him and she'll be on her feet, I'll bet."

How long did I sit on that bench? I don't know. It only seemed like a second before I saw Doctor Kane come through the door with his black bag. He was apologizing to one of the officers for being so long because he had been down to the quayside where a man had been hurt in a winch. And then he turned and looked at me, and all the hairs on his face spread out, his mouth opened wide, and I saw his tongue. It came out twice before he clamped his teeth shut. Then coming slowly towards me, he said, "What in the name of God! has happened to you?"

The kindly policeman was at his side now and he said, "Doctor, can you spare a minute, just a minute?" And my dear friend turned from me, because he was a dear friend. And I was so pleased to see him, yet I didn't show it. But he went with the kind policeman to the counter, and there he stood listening to the man behind the counter and the kind policeman and the one with the blood on his brow which by now had congealed. It didn't look a very big cut, not from where I was sitting. And all the while the conference was going on, the doctor kept turning and looking towards me, and the hairs kept moving on his face. Then I saw that he was talking, and the policeman was looking towards me, and their eyes were stretching.

When Doctor Kane eventually came over to the bench, he first bent down and patted Bill, saying, "Hello there, old fellow. Bet you never expected to be in the clink." Then sitting down beside me, he took hold of my hand and he said, "Well, you did something at last, Maisie; but you needn't have made it so drastic." He leant forward towards me now and, his face close to mine, he said, "Don't worry. Something had to happen. Just take everything quietly. But I'm afraid, Maisie, you'll have to stay here for a time. You understand that?"

Yes, yes, my mind was saying; definitely, yes, I understand that I have to stay in . . . I hesitated at the word, gaol. But that's where I was, I was in the police station and they would keep me here until somebody could take me out. He said now, quietly, "I'll bring your granny, and she'll take the dog. He likes staying with her, doesn't he?"

My eyes answered him, but still I said no word. He put up his hand and stroked my hair, and his touch brought a flood of tears. Like a spring bursting from a rock, they flowed out of my eyes and nose and mouth. Yet unlike a spring, they didn't make any gurgling sound, no sound at all. And the doctor got up and abruptly walked to the counter, and he said something to them, then went hastily out.

The three policemen and the police-woman all looked towards me. Their faces had a quiet look.

There followed a period during which different people came in. One lady had lost her cat; but the greatest commotion was when two policemen brought in an old lady who was singing, and when she tried to stop and speak to the policeman behind the counter, he yelled at her, "Get goin', Mary Ellen! Get goin'!" And she called back at him, "Okay, darling. Okay. See you at the 'sizes."

It was all very cheeky and I was beginning to feel very quiet inside, but then the door opened and in came Doctor Kane and Gran. It seemed that the doctor had to push Gran towards me, because she kept hesitating and looking at me as if she didn't recognize me. And when she eventually sat down beside me, her remark was typical: "God in heaven! lass," she said. "God in heaven! You needn't have gone and killed him."

Had I killed him? Well, that's what I'd wanted to do, wasn't it? When I lifted that first bottle I wanted to obliterate him like something that was festeringly evil.

"Say something, lass," she said.

I stared at her and my mind said, What can I say, Gran? It had to come. If only you could have heard him. I'm not a worm, Gran. I'm not a slug. I am a person. Mr Leviston knows I am a person. Mr Leviston is the first one who has ever recognized that I've got a mind. You're kind, Gran. You're a lovely woman, but you never recognized that

I'd got a mind. And neither did George. You both loved me through pity. But Mr Leviston . . . well, he likes me. He likes my turn of phrase. He likes what goes on in my mind.

"Why won't she speak?" Gran had turned to the doctor now, and he said, "It's a kind of shock. She's retreated into herself because she can't stand any more."

"What'll they do with her?"

"Oh, they'll likely keep her here . . . well, until she's charged, and then she'll get bail. We'll have to arrange that some way."

"Keep her in the cells?"

"Yes, yes, in the cells." His whiskers were bristling now. "She's almost killed him. If he survives, he'll bring a case against her. By God! he will. He'll do his best . . ." He turned away now and, helping Gran up from the seat, he walked with her to the counter, his voice low, and although I couldn't hear with my ears the end of that sentence, my mind knew what it was: after this to have her put away. "Anyway —" His voice came to me now, saying, "the police will charge her. It's really their case."

Dear God. That would mean he would achieve his aims in the end. But then, there was the tape. What he said was on the tape. If I could tell the doctor about the tape.

But I couldn't.

Gran and the doctor seemed to be a long time at the counter talking to the man behind it, and bits of the conversation drifted towards me, such as when the man behind the counter said, "She could have knocked his eye out." And the doctor answered, "Oh, it's only a scratch: a couple of stitches and that'll be all right."

"Nevertheless, the charge will be bodily harm, you know that yourself. And I've got to charge her in the normal way, dumb or not dumb as she makes out to be."

Of a sudden I felt tired; all I wanted to do was lie down, even on this form.

I was only dimly aware now of Gran coming and putting her arms around me and kissing me, then leading Bill away; and of the doctor, his hand once again on my hair, saying, "It's going to be all right, Maisie. Don't you worry; it's going to be all right. I'll see to it. Trust me. It's going to be all right."

When the policewoman took my arm, I went quietly with her, but when she put me in a small room and closed the heavy door, the tiredness for a moment left me and a great yell spiralled up, seemingly coming through the stone floor and up through my body and out through the top of my head.

Yet I didn't make a sound. Instead, I lay down on the wooden bench that had a mattress on it and I drifted away into a kind of sleeping wakefulness in which the voice of the singing woman came through the wall and bottles of all kinds floated round the room. I started naming them: There went a big one. It hadn't any neck; that had broken off when it hit the ground. I could see the label: "Allsop's Indian Pale Ale". And there were his precious blues, some of them dark blue, some of them pale blue. Some of them with the word "Poison" raised in the glass. And, oh, there went a variety of the soda-water ones, the marbles all rattling in the necks. Funny, but few of those had broken. They were very solid bottles. 'Twas a pity I thought. And there went a row of little medicine ones, patent medicine ones: "Veno's Cough Cure", "Glycerine and Honey". And now the beer bottles started passing each other as if in a dance: "Guinness's Double Stout", "Guinness's Extra Strong Stout", "Australian Pale Ale". That was a funny one, why Australian? He had prized that one. Some of them were quite whole and bright and looked just as they did when he used to hold them up to the light after washing them in the kitchen sink. If he had only treated me as gently as he had done those bottles.

When the bottles started to mark time to the woman's singing voice coming through the wall, a hand came on my shoulder and I shrunk instinctively from it and crouched against the wall. But as a quiet voice said, "Sit up and have this drink," I opened my eyes, and there was the policewoman. And I sat up and I thankfully drank the mug of steaming tea.

"How are you feeling now?" she asked.

I looked at her and shook my head.

"I'll bring you another blanket," she said, and she did.

When she left me and the door clanged again, I shuddered, and the shudder told me I was back in my senses, for I seemed to have been out of them for some time. I drew in a long breath and looked about me. This was terrible; I was in a cell. It doesn't matter, I told myself, you've done it. And I answered, Yes, yes, I've done it. But where was the exaltation I'd felt earlier on? I wanted someone, company, the doctor, Gran, anybody. I got up and started to walk about in the narrow confines, then sat down again, and as I did so, the door opened yet again and there entered the doctor and the solicitor. I almost threw myself upon Doctor Kane and he, gripping my hand, said,

"There now. There now." And looking intently into my face, he said, "You feel better?"

I shook my head, and for the first time in what appeared to me years my voice came out of my mouth, and I said, "No. Terrible."

"Well, that's better than your dumb show anyway. Now, here, as you see, is Mr Pearson. I'm going to let him do the talking."

Mr Pearson now asked me to tell him exactly what had happened, and I was telling him when, half-way through, he stopped me and said, "You had a tape recorder running through all that he said?"

"Yes, at least I switched it on; unless in the excitement I ran it back and rubbed it off."

"Pray God that you didn't, then."

Yes — I nodded at him — pray God that I didn't.

When I had finished telling him all that had happened, I asked pathetically, "Will they let me go out now?"

The two men exchanged glances, and Mr Pearson said, "My dear Mrs Stickle, I have no doubt that your husband deserved everything you gave him, but as yet I don't know how serious his injuries are. I'll have to visit the hospital to find that out. Let's hope they are not as serious as some people seem to think. And then, don't forget, my dear, that you also left your mark on a policeman."

I closed my eyes tightly and looked down and muttered, "I'm sorry about that; but" — my eyes opened as quickly as they had closed — "I'm not sorry about what I did to him . . . Howard, and never will be, not even if he dies. I'm only wondering now how I resisted doing it before. But . . . but when he kicked the dog, and he isn't well, Bill, that seemed the last straw."

"He kicked the dog?"

"Yes."

Mr Pearson turned now and looked at the doctor, saying, "I suppose I could get the key from the police to enter the house. You could come with me and pick up that tape because" — he turned now and looked at me — "if that conversation is recorded, it's going to be your main witness. No matter what the doctor or I might say, or your counsel, and you'll have to have a counsel, if your husband is condemned out of his own mouth, then that should carry great weight with the judge."

I felt sick from the pit of my stomach. I'd have to go to court, face a judge? Well, I wasn't stupid altogether; of course, I'd have to go to court and face a judge. I said on a gulp, "Will they let me out now . . . I mean, until the time comes?"

Mr Pearson pursed his lips for a moment. "I'm sorry, my dear," he said, "procedure is: you will have to go before the magistrates in the morning, and it depends on how you plead whether you get bail straightaway or not. If you plead not guilty, you'll be allowed out on bail, but if you plead guilty, I'm afraid you'll likely be kept . . . be kept in custody until your case comes up."

"But . . . but I am guilty. I did do it. I did hit him. Well!" My voice was shaking now, not with laughter, but at the silliness of his suggestion: guilty, or not guilty. Everybody knew I was guilty and I said so: "Everybody knows I did it. There was a big crowd there; they saw me."

"Yes, I know that. We all know that. But I'm telling you that you must plead not guilty if you want to get out of here and stay out until your trial."

Doctor Kane had hold of my hand and once more patted it as he said, "It's difficult to understand, but that's the law. Now tomorrow morning we'll be around here like a shot, and all you've got to do when you go before the magistrates and they ask if you're guilty or not guilty, you've just got to say, not guilty. Anyway, we'll go into the procedure more tomorrow morning. Now"

— he got to his feet — "try to get a night's rest."

As they went to leave I caught hold of Doctor Kane's arm and said, "You will come? I mean . . ."

"Of course I'll come. I'll skip surgery. My lazy good-for-nothing partner can do some work for a change." He grinned, but it was a weak grin, an anxious grin; and I nodded at him, then at Mr Pearson, and they went out. The door clanged again and I put all my fingers in my mouth and bit down hard on my nails.

CHAPTER 5

I was in the street. There was the sky above me. It had never looked so wide, nor so high, nor had the air tasted so wonderful, it was going down my throat like the wine I'd had that time in London. I stood and looked about me as if in wonder, and the doctor was standing on one side of me and Mr Pearson on the other, and Mr Pearson patted my shoulder and smiled at me now as he said, "You did very well."

"I only said, not guilty."

"But you said it with some conviction."

"Did I?"

"Yes, you did."

"By the way, two hundred pounds. Who stood all that amount?"

"Never you mind." Doctor Kane now caught hold of my arm, saying, "I don't know about you, but I'm frozen standing here. The quicker we get to your granny's the better. And I hope she's got the teapot on the hob."

"You put up the money?"

"Yes." He now poked his head towards me. "And don't you go and scarper."

"Oh, Doctor Kane."

"Never mind, oh Doctor Kane." His voice was impatient. "Come on, get into the car . . . You following?"

Mr Pearson nodded, saying, "Yes, I'll come along; I'll have to see where I can find you." He now smiled kindly at me and walked back to his car.

As soon as we entered the door of Gran's house, and not without curtains being drawn aside in the street, Bill scrambled towards me, and Gran put her arms round me and, the tears running down her face, she said, "Doctor thought it better that I didn't come. Aw, lass, I've been worried sick in case you said the wrong thing and didn't get out."

"Don't let's have so much palaver, Hannah. What about that teapot?"

"Oh, aye, the teapot." She looked from one to the other as if in a daze, then went to the kitchen, only to return almost immediately to the doorway and ask the doctor, "How is he, Stickle?"

"Oh, he'll survive. But no thanks to this one here." He now looked at me and added, "You did a good job on him. And after listening to that tape" — he nodded at me now — "oh yes, we found it —" He glanced at the solicitor, then turned his gaze on me again as he went on, his voice quiet, "I don't blame you, nobody would."

"Where's the tape now?"

"I've got it." Mr Pearson held up his index finger. "And as the doctor just said, it's understandable, your reactions; but I must add, you are very lucky that you succeeded in taking down what he said, because without this evidence, had your husband produced the . . . well, writings about this horse that the doctor tells me here is a sort of" — he paused — "companion, he might have, after all, succeeded in his claims." As he finished speaking, Gran came out of the kitchen carrying four cups of tea on a painted tin tray, and just before she put it down on the table she glanced towards the window, saying, "There's a taxi just pulled up. That'll be another of 'em. They were swarmin' round here last night like flies on a midden. All the way here from Newcastle and Sunderland, they had come. At the finish, I clashed the door on their faces and told them to get the hell out of it. An' that's what I'll say to this one an' all."

She marched to the door now, and when I heard the voice say, "Are you Mrs Carter?" and Gran's reply, "Yes; and what of it?" I got up from the couch and pushed past Mr Pearson and the Doctor and went to the door; and there, pressing Gran aside, I looked at the visitor and said, "Oh, Nardy."

"Maisie." He held out his hand, and I looked about me in bewilderment back to the two men who were looking towards us down the passage, then to Gran, and I said, "Gran, this is Mr Leviston, you know, from London."

"Oh, aye. Aye." Gran's whole manner changed, and she now extended her hand, saying, "I'm pleased to see you, sir. Come in. Come in."

He came in, and in a fluster now I looked from the Doctor to Mr Pearson and said, "This is a . . . a friend of mine from London, Mr Leviston." Now I turned and looked at Nardy and added, "This is my solicitor, Mr Pearson."

The men shook hands, then stood looking

355

at each other, and it was evident to me that the doctor was definitely wanting to know how I'd come by this friend from London, this well-dressed, city-looking gent. Then as I was about to speak, Gran said, "Would you have a cup of tea, sir?"

"Yes, yes, Mrs Carter; that would be very acceptable." Once again the men looked at each other, and now I said to Nardy, "I'd better tell them."

And he answered, "As you wish, Maisie. As you wish."

I looked pointedly at the doctor as I said, "This is my publisher." I indicated Nardy with my hand, and when Doctor Kane's eyes became lost in his hair, as they were wont to do when he was puzzled, he said, *"Your what?"* And at this I said, without a smile because there wasn't a smile in me, "You've got that habit now. You heard alright, my publisher. I've written a book."

I saw him look at the solicitor, and they exchanged glances that, a few minutes earlier, if Nardy hadn't been present, would have read, Poor thing. It's a pity, but he was right. Yet, still their glances exchanged incredulity.

I think it was the first time in our acquaintance that I found the doctor absolutely stumped for words. It was Mr Pearson who said, "A book . . . you have written a book?"

"Yes, that's what I said, I've written a book. And it's to be published. . . . When?" I looked at Nardy, and he, now seeming to enjoy the situation, smiled from one to the other as he said, "It should be out in the first week of December."

The doctor now spoke. "A book about what?" he asked.

I looked directly at him as I replied, "Hamilton, the horse I told you about."

"Hamilton?"

"Yes, the horse."

"And you've made it into a book —" He cast a glance at Nardy now before he added, "that will sell?"

"We have every hope that it will romp, and keep pace with Hamilton himself."

Gran now brought all the attention upon herself by saying, "She's been tellin' me for ages about this horse that's been rompin' round me kitchen, an' I've said, well, it's a pity it couldn't be of some real use and leave some manure on me patch of garden."

"Oh, Gran." Once more I wanted to laugh, but I couldn't. I had the feeling deep inside me that I'd never laugh again, nor would I ever think anything funny again, Hamilton or no Hamilton. I felt that, since twelve o'clock yesterday, my whole person-

357

ality had undergone a strange change. First, I felt much older, and adult with it. I knew that some people could reach seventy and never be adult, but now I felt adult. I felt that in a way, whatever lay in the future, I would be able to cope with it. But I added a proviso to this thought, and it was, as long as I had friends such as these to support me. Part of my whole being, I knew, was still in that cell in the police station, and the thought that I might have to return there created a blackness shutting off some section of my mind wherein lay my future.

"Maisie, it sounds trite, but you amaze me. You always have." I was looking at the doctor, and he went on, "There you've been, pestering me morning after Monday morning, with one thing and another, and all the time you've been living another life, because you must have been if you've written a book. So I'm going to ask you this, woman: why, if you are capable of writing a book that's going to be published, and it must have some quality if that's the case, because from what I've heard of publishers" — he glanced at Nardy — "they don't act like a charitable organisation; that being so, why the devil couldn't you take yourself in hand before now?"

I let a pause elapse before I answered him,

and then I said, "When you read the book, you'll find out."

"We've got another situation here." We all looked at Mr Pearson now and watched him take a drink of tea from his cup, which from his veiled expression I didn't think he found palatable, as Gran's tea always looked like ink and she put very little milk in it, because that's the way she liked it herself. Then he went on, "You have written this book under a pseudonym, I presume?"

"Yes."

"And no one up till now has known about it except Mrs Carter" — he inclined his head towards Gran — "and your publishers?"

"Yes, that's right."

"Well, that being the case, if you want my advice, I would leave it like that until the case comes up. And of course, the timing of that will depend upon how quickly your husband recovers. Anyway, it might not come up for months. In the meantime, your book will have come out and have been read. When you say it's about a horse, I presume it deals with your imagination, you just imagine you see this horse. Is that so?"

I paused before I answered, because I expected Hamilton to appear rearing on his hind legs in denial of his immaterialism, but there was no sign of him, so I said, "Yes, you could say that."

"Well, as this seems to be one of the main points on which your husband will press his case, which, putting it plainly, is that you are mentally unbalanced, and if it appears that this is carrying weight, and with some judges it certainly could do, even with the evidence of his conversation on the tape recorder, the fact that you've written this as a book could influence the proceedings. But then, we must remember, the real case concerns your attack on him."

As he pursed his lips in a jocular fashion I bowed my head, but it wasn't with any feeling of remorse because I felt not one tinge of regret at what I had done. I wasn't even interested in the extent of Howard's injuries. Yet when Doctor Kane said, "Anyway, what's twenty-seven stitches here and there between friends?" I looked up and at him, and he nodded back at me, adding, "It's a good job you spread those bottles around. If they'd hit the one place, things might have been serious." He now turned to Nardy and said, "I suppose you know all about it? Have you been to the police station?"

"Yes. I . . . I called there, naturally after

I'd read the morning papers."

"But how did you get from London to here in this short time?"

"I flew up. Anyway, the news really didn't surprise me."

It seemed that both Doctor Kane and the solicitor spoke at once, and he repeated, "No, not after having read Maisie's story. It is intended, I think . . . at least you would say, wouldn't you, Maisie, that it is a funny book? Yet running through it is the story of a sadist and his treatment of his wife Rosie. That's the girl in the book. Anyway, I felt I came to know Mr Stickle very well before Rosie" — he now inclined his head towards me — "gets rid of him towards the end."

"Gets rid of him?" Doctor Kane poked his head forward. "You mean . . . you mean, actually?"

"No. Maisie was kind: she let Rosie divorce him, but not before Rosie's supposed brother has a go at him; and also Rosie's dog, which didn't happen to be a bull-terrier, but a small Highland terrier whose chief occupation was chasing rats; and he recognized a big rat when he saw one and so he went for Rosie's husband. There is a court case at the end of the story, too, where the man is trying to have the dog put down."

"Does he succeed?"

Nardy shook his head and smiled at Doctor Kane as he replied, "Of course not."

"And how, may I ask, does that story end?" Doctor Kane's face was straight now.

"Oh" — Nardy turned and smiled at me as he said — "Rosie achieves her heart's desire. She goes on a sea cruise, dressed up to the nines. And there begins the sequel . . . we hope."

"Well, well." The doctor got to his feet, adding now, "And we all lived happily ever after." Then looking down at me, he said, "I hope your own story turns out as well as the one you've written. Anyway, we'll do our best to see that it does . . . Do you want to go on a sea cruise?"

"No." I shook my head. "I'd be seasick; I heave when I cross the ferry."

As the doctor buttoned his coat I said to him, "Will it be all right if I go home?"

"No, it won't!" His words came from deep within his throat. "You'll have the place infested with reporters once they know you're there. What's more, you'll have to put up with the neighbours. You stay put, here with your granny for a few days." And he added, with a laugh, "The neighbours around this quarter will be more in sympathy with you, because if some of them had been with you, they would certainly have helped you with your pelting, imagining they were getting one back on their own men. Isn't that so?" He looked at Gran, and she said tartly, "If you say so."

Doctor Kane and Mr Pearson shook hands with Nardy, and the moment the door closed on them, Gran said, "Now that you've got company for a bit, I'll get out and do me shoppin'. That all right with you?"

"Yes, Gran."

I knew the shopping idea was a pretext; she wanted to leave me alone with Nardy so we could talk. She'd had her own ideas about him and me long before this morning, and as I said, it was no use telling her that, as I saw it, she was barking up the wrong tree.

Once we were alone, we sat quietly on the couch looking at each other. I broke the silence by muttering, "I'm not sorry."

"I'm not either. I'm glad."

"He kicked Bill. That was the breaking point. But I'd meant to do something, anyway, even before that. I didn't know what. And then there were the bottles right to my hand as if they had been placed there on purpose."

"Perhaps they had; God works in strange ways His miracles to perform."

"Oh" — I turned my head away — "I don't think anything I did could have been under the directive of God. I know now that I went mad, I did really, I went mad for a time. It seemed as if I was jealous of the bottles, because he was always tender with the bottles, washing them carefully, drying them, polishing them, arranging them in sizes and colours . . . What do you think will happen to me?"

He hitched himself towards me and caught my hands and, pressing them firmly, he said, "Nothing that cannot be overcome. You seem to have a very good man in your solicitor . . . and your doctor; well, he's just as you described him in the book. And when he says his piece, and that tape is played through . . . By the way, that was a brilliant idea." He nodded at me. "That, I'm sure, was God-inspired. And then the fact that you are a writer, and I, and everyone else in the office, think the book is going to be a great success. Well, when that is revealed, it should quash any ideas that your husband has with regard to your mental deficiency." He ended by pulling a face.

"Do you think he'll try to get back into the house?"

"No, I don't think there'll be a chance once the judge knows of the woman and the children . . . if they are his. Anyway, your solicitor saw to that side of it; his personal belongings have been sent to him."

"But . . . but what —" I found that I could hardly speak the words that I was thinking now, and when they did come out they were low and muttered, "But what if things don't go as you think they will and I'm sent to prison?"

"Maisie." He had lifted my two hands and was holding them against his chest, and slowly he said, "Look at me." And when I looked at him, he went on, "Whatever happens, do you hear? Whatever happens, just remember this, I am your friend . . . and more than a friend. You understand?"

I did and didn't, because what I thought his words meant conveyed something that was really beyond contemplating. This man, an educated man, well-born, because that much I had gathered from his house and his style of living, which was as natural to him as breathing, this man was suggesting . . . What was he suggesting? No, it was impossible. I wasn't going to dwell on that with all the rest of the things raging in my mind. He said he was a friend, more than a friend. That meant a dear friend, and that was enough, quite enough. *I wasn't going to bark up the wrong tree.*

The leading northern papers had carried headlines of my escapade. The Battle of the Bottles, it was called. They had described, each in a different way, my raining the bottles down on to a crowd in the street.

"The neighbours say the victim was a quiet, gentlemanly man," said one paper. Another heading was: "Little termagant wages bottle battle against husband". And the third one began, "Virago goes berserk with bottles. Husband in dangerous state in hospital. Policeman's head split open".

Then on Saturday morning came the local paper. Gran had gone out to the butcher's and she brought it back with her. She almost burst into the room and threw the paper at me, crying, "Read that! Read that!" She pointed to the right-hand corner and the last column on the front page. The headlines were: "A Reason for the Bottle Bashing". Then followed the words: "So far no one seems to have got to the bottom of why a wife should attack her quiet gentlemanly husband, a man who was well-known in the business centre of the town, but new light was thrown on the situation yesterday when a woman visited Mr Stickle in hospital. She was accompanied by two young boys who spontaneously addressed the patient as Dad. A reporter, who happened to be visiting a patient in an adjoining bed, took the matter up with the woman when she later left the hospital and she aggressively stated that she had lived with the man for over twelve years. Moreover, she had been engaged to him before he had married his present wife, whom she said, he found it difficult to live with because she was unbalanced."

There was more but I didn't read on. I looked up at Gran, and she said, "There's your divorce, lass. There's your divorce." And I said, "Yes, from an unbalanced woman."

"Oh" — she jerked her chin upwards — "that will be knocked on the head when the case comes up and they find out what this so-called unbalanced woman has done and is now the famous writer . . ."

"Oh, Gran! Gran!"

"Well, you will be. You know I don't read stuff like that, but when I read that copy you brought back, well, I was laughin' one minute and cryin' the next. It's that kind of a book, 'cos in a way it explains things, you know, like talkin' to yourself. I never realized that I've been talkin' to meself all me life. That's when I had nobody else to talk to. And that's just what you did. You had nobody to talk to, so you made up a horse. By the way" — she looked about her — "where's he got his big feet now?"

"I haven't seen him for days."

She seemed to recognize the sad note in my voice and she said, "Well, the quicker you get back in touch with him the better if you're goin' on writin' about him. Eeh" — she wagged her head — "didn't those men laugh when I said he should have left some manure for the garden . . . I think I could write a book meself." She turned about and took off her coat and the silly woolly hat with the red pom-pom, that from the back made her look like sixteen; more and more she was wearing younger type clothes, even going out in trousers. I often thought some young lads must have received a shock when they got round to her front.

As she went into the kitchen I said, "I've just made the tea." And to this she answered, "Good."

Then she called, "What d'you say, lass?"

And I called, "After reading this" — I tapped the paper — "I think it would be all right to go back home, because the neighbours might now be thinking a little differently and seeing things perhaps from my point of view."

She came to the kitchen door. "Well, it's up to you, lass. I know this place must be getting on your nerves, only being able to creep out at night with that fella." She pointed to Bill.

"You won't mind?"

"Don't be silly, lass. Anyway, once you're gone I'll be able to get out and to me bingo. I've never won anything this week. Well, I wouldn't, would I? 'cos I haven't been."

"Oh, Gran."

Two hours later, as I was about to leave, she said, "I'd better tell you that I wrote to our Georgie, telling him about it, 'cos I don't suppose they get our news down that end of the country, so don't be surprised if he's on the doorstep any day from Monday."

Funny that. I hadn't given George a thought in days. Was it possible that people once loved could take a back seat in your mind? I'd thought of George as my protector for years, whether he was with me or away from me. But now I thought of him no more, not in that way, because his place had been taken by Nardy.

CHAPTER 6

It was the day of publication. I received two telegrams, one from Mr Houseman and Mr

Rington, and a separate one from Nardy saying simply, "Congratulations". Then followed two bouquets. The man who brought the flowers said, "Is it your birthday?" And I said, "Yes." I left the flowers as they were, all wrapped up, in a bucket of water. They were bringing no joy, for my heart was like lead.

I went back into the sitting-room where, before a big coal fire — I had discarded the electric one — on the rug lay Bill. On each of the past three days the vet had called, and he said there was nothing that could be done: Bill had kidney trouble. What was more, he was having hallucinations, when he would urge his weakened body to rise and go for something on the wall.

I knelt down beside him and stroked his dear head, and he turned his eyes towards me, and his tongue came out, but he couldn't lick me. "Oh, Bill. Bill. What am I going to do without you?" I was moaning aloud. At this moment I had nobody in the world but Bill. Gran, Nardy, the doctor, the solicitor, George, they didn't matter, only this animal which had been the only creature I had been able to hold tight to me during the past long years. I began to plead with him now, "Don't go, Bill. Oh, please don't go. Don't leave me."

And when I knew his breaths were numbered I crouched low down until my head was on a level with his, and his round dark eyes looked deep into mine and they were full of love. Slowly he lifted a fore paw — it was a form of shaking hands — and when his whole body jerked as if he was going to get up and run, I put my arms about him and he became still, so still, that his head fell on to the side of my arm.

I sat rocking him and crying, and Hamilton came and sat by my side. He had been with me all day, that is, as long as I was in the room with Bill. He never followed me out of it, but when I returned, there he would be sitting on his haunches, his head drooped, looking down on Bill. I looked at him now and cried brokenly, "There'll never be another Bill." And he answered, No, there'll never be another Bill. There might be a Simon, or a Sandy, or a Rover, but there'll never be another Bill.

"No! No!" I knew my voice was almost a yell. "I'll never have another. Do you hear? *Never. Never.*"

All right. All right, he said. Calm yourself, or you'll have Mrs Nelson in. She is very attentive these days.

"Yes, yes" — I nodded at him — "she's very attentive these days when I don't want

371

her to be. If only she or one of the others had given me their attention or even noticed me eight or ten years ago, I wouldn't have had to rely on you so much, would I?"

No, no. He nodded at me. That's true; but there again you wouldn't have had a book out today, would you?

Oh, a book, a book. What did it matter? What did it matter? I'd lost Bill.

I was unaware that the back door had opened or that someone had come across the hall, until the sitting-room door opened and there stood Gran. She came towards me slowly, and I looked up to her through a blur and I said, "He's gone."

"Well, you knew he was going, lass. You knew it was coming."

"I can't bear it, not any more. I've had enough; I can't bear this, Gran."

"Lass —" She bent down to me as if she was going to take Bill from my arms as she said, "He's only a dog, lass. Now look at it like that, he's only a dog."

"*Shut up, Gran. Shut up.* He wasn't just a dog to me. He was the baby I lost; he was the husband I never had; he was the friend I never had. Don't you say he was just a dog, Gran. He had more consideration for me than anybody else in my life."

"Aw, lass, that isn't fair. You're not thinkin'

of me or Georgie when you're sayin' that. Well now, come on. Come on. Put him down."

"No, no, I'll not put him down."

I wasn't surprised when she walked straight out. When presently she came back, she said, "Let me hold him while you drink this cup of tea."

"No, no. I can manage."

But when I lifted my arm from him to take the cup, he slipped gently from my hold and on to the rug again.

I found myself gulping at the tea because it was the first drink I'd had that day.

During the following half-hour, Gran kept walking from the sitting-room into the hall and back, in and out, in and out. And then, when the bell rang, she hurried to the door, and the next minute there was Doctor Kane looking down on me. So that's what she had done. Well, what could he do for Bill? Nobody could do anything for Bill now. I said that to him. Looking up at him, I said, "You can't do anything for him."

"No, I know that, but I can do something for you. Come on, get to your feet."

"No, no."

"Maisie. Look, behave yourself." He was talking to me as if I was a child, and now he gripped me by the arm and hauled me up.

Then pointing down to Bill, he said, "You've got two choices: one, he goes to the vet and they'll dispose of him; two, we bury him in the garden." And now his voice softened and he said, "In that way you can make a little grave and you can tend him every day. What is it to be, he goes to the vet?"

"No! no! no!"

"All right then, let's see about it."

I wrapped Bill in his rug and laid him in a large packing case I'd brought down from the attic. I put his rubber bone and his toys by his side, and when that was done, the doctor forced me to close the lid. He himself dug the hole at the bottom of the garden. I realized, even as I watched him, that he wasn't used to digging, but when I went to help, he thrust me aside. Although it was an icy cold day the sweat was dripping from his beard.

It took us all our time to lift the case down the garden, even with Gran helping, and when it was in the hole and covered over, he had to pull me away back into the house.

Gran made more tea, and I sat staring into the fire, the tears raining unheeded down my face.

"So it's come," he said. He was holding out my book to me. That morning I had received the six free copies that I was told were allotted to every writer on publication. His voice held an excited note as he said, "It's a splendid cover, isn't it? A horse sitting at a table, its forelegs crossed on it —" and he chuckled as he added, "as if he was talking to you. And I suppose that's you sitting at the other side. It isn't unlike you, you know."

There was a pause, and now he was reading aloud from the back cover of the book.

"This is a funny book. It will make you laugh. But there are places where it may make you cry, because many will identify with the woman in this book who is so lost and lonely that she conjured up a horse and clothed it with flesh and bone until it became real. And this story tells what happened to Rosie and Hamilton. Take it to bed with you, but don't expect to sleep."

Nardy had written that. They called it a blurb.

"Aren't you proud of yourself?"

I looked up at him and said simply, "It doesn't matter."

"Don't be silly, woman. Look, you'll get another dog. In fact I know where there's some pup . . ."

"I don't want another dog. Bill wasn't just a dog."

"Bill was a dog." He was shouting as loudly

as I had done.

"All right he was a good companion, but nevertheless he was a dog . . . an animal. What you've got to do now, Maisie, is to concentrate on human beings."

"I've never found any worth concentrating on."

"Thank you." His voice dropped now, and when he added "Thank you very much," I put my hand to my head and stood up and whimpered. "I'm sorry. I'm sorry. I didn't mean that. But can't you see, I'm . . . I'm so distressed."

"Yes, yes." His voice was soothing now. "But you will soon have other things to think about that will certainly take your mind off Bill. I happened to meet Mr Pearson this morning and he thinks your case will come up early in the New Year, and you will be charged with grievous bodily harm, and from what I gather, your husband is going to sue you for everything that he can think of with regard to the damage you've done him. He's suffering headaches, impaired memory, loss of work, facial scarring, et cetera, et cetera. But, as I understand, you would have to take his cap off to see the evidence of the last. Anyway, as I see it, he knows he stands no chance of getting the house, but he does stand a chance

376

of making you pay so much compensation that you would likely have to sell it. Now think on that."

I couldn't think on it, not then, I could only think of Bill lying out there in the cold ground.

I started to cry again, and he left me, saying, "It will do you no harm to cry it out."

But when the following day Gran came and found me still crying, there he was again, in the bedroom this time, and he stuck a needle into me and I went to sleep, and slept for two days, and when I eventually woke up fully I knew that tears would not bring Bill back, but that I would carry the weight of him in my memory forever.

CHAPTER 7

My case came up in February. It was to extend over two days and I returned home after the first day slightly stunned and very apprehensive.

Nardy was with me, as were George and the doctor, and no sooner had we got indoors than George demanded of Nardy, "What did she need a bloody counsel for? What did he do? When that swine was on the stand, he treated him as if he was defending him, not against him." And

Nardy said quietly, "Wait until tomorrow; he'll spring a lot of surprises tomorrow."

"He'll bloody well need to. To my mind the defence and the prosecutin' counsels should change places 'cos that fellow Taggart had some force . . ."

"Wind."

George turned to the doctor, who repeated, "Wind. As Mr Leviston says, wait until tomorrow, and there'll be a lot of surprises all round; even you might get one."

"That'll be the day when anythin' surprises me, Doctor."

"And stranger things have happened, George. Well, I must be off." He turned to me and stood looking at me for a moment quietly, before he said, "This time tomorrow it'll be all in the past."

"One way or another," I said.

"Yes, as you say, Maisie, one way or another. But don't forget Hamilton."

He now nodded towards Nardy, saying, "See you sometime tomorrow."

"Yes, Doctor."

George now turned to me and said, "Aye, what's this about this thing called Hamilton? We got in court late, an' just heard the last bit on it." Then changing his tone, George bent over me, saying, "I just had to be here, Maisie. We set off last night. It was a hell of a journey. We stopped for three hours on a lay-by, and the bairns were nearly frozen in that van."

"Serves you damn well right." This was from Gran as, coming from the dining-room, she passed us on her way to the kitchen. "Whoever thought of packing four bairns into that thing in weather like this."

"Well, what did you expect me to do? Leave them there?"

"Yes, yes."

"Aw, Ma." He followed her now to the kitchen, saying, "I didn't know how long I was gona be here. And Mary doesn't like to be left on her own."

"Did you ever hear the like?" The voices faded away as I walked with Nardy into the sitting-room, and there he smiled at me, saying, "You get your characters dead on. He's exactly like you portrayed him in the book."

"He won't recognize himself." I smiled wearily at him.

"Oh, I don't know. I think there's quite a bit of sense behind that blustery manner, and a very big heart. The children, are they his?"

"No."

"Well, it's as I said, he's got a very big heart."

I looked at Nardy. He was so nice to look at: his eyes were always kind and he had such a nice face. I said, "Thank you for coming up."

"Don't be silly. As if I could stay away. And Bernard will be here tomorrow. He's delighted with the way the book's going, and that's before there's any further publicity. The whole house is really on tiptoe, and when there was an order came in last week for another two hundred and fifty from one store I understand the packers yelled hooray."

"They are all very kind."

"They are all very fond of you."

"Only perhaps because I'm . . . well" — I smiled deprecatingly at myself — "because I'm different from the usual type of novelist."

He was leaning forward as he said slowly, "And let me say that in some cases that's a very good thing, and right through the house, they are not slow to recognize it. As I've said before, first novels are often very heady medicine to some people. How's the second one going?"

"I'm stuck, and will be until . . . well, until I know what's going to happen. Nardy" — I caught hold of his hand now — "it's right what George said: Mr Collins didn't seem to make any impression on anyone, and when he started putting words into Howard's mouth, like him having compassion for me all these years and being very worried about my mental state, well, I couldn't . . . well really, I don't know what he's up to."

He now pressed my hand tightly, saying, "Maisie, if we knew what these fellows were up to, there wouldn't be any cases for defence counsels, the matter would be simple and we would defend ourselves. Some people try, and a few manage to come out on top. But it's a very tricky business. Counsels such as Mr Collins are devious men. They've got to be. They're actors: in fact, you could say they're con men because they con those in the stand to make liars of themselves, as you will find out tomorrow. I'm not in the least perturbed that our Mr Collins appeared to be a soft touch. And from what I've heard about him, he is a very clever defence counsel, and in this case the right man for the right job. You'll see, tomorrow. He'll make your husband eat the words that he has spoken today about his consideration for you; about the facts of his taking up with another woman mainly because you refused him your bed; how he tried to get you interested in outside games such as tennis. Oh my! Maisie" — he pulled a face at me now — "wait till tomorrow."

At this point Gran came bursting into the room, saying, "Well, there's a meal ready such as it is in the dining-room, lass." Then looking at Nardy, she said, "It'll likely be nothin' what you're used to, but the parts of you it doesn't fatten, it'll fill up. An' what do you think of that stupid bug . . . big lump of nothin' out there?" She jerked her head towards the door. "Bringing his woman and four bairns!"

I stopped her. "Don't call her his woman, Gran, it maddens him, she's his wife."

"Aye, well, here he is landed, as you say, with his wife and her four bairns. And where, may I ask, are they going to sleep the night? In that covered wagon that looks as if it had come out of the films, an' been half across America an' through the gold rush an' all? It's a wonder those bairns are alive, havin' slept in that."

"Well, Gran" — I was walking towards the door now — "as you say, they can't sleep in that tonight. So where do you propose they should sleep?"

"You tell me where I'm going to put six of 'em. I ask you. He said he and the lads would sleep in the van if her and the lasses can sleep in my place. But there's only a

382

single bed in that back room. And, anyway, it's never been used for years."

"Gran." I caught hold of her arm and endeavoured not to look at Nardy who was standing behind her, his head bowed as he tried to suppress his laughter. He had become very fond of Gran. "Gran," I said slowly, "there are four empty rooms upstairs; they haven't been put to use for a long time. They can all come here."

"You must be up the pole. Once you get them in, you'll never get them out."

"That'll be nice because I like them, I like them all, especially Betty." Betty was fifteen and seemed to have a sweet disposition. "And I could do with some company. And, don't let us forget" — I bent my face down towards hers now — "the house might need a caretaker for some time from now on."

"Aw, lass" — she backed from me, her face trembling — "don't say that. Just don't say it. If that happened it would put the tin hat on everythin'. You've knocked the stuffing out of me for enjoyment over the past weeks, but if you went along the line . . . oh, my God!" She almost rushed into the hall now, her head wagging, saying, "I shouldn't have this worry, not at my time of life."

Nardy, his head still bent, took my arm

now, saying, "Come on, and let us get through that which doesn't fatten but fills up."

I let myself be led towards the dining-room, thinking as I went. He's wonderful; he can adapt to anyone and any place. But then, gentlemen usually could. And for a moment a weight lifted from my heart and I thought that, no matter what happened tomorrow, if I did go along the line, as Gran had said, he'd be there when I came out.

CHAPTER 8

The court-room was crowded, but from where I sat in the dock I could see the whole court. There below me was my counsel, Mr Collins, and next to him sat Mr Pearson; in a balcony to the left were seated the doctor and Nardy and Mr Houseman, and behind them were George and Gran and Father Mackin; and seated at the end of a row was Mrs Maddison who only that morning had done my face up. That had been Gran's idea. And vaguely, seated at the back of the public gallery, I took in known faces from the terrace as I'd seen them last night from behind their curtains when I returned home after my counsel had got my bail extended.

The reports in the city papers last night

had been relegated to inside pages. One such said: Husband emphatically denies ever being cruel to wife. Another: Patient husband had to recognize that she was mentally unstable when he discovered she was talking to a horse that wasn't there, and her instability was emphasized when she attacked him with his precious collection of bottles, cutting his head in several places.

The only report that seemed anywhere near the truth was: The policeman said the accused didn't actually hit him with a bottle; it bounced off the stone wall and struck his head while he was attending to the prostrate man.

Across the far side of the court sat Howard. He was quietly but sprucely dressed, as always. He had half turned towards me as I entered the dock, brought up from below by a policeman and, at first, his expression, I saw, was one of pained injury. Then, his eyes fully on me, his face underwent such a quick change one could imagine he had been prodded with a pin . . . or my elbow. And certainly, my appearance must have prodded him, for yesterday I had come into court drably dressed, wearing a grey coat, a grey felt hat, and no make-up. Now, this morning, I had on my London rig-out — this, on the advice of my counsel and a suggestion of Nardy's, and I knew I had literally turned the heads of those people who had been here yesterday.

When the judge entered we all stood up, and when we were seated his eyes came to rest on me, and I think it was a few seconds before he connected me with the accused who had come before him yesterday.

So the second day began. My heart was beating so rapidly at times that the noise of it seemed to shut out the voices and the legal jargon that was going on to the side of me. And when someone said, "Will Mrs Stickle take the stand?" the policeman had to assist me to rise, and guide me out of the dock and down the side of the court, past Howard and into the witness-box, where I seemed to be standing eye to eye with the judge.

The prosecuting counsel was a huge man. He had a round face and heavy-lidded eyes. He had the habit of moving one lip over the other before asking a question. "You are Mrs Maisie Stickle?" he said.

"Yes." Of course he knew I was Mrs Stickle. It seemed all a waste of time.

"And you live at 7, Wellenmore Terrace, Fellburn?"

"Yes."

"You have been married to Mr Howard

Stickle for thirteen years?"

"Yes."

"How would you describe your married life?"

"Hell."

There was a slight rustling in the court; then everything went quiet.

"Would you deny that your husband swore yesterday, where you are standing now, that he was most kind and considerate towards you?"

"I would emphatically. He was never . . ."

"Please answer yes or no. I will repeat the question: Would you deny that yesterday your husband stood where you are standing now and under oath swore that he was most kind and considerate towards you?"

"No, I wouldn't deny that he stood here and said that, but I would deny that it was the truth and . . ."

"I would be obliged if you would answer yes or no, to my questions."

"One could not answer yes or no to the way you phrased that question, sir."

I heard a lot of clearing of throats from the people sitting in the first two rows now.

Then the judge's voice broke in, saying, "The defendant has a point there, Mr Taggart, if you have time to analyse it."

And Mr Taggart replied, "I'm obliged to

your lordship." Then he turned towards me again. His expression had altered slightly. I saw him draw in a sharp breath now before he said, "Is it true that you are in the habit of addressing a horse?"

"Yes."

"And that you have been doing it for some long while?"

"Yes."

"Do you not consider it an odd habit for a grown woman to converse with a horse . . . an imaginary horse?"

"Not when the horse is as sensible as Hamilton."

I felt a stir going through the court, but for some strange reason all fear had left me. Perhaps it was because there he actually was, sitting up on the bench next to the judge, leaning forward, his forefeet crossed in front of him, his whole attitude one of attention.

The counsel now took three steps away from me and picked up some papers from a table to the side, and I recognized them as the discarded sheets that Howard had stuck together and waved in my face. And he looked at me before he began to read, saying, "Would you consider this sensible conversation, or at least sensible talk? From what I gather you and the horse are in church and you go on to say here —" He now began to read: "Hamilton left the pew, genuflected deeply, walked up the altar steps and stood by Father Mackin, and before the priest had time to raise his hand, Hamilton gave the blessing, saying, 'As it was in the beginning, is *not* now and *never* shall be.' "

When the judge's hammer banged on the bench the laughter faded away and counsel stared up at me as his hand gently waved the patched sheets backward and forward.

Now I knew this was the opening that my counsel said would come and I took it. "Oh, that!" I said airily. "That was a funny part of the second book."

My answer brought counsel's eyes wide and there was almost a look of triumphant glee on his face. I could almost read his thoughts: I had won his case out of my own mouth.

He leant towards me. "You have written a book about the horse?"

"Yes, about the horse called Hamilton."

"Well, now. Well now. Correct me," he said, "if I'm mistaken. Isn't there a book already achieving some success with a title of that very name?"

I let a long pause elapse before I said, "Yes."

"And" — his thick lips moved one over the other before he went on — "you said you had written a book, a similar book about a similar horse?"

"No, about the same one."

"Now, now, Mrs Stickle."

"My name is not only Mrs Stickle, it is Miriam Carter."

"Oh. Oh, yes, I remember, that is the name of the author of the book about the horse called Hamilton. And you are Miriam Carter?"

"Yes, I am Miriam Carter."

There was a great stir in the court. I kept my eyes on the counsel, but I felt the rustling and the moving of people. Then the counsel left me for a moment and went to the bench and said something to the judge, and the judge looked towards me. Then he spoke to me and there was behind his question another question: Was I or was I not the person I was saying? Because I'm sure he was remembering me from yesterday and today I certainly didn't look like the Mrs Stickle of yesterday because she possibly could have been a little deranged in her mind. What he said to me was, "Have you any authority for that statement, Mrs Stickle, that you are the author of the book *Hamilton?*"

"Yes my Lord. My publishers are present, Mr Houseman and Mr Leviston."

I pointed, and all eyes turned on Mr Houseman and Nardy.

I saw my counsel go up to the bench now, where the prosecuting counsel was still standing, and he spoke to the judge who was leaning forward, and then to the prosecuting counsel, whom I noticed held the palm of his hand to the front of his wig for a moment. Then I saw him talk rapidly to my counsel before returning to me. And now the oily smooth look had gone entirely from his face. It was flushed and his lips were working at speed, and he began, "Well, it is established that you have written a book on what appears your pet hobby of talking to a horse, but as I see it, this only goes to prove that you were of a deceitful and unbalanced . . ."

My counsel was protesting strongly now, and the judge, speaking to the prosecuting counsel, said, "Objection sustained."

"Well, I shall rephrase my question." And he did, saying, "Was it the action of an ordinary thinking person to make out that she was a null, ill-treated, poor little woman, while at the same time having the intelligence to write a novel that seems set, to use the common term, to become a best-seller?"

"If, as you say, sir, it takes intelligence to write, then my intelligence goes back to when I was a child because I have always written bits and pieces, and all I did last year with my bits and pieces was to compile them."

He stared at me in hostility for a moment, then said, "And when your husband found out what you were doing, you became so enraged that you attacked him, not with your hands but with implements, glass implements, heavy bottles, and occasioned him such bodily harm that he will never again be the man he was."

"If that is the case, sir, there can be nothing but improvement."

"Madam."

I turned to the judge who was speaking to me now. His face straight, he said, "Kindly endeavour to keep your answers brief."

The counsel was at me again. "Then you admit to attacking your husband?" he said.

"Objection." My counsel was standing again; and this time the judge said, "Objection overruled."

"Did you or did you not throw a number of bottles at your husband?"

"I did."

"With the intention of maiming him?"

"No."

"What then?"

Of a sudden my throat was tight, I was seeing back down the years, and my voice came out now as a sort of whimper as I said, "In retaliation for years of humiliation and fear, and because he kicked my dog who was ill, dying."

The counsel stepped back from me. He looked at me almost like Howard used to. I stood with my head bowed as I listened to him speaking to the jury, telling them they had been listening to a devious woman. Could anyone imagine looking at her and listening to her that she had been made null and was browbeaten? Wasn't the boot on the other foot? Hadn't they listened to her husband yesterday, a quiet sensitive man? And could they imagine him kicking a dying dog? They must not forget that here was a woman who used her imagination.

I was saying, Oh, my God. Oh, my God, inside myself when the voice of my counsel came to me, "Tell me, Mrs Stickle, what were you doing about a quarter to one on the day in question?"

I again swallowed deeply before I said, "Typing, in my study."

"What were you typing?"

"I was doing an article for a member of the Writers' Circle."

"What did you happen to have on your desk at the side of your typewriter?"

"A little tape recorder."

"And what did you use this tape recorder for?"

"For making notes."

"What kind of notes?"

"Well, funny little things I might think of to put in my book, because I couldn't always remember them later."

"And you had just stopped typing and switched it on to record something when the door burst open?"

This was a piece of invention advised by my counsel.

"Yes."

"And your husband came into the room?"

"Yes."

"What did he say to you?"

"He . . . he told me how he was at last going to get my house, by making me out to be of unsound mind because he had found pieces of my writing in the wastepaper basket."

"Could you remember everything word for word?"

"No, but the tape was running and everything he said went down."

My counsel turned from me, and now he went to the table and picked up my tape recorder and, taking it to the bench, he spoke to the judge.

The prosecuting counsel was standing once again beside him and there seemed to be some slight argument. Then the judge said, "We will hear the tape."

At this my counsel said, "It isn't very loud, my lord, as it is only a pocket tape recorder, but I have brought an attachment that will make it much clearer . . . With your permission."

He went back to the table and opened his case; then returned to the bench and, placing my tape recorder on it, he attached a sort of amplifier to it.

Then my voice filled the court, saying, "If anything happens to Bill, I don't know what I'll do. Gran says I should get another dog straightaway, but I'll never have another dog. There'll never be another one like Bill. I've felt lost when I've had him, but that will be nothing to what I'll feel when he goes."

There was a silence now. Then as Howard's voice burst into the court-room, I saw him swivel round towards me and the look on his face was similar to that which it had held when he had first spurted the words at me.

"Well now, little Maisie, so you've been snooping around, eh? And what did you find, eh? Nothing. You just had to take the word of your friends, hadn't you? You've had nice little journeys out there on Saturdays and Sundays, haven't you, Maisie? You think you've got me where you want me now, don't you? But what proof have you? None whatever. I was visiting a friend the day Maggie Talbot happened to come to the door. My friend's name is Mrs Ribber, and her two boys are called Ribber. No, Maisie, you've got nothing on me, but by God, I've got something on you. Something that, if it doesn't fix you for good, it'll prove that you are in need of psychiatric treatment and should be put away for a time. And while you're away, I'll have to have someone to look after me, won't I? So I'll bring in a housekeeper, all very proper, and who better than Mrs Ribber and her two boys. And should you ever come out of wherever they send you, you'll have to have someone to carry on looking after you, won't you, Maisie? And Mrs Ribber will see to it, and I will see to it, for as long as you care to stay. Do you understand me, Maisie?"

"You can't do anything like that, as much

as you would like to. I have my doctor and
. . ."

"But has he seen these, Maisie? . . . This
is just a sample. I've got dozens of them,
telling about a woman who's so barmy she
talks to a horse that crawls around this
house and gets on buses with her and goes
into the supermarket and stands on its hind
legs in indignation when it sees women
shop-lifting. Oh, Maisie, Maisie, what have
you put into my hands, eh? Well now, can
we come to terms, eh? Will I have to have
you exposed and put away, at least for a
time in order to bring my wife . . . And yes,
she is my wife. And if you hadn't been
mental you would have suspected something
long ago. What did you think I got the seven
hundred and fifty out of you for? To give to
old Hempies in order to become manager?
Huh! I wouldn't give that old sod the smoke
that goes up the chimney. As for him inviting me for the weekends there . . . Eeh!
God, when you swallowed that, I realized
you'd swallow anything. No, that money
went to buy the cottage. And the rest of
your four thousand to get my first car and
add a bit on to the end of the house. Oh,
anybody that wasn't mental would have
seen through it years ago. But you are,
aren't you? You're bats. You've not got one

scrap of brain, except to copy what other people think, and any idiot can do that, any idiot. And write down your madness. Well now, am I to expose you, or are you going to sit quiet and let me bring in her and the boys? It's up to you, because, let me tell you this, I'll have this house in the end. May persuaded me to marry you in order to get it and get it I will, because by God, I've bloody well worked for it. Just seeing you day after day has been a heavy mortgage. Now I'll give you till this evening to make up your mind, no longer, then I'm going to the doctor. And, by the way, for some time now I've taken the precaution to mention your oddities to him. I've also said you've denied me your bed for the past ten years or more. Huh! and by the way, I can tell you this, that you can thank my woman on that score, because without her, by God! I would have taken it out of your limbs. What I did to you in the beginning would have been nothing to what I would have done if I hadn't had her. Anyway, there it is."

When there sounded on the tape a little click which was the door closing, there was silence in the court. It was like the silence that follows a marvellous play or concert. Then the noise became almost deafening and the judge had to bang his hammer three times before the last voice faded away and he said, "Any more of this and the court will be cleared."

Now, he turned to me where I was standing, but standing with an effort for my legs felt like jelly, and in the complete silence he and I looked at each other. And then he began to speak, partly to me and partly it seemed to the jury. "I see before me," he said, "a woman who has been physically handicapped since she was a child. I see before me an intelligent woman, whose intelligence was battened down by circumstances of her life, and she became so lonely that she resorted to fantasy in order to gain a friend. And for a friend who does she pick but a noble animal, a horse." He paused here; then went on, "I think that if a priest was attempting to explain her choice of a friend in whom she could confide, he would, in my opinion, say that she had been really communicating with her spirit. Or on the other hand, if an atheist was endeavouring to explain it he would say she was communing with the 'I' in her . . . the 'I' that is in each one of us."

Again he paused, but his eyes never left my face; then he went on, "Now, if it was Rabindranath Tagore or — say — Sai Baba, either of these Indian mystics, they would undoubtedly put the name of soul to Hamilton, but with whatever name you care to explain her friend, she was I think . . . no, I am sure, communing with her better and wiser self. And who among us, except the utter fools, do not at some time have the sense to look deep inside ourselves and find that small spark which is really the core of all that is in us. This thing that never lies.

"So, as I see it, far from Hamilton being the evidence of a disordered mind, I would say he is proof of a deep spirituality, which" — he paused now and shook his head — "I'm afraid must for a short time have deserted her when she resorted to an old-fashioned ginger beer bottle as an implement of retaliation for what she says she had suffered from both the hands and the tongue of her husband for thirteen years. And her husband has just, for all to hear, endorsed her statement." He paused a long moment here and his eyes turned from me and moved to the jury, and he went on, "You will, I know, judge this woman as your minds direct, but I would point out to you . . . and the press, who will no doubt make tonight's headlines out of this case, that it is nothing new for the human mind to take an animal into its consciousness and to talk to it, because, while being unique, we are nevertheless lonely creatures at best, and I feel it was the deep awareness of this knowledge that prompted an eminent American doctor to write a book called, *Feeling Fine.* This book states it is a twenty-day programme of pleasure for a lifetime of health, and I can vouch that if you read it and follow the advice therein, you cannot but help feel better. By the way, the doctor author himself talks to a rabbit, called Corky, and in doing so, taps his inner wisdom. And, I may add at this point, this particular doctor is not considered to be mad. They don't usually give great lengths of television time in the U.S. to madmen. I myself enjoyed reading this book because it confirmed in my mind that I wasn't any different from the rest of youth when from five to fourteen years old I talked to a she-wolfhound.

"But when my father remarried, after being a widower for seven years, I didn't need my canine friend any more. And I don't think after this Mrs Stickle will have further need of Hamilton, except as a subject for her books."

Did he smile at her? The muscles of his face moved. But then I could hardly see him. Somebody said, "Stand down." Somebody else led me into the dock again. I knew the Doctor and Gran and George and

Nardy and others were all looking towards me, yet I couldn't distinguish their faces.

The jury was out for only fifteen minutes. The man at the end stood up and when he was asked, "Do you find the accused, guilty or not guilty?" He said, "Not guilty, on all counts."

Again the judge's hammer banged on the bench. And now he was speaking to me, "Mrs Stickle," he said, "you have been found not guilty. But you did cause what's called an affray. May I suggest that in future you rely more on your spiritual self to guide your behaviour." And now he smiled quite broadly.

I had seen the devil in Howard when he stood looking at me over the desk that fateful day, fateful for him, but that look was nothing to the expression on his face as he turned and looked at me across the courtroom before his solicitor took his arm and almost pulled him up the aisle.

Then Father Mackin pushed his way towards me, and he said, "I'm happy for you. Yes, I am, but there's no getting away from it, you are a dark horse." This caused general laughter, until he said, "As it was in the beginning, is not now, and never shall be. Well, there's a lot of truth in that, and more's the pity." Then almost whispering in my ear, he said, "We're very tolerant people, we R.C.'s, and we laugh at ourselves until we bust, but we don't take too kindly to it coming from the outside. So, why don't you bring your horse into our stable, eh?"

I laughed and he laughed as I was tugged away. He'd never let up, would Father Mackin. But I liked him. And after all, it was he who had sparked off the idea of making Hamilton into a book. I must tell him that next time I see him, I thought.

It was only through the efforts and protection of the men around me that I got through the crowd of reporters and clicking cameras outside the court-room. And then I was home. We were all home, and Gran was hugging me, and George's Mary was hugging me, and the children were jumping about, and everybody was talking and all seemingly at once. Then George's voice rose above the rest and he, with his big hands under my oxters, lifted me up off the floor, crying, "A bloody novelist of all things! I knew you had it in you. Eeh! But I couldn't believe it. Eeh, by! but I was proud of you. You showed 'em. By! you showed 'em."

"Shut up you! An' put her down. An' look," Gran cried; "get yourselves into the sitting-room. There's something in there to wet your whistles, and I'll bring the tea in in a minute."

And there was something in the sitting-room to wet the whistles: two bottles of whisky, a bottle of sherry, and a bottle of port. It crossed my mind that it wouldn't have gone to waste if I hadn't come home.

George did the honours and they all drank to me: The doctor, Mr Houseman, George and Nardy, Gran and Mary, and I still continued to cry even while I was smiling.

About half an hour later, Doctor Kane said he would have to go as he had a surgery and that fool of a partner of his would be killing the patients off two at a time. He was very fond of his partner, I knew that.

I walked with him to the door and I held his hands, and when he leant forward and his bushy face came close to mine, closer than ever it had been before, and he kissed me, I put my arms around him and said, "Thank you, my dear Doctor, thank you for giving me Hamilton."

"Oh my God!" He pushed me away from him. "Don't you lay the blame on me for him." Then he said softly, "You know what I would like to do?"

"No?"

"I'd like to bring the wife around later on if I may?"

"Oh, I'd love that. I've never met her. Oh,

I'd love that."

"And you'll love her; she's a canny lass."

When he was gone, Mr Houseman followed, but not before telling me that my book would have runaway sales from now on. When Nardy said he would see him to the station, I was surprised, yet so pleased he wasn't returning to London until tomorrow. He said he had some unfinished business to attend to.

When they had gone, I said to George, Mary, and Gran, "Nardy's coming back, and you know what? The doctor's bringing his wife round tonight."

"Oh, my God!" said Gran, getting up. "The doctor's wife? Eeh! that'll mean we'll have to get somethin' in, bits and pieces to make sandwiches an' such." And at this she hurried out of the room, saying to Mary, "Come on, lass, get your coat on. We'll have to do a bit of shoppin'."

Left with George, we sat close together on the couch, and quietly now he said, "Well, it's over, lass. Your purgatory's over."

"Yes, George, my purgatory is over."

"You're puttin' in for a divorce?"

"That's already in hand."

"Well, with what's happened these last few days, it shouldn't take long. By the way, he's a nice fellow, that Nardy."

"Yes, he is."

"You like him, don't you?"

"Yes, I like him."

"He likes you."

I turned and looked at him as I said, "Yes, I know he likes me. But he's a bachelor of forty-five, and settled in his ways. Moreover, he's a gentleman. So, we both like each other and that is as far as it will go."

"You never know. No, you never know where a blister might light."

"Oh, George. I'll tell you whom I more than like."

"Who?"

"You."

"Aw, lass." He put his arms around me and hugged me.

He seemed to have his arms still around me at ten o'clock that night, when with the doctor and his wife Jane, Nardy, Gran and Mary, he sat singing, "Now Is The Hour", an old Gracie Fields song, and we were all joining in. It was past eleven o'clock and the drinks had been flowing from shortly after eight. We were all very merry. There had been another addition to the company earlier on, for my solicitor, Mr Pearson, called in. He had congratulated me, and everybody had congratulated him on his choice of counsel, and when he had left me an hour ago, there was no sign of the formal man I had come to know. Three large whiskies had, in George's words, slackened his face.

The doctor had added to the liquor store a bottle of brandy and a bottle of whisky, and Nardy had gone out with George and returned with bottles of beer and more spirits.

What not only I but the whole company had discovered in the last few hours was that Nardy had a beautiful tenor voice. Apparently, from what I remember him saying to the Doctor, he had been at a sort of choir school in his youth and had been weaned on the usual "O For The Wings Of A Dove".

George was now crying towards him, "Come on, let's have another one of them ballads! It's a night for sweetness an' light."

These last two words, sweetness and light, said in George's broad Geordie twang, sent the whole company roaring. And Gran, thumping her son on the side of the head, cried, "Did you ever! Him comin' out with things like that, sweetness an' light."

Nardy was on his feet now: standing with his back to the fire, his face was flushed, his eyes were bright. He had, I had noticed, drunk as much as anyone there, yet seemed the least affected by it. He didn't sway on his feet, nor was his voice fuddled, as was the doctor's when he cried, " 'I Hear You Calling Me,' or 'Love, Could I Only Tell You?' They're lovely. They're lovely."

Before anyone could answer, Nardy said, "Let it be this one."

I hadn't drunk anything near the quantity that the others had imbibed because I was wanting to remember every detail of this night. I'd had two sherries and I was glad at this moment that the emotion that Nardy's voice created in me did not come about through spirits. His voice was clear and warm, the cadences rising and falling, and his eyes were fixed on me as he sang:

"One day when we were young,
One wonderful morning in May.
You told me you loved me,
When we were young one day."

My emotions became almost unbearable. If only he was younger and I was older. If only he did not look upon me just as a friend, a dear, dear, friend. If only I could see him in the same light and not as I did. If only . . . if only.

"Remember, you loved me

When we were young one day."

He was looking at me, his face soft, yet aglow. The tears were streaming down my face, but I was the only one who wasn't shouting his praise and clapping.

" 'I Hear You Calling Me'." It was the doctor shouting again. "My mother used to sing that. Go on, Nardy." Everybody called him Nardy now. "Go on, Nardy," he said. "Go on, give us, 'I Hear you Calling Me'."

And so, still standing, he sang,

"I hear you calling me.
You called me when the moon had veiled
    her light
Before I went from you into the night;
I came, do you remember, back to you
For one last kiss beneath the kind star's
    light."

The beauty and the sweetness and the sadness of his voice was too much. And as he finished drawing out those last four words, "I hear you call——ing me", I could bear it no longer and I went out of the room.

I had broken up the party and I was sorry. The Doctor and his wife came into the hall and he was saying now, "Look at the time. And there they'll be, in the morning, rows and rows of 'em. And where will I be? Stuck in the bathroom with my head under the tap. Isn't that so?" He leant, swaying, towards his wife, and she, putting one arm around his waist, said, "Yes, as you have been so many times before, dear."

And now the doctor turned to Nardy and said, "Where you staying? You staying here?"

"Oh, no, it's a full house here. No, I booked a room in the town."

"Well, come on, we'll take you there."

"I think it would be safer to walk."

"Who you insultin'?"

There was laughter now as the doctor's wife said, "I'll be driving. You'll be safe with me."

There followed the business of putting on coats and of wrapping up, then handshaking all round; and when Nardy took my hands, he bent towards me, saying, "Get yourself out first thing tomorrow and try to find some summer dresses. You'll need them."

"Need summer dresses —" I screwed my face up as I ended, "In February?"

"It won't be February where you're going, miss. It's all settled. At least it will be in the morning. Remember what Rosie did at the end of your book?"

Yes, of course I remembered what Rosie

did at the end of my book. We had discussed it before. She went on a cruise.

I didn't answer him, and he said, "Well, that's where you are going shortly. We'll see that you get your passport in time. And Doctor Kane will jab you."

"What's this? What's this?" George and the doctor and Gran were all speaking at once. And Nardy, opening the front door, turned for a moment and looked at them as he said, "She's going on a month's cruise to the West Indies. Anyway, I'll be round in the morning."

When the door was closed again, George and Gran turned to me, saying, "What's this about a cruise?"

"You know as much about it as I do. And anyway" — I laughed — "I'm going on no cruise: I don't like the sea; I'm always seasick. But where I'm going now is to bed. Will you lock up, George?"

"Aye. Aye, I'll lock up. It's been a wonderful night, hasn't it? The best I remember. Eeh! they're a fine lot of people. And" — his voice dropped — "a wonderful day. Aye, lass, a wonderful day." He gave me a smacking kiss and I turned from him and called to Gran and Mary, "Good-night, Gran. Good-night, Mary." And they answered softly, "Good-night, lass."

Going on a sea cruise? Not me. What did he mean anyway, it was all fixed? Really!

The following morning Nardy was round at the house by half past nine. He showed no signs of a hangover; whereas George was suffering from a severe headache. "That's the bloody spirits," he had informed me when he staggered downstairs. "I should have stuck to beer. I've never felt like this in me life afore, even after I've had a skinful. Have I, Ma?"

"Of course you have," replied Gran. "There's times when you haven't seen daylight until the bars opened again."

Gran and George tactfully left me alone with Nardy in the sitting-room, and immediately I said to him, "I haven't got a hangover and I remember clearly your last words to me, that I had to buy a summer rig-out, dresses you said, for a cruise."

"Yes" — he nodded at me — "you're right. I haven't got a hangover either, and those were my very words: You're going on a cruise."

"Oh, no."

"Oh, yes, Maisie." He now pulled me down to the couch, saying, "From now on, for weeks ahead you will be eaten alive by reporters and all their kin: Smart ladies

412

from magazines asking you to tell the world how you began to write; feminist women wanting your opinion on man and his subtleties. After yesterday's business you'd be eaten alive. Just go to the window now, my dear, and you'll see three men at different points along the railing bordering the field."

"No."

"Yes."

"But I've got no need to go on a cruise to get away from them; I can go on a holiday anywhere in England."

"Maisie, your picture has been splashed over all the morning papers. Every word that came over on the tape, every word that the judge said. And my word, he did say some words, didn't he?" He grinned at me now. "And all kindly. So you'd be recognized in any hotel the length and breadth of the country, unless you went and hid in the Welsh hills or in the depths of Cumbria. No; I thought about this some time ago, and I have a friend who runs a travel agency. I put the situation to him and they had a cancellation and he held it until last night to see how things went in court. And so my dear, you're booked on the *Oriana,* sorry! not the *QE2,* heading for Madeira and then the Caribbean islands. But in the meantime you'll be staying with a friend of mine in Carlisle."

"Oh, Nardy." I sat back against the end of the couch and, like a child now, I said, "But what will I do on board ship? I won't know anybody."

"Everybody knows everybody within the first few days on a cruise."

"Well, if that's the case, won't they know as much about me there as they would on dry land?"

"No, not really. People who are going on cruises are so taken up with excitement for days ahead that half of them haven't time to read the newspapers. And if the other half do and you're recognized, well, my dear, you've got to get used to being a celebrity, and making friends."

"Celebrity my foot. Here, I've got Gran, and perhaps George and his family because Gran tell me George doesn't want to go back to the West Country and is going to try and get a job here again. And then I have my trips to London." I now pulled a face at him. "But on board ship, how will I spend my days?"

"You'd be surprised."

I stood up and walked to the fire and, my forearm resting on the mantelpiece, I looked down into the flames, and his voice came to me quietly, saying, "You need a change. You need to get away from this house for a time and all the memories it contains."

I knew he was right, I did need a change. And I needed to get away from this house. This house that was totally mine now had of a sudden taken on the appearance of a cage, a cage I had made for myself and was afraid to leave.

I turned towards him, saying, "I'd be terribly seasick."

"I'll see to that. I'll get some special pills."

"A month's time you say?"

"Yes, a month's time. You'll sail on Saturday. That's four weeks including today, so you'll have to get cracking."

"I'll have to close up the house."

"I'd thought about that. But you've just said that George would like to come back to the north again. Why not let them stay on here the time you're away, and he can look around. And these friends that you are going to, they're an old couple. Anne is my mother's cousin — you'll like her, and the house in the country."

"You think of everything, don't you?" I know my tone sounded a little terse, but then I was feeling a little terse, because this friend of mine, this dear, dear friend of mine was quite willing that I should go on a month's cruise and meet lots of other people. It signified something in my mind that I didn't like. Then he rose from the couch and came towards me and, holding my hands, he said, "I must tell you that after I get you settled at Anne's I won't be able to see you for a while, in fact, I don't think I shall be on the dock to wave you off."

"You won't?"

"No, I won't. You see" — he put his head to one side then bit his lip — "I . . . I have a little business. Well, not a little business; it's quite a big event in my life and it happens to fall on that same Saturday. But once I get back to town today I'll get cracking on those tickets and, of course, your passport. You'll have to fill in a form, but with a little prodding you should have it back well in time."

I stared at him. There was a big hurt inside me which all the good things that had happened to me of late couldn't soothe. I was soon to be divorced from that man; I had my house; I was acknowledged as a writer; but here was my dear friend telling me he couldn't come and see me off on a trip he had planned for me because he had other business on that day. When he took my hand and pressed it to his lips it meant nothing.

"Happy days, Maisie."

This created no response in me, and he went out of the room.

I knew he had gone into the kitchen to say good-bye to George, Gran and Mary. And I sat down and waited to hear him leave by the front door.

I looked at the clock. He had been in the kitchen over fifteen minutes.

I looked at the clock again. He had been in the kitchen over half an hour.

When at last I heard him leave, I turned and looked towards the door, and there walking through it, of all people or creatures or whatever he was, came Hamilton. And he was doing a slow waltz while singing,

One day when we were young,
One wonderful morning in May.
You told me you loved me,
When we were young one day.

I turned to the fire again and almost bitterly I said, "For God's sake, go away! Don't start that again. I don't need you any more. I've got Gran and George and Doctor and Mary and the children . . . and the neighbours are all nice to me, and I'm no longer looked upon as some sort of freak. And I'm shortly going on a cruise. Do you hear? a cruise!"

I turned to him as I asked the question; but he was gone, and I felt more lonely and rejected than ever I'd done when I'd lived with Howard.

CHAPTER 9

How did I manage to come here, sitting in a first-class cabin on the promenade deck of a ship loaded down with people all excited about going to islands where the sun shone all the time and the surrounding sea apparently hadn't any angry waves.

The weeks had passed like a flash. I hadn't gone to Nardy's friends as he had planned; something had made me perverse. It was, I think, all to do with his not coming to see me off after he had arranged to have me sent packing, as I now thought of the trip. I told him that George had offered to be my bodyguard, and would deal with reporters; and to this, all his reaction had been was to laugh and say, "Okay."

Gran and Mary had hustled me here and there, even to getting Peg Maddison to do a long job on me. I hoped her efforts would last during the cruise. She said they would if I followed her advice and applied the five layers as directed. I had found it a time-taking business, making up one's face. I was asking myself now, as I caught a glimpse of my slumped figure in the long mirror in the wardrobe to the side of me, if it was worth it. I guessed I must be the most dejected and reluctant holidaymaker on this ship.

Yet everybody, without exception, had been so kind, and they all praised Nardy for his brainwave, even Mr Pearson saying he thought it was a splendid idea: I had to go off and enjoy myself and not worry about a thing, and they would do their best to rattle my divorce through.

At times during these last few days I'd let my mind dwell on Howard, because the latest retribution he was suffering, I understood, was his dismissal from the shop. Mr Hempies apparently hadn't liked what he had said about him.

Did I feel sorry for him?

No . . . Oh no. I wasn't a fool any longer.

Looking back, I realized I hadn't believed in devils or evil, but my experience had taught me, and painfully, that there were people who were born evil. These people had two distinct personalities, and I felt now that Howard hadn't been alone within this category. I thought back to the days when I sat in the surgery waiting-room and heard snatches of conversation from weary women with regard to the lives they were being forced to lead, just a few words here and there, but so telling if you had the key, and I'd had the key.

I looked around my cabin and I had to admit it was lovely. And all those flowers. One bouquet had come from the doctor and his wife. Oh, he had been so kind. They had both come to Newcastle to see me off, and after I'd been hugged by Gran, Mary, George and the children, the doctor was the last to take my hands as I stood on the steps of the train, and what he said to me was, "I'm sorry, Maisie, I'll never see you sitting in the surgery again."

"Oh" — I managed to laugh — "don't be too sure."

"Well, I can be, at least on one point, it won't be for your old complaint. Now go and enjoy yourself. Life's going to open up for you." Then he reached up to me and his bushy whiskers were tickling my cheek as he whispered, "I'll take care of Hamilton for you; in fact, I'll adopt him."

Oh, the doctor. The doctor. What would I have done without him all these years; his concern, his understanding, all hidden behind that bushy hairy hedge and bullying manner.

When the train had gone round the curve as it went out of the station and I had seen the last of the waving hands, I sat back in that first-class compartment. Yes, Nardy had sent me, among other things, a first-class ticket to Southampton, and I felt more miserable than I'd ever done in my life before. And when eventually I reached the dock and, with the guidance of a porter and a steward, came on board, I think I was the only one on this trip without a friendly face to see me off or a hand to wave good-bye. There was a card attached to the bouquet from Mr Houseman and all in the publishing house wishing me a happy holiday. There was a card attached to another which read very characteristically: 'Live it up, lass. George, Gran, Mary and the bairns'.

How does one live it up on one's own? Nardy said I would make a lot of friends on board, but in order to do so I would have to go out there and parade the decks, or go into the recreation room, or the saloon, or the dining-room . . . Well, I'd have to go into the dining-room, wouldn't I?

Oh, dear me. I got up and went to the window. There was the sea stretching away for miles, as yet looking quite smooth. Still standing looking out, my ear picked up the soft, soft hum that could have been the sound of the engines, and I thought for a moment, it will be all right if it keeps like this. But I knew it wouldn't. Anyway, I grabbed at the next thought, if I was seasick that would give me an excuse to stay tight put here in the cabin and be looked after by the steward. He was very nice. He told me he would be caring for me during the journey. He had said it in such a nice way, as if I was somebody special. I had just to ring if I wanted anything, anything at all.

Oh, my, what was I to do?

There came a tap on the door. That would be him.

"Come in," I said. And somebody came in and the door closed.

There he stood with his back to it. The shock was such that I grabbed at my ribs as I thought, Eeh no! It's all right conjuring up a horse, but not people that you miss. I don't think I could have been more surprised if I'd seen Howard standing there.

"Well, aren't you going to say anything?"

He came slowly towards me and held out his hand, but I didn't take it. What I did was to flop down into a chair. Then, my voice a squeak, I said something silly: "What are you doing here?" And he answered, "I'm starting a long anticipated holiday in the West Indies. I haven't seen them for ten years."

My voice still a squeak: "Why . . . why

had you to do it like this? Upsetting people. I mean . . . well, making me think . . . It wasn't nice; it wasn't fair."

He sat down beside me now, his hands on his knees. And he leant towards me as he said, "It mightn't have been nice for you, but it was fair. What do you think would have been said if I had announced that I was coming on holiday with you? Even if I'd accompanied you to Southampton? As I told you, your face is well-known over the country. Things being what they are, it will be replaced shortly by someone else who has caused a sensation. But there was bound to be reporters on the quay, and I think you've had all the publicity you can stand for a while. So here am I. Here we are. And you don't look very pleased to see me."

"Oh, Nardy; you are a funny man."

"Oh, my dear. Me . . . a funny man? Anyway, are you pleased to see me?"

"Do you need to ask?"

"No; but I do need to ask you something and tell you something, and I think I'd better tell you the something first. And it's just this, Maisie." He now brought my hand up to his cheek as he said softly, "I love you. I love you very much."

No one in my life had ever said they loved me; not one, not even George, and here was this man . . . this gentleman saying these words to me, and meaning them, for the essence of them was in his eyes. There came over me a feeling of emerging, as if I was being born again; I felt my body growing, swelling, pushing out, away beyond this cabin, this ship, this great sea. My mind was singing beautifully but in his voice:

You told me you loved me,
When we were young one day.

"Maisie." He was patting my cheek now. "Don't cry, my dear. Oh, please don't cry."

"I love you, Nardy. I've loved you for a long time," I said, as the tears ran from my chin. Then I muttered, "But how can you love me . . . me?" I thumbed myself in the chest. "You could have anybody; you're so . . . so . . ."

"I don't want anybody, I only want you. I've only loved two women in my life."

My mouth fell open. He had loved before! Of course he had loved before. Don't be such a fool, woman! He's forty-five. Oh, you are a fool.

"We were engaged," he was saying. "It was in '65. A week before our wedding she had a car accident. She didn't die; she lived for eight years, and she never knew anyone again."

"Oh, Nardy."

"It's all in the past. I loved her, and I love you. And perhaps for the same reason" — he smiled softly — "she was a real person and had a great sense of humour . . . Will you marry me, Maisie?"

No words came. I simply threw myself into his arms and howled and howled his name over and over: "Oh! Nardy. Nardy. Oh! Nardy. Nardy."

When for the first time in my life I was really kissed I had the most odd and really ridiculous feeling: I felt beautiful.

Then to cap it all, there *He* came squeezing through the window, and he stood on his hind legs, his mane waving, and his white tail lashing from side to side.

We were standing, Nardy's arms around me, my arms around him when I said, "Will you take on Hamilton an' all?" And when he drew himself up and said in dignified tones, "Of course, I'll take on Hamilton; your people are my people," I answered through choking laughter, "That's a good thing, because he's prancing behind you now with mane and tail flying."

Again we fell against each other, and we laughed until we ached. Then holding me from him, he said, solemnly, "God bless Hamilton." And I said, "Amen to that. Oh yes, amen to that, because without Hamilton I'd never have met you."

ABOUT THE AUTHOR

Catherine Cookson lived in Northumberland, England, the setting of her international bestsellers. She was born in Tyne Dock, the illegitimate daughter of an impoverished woman, Kate, who she was raised to believe was her older sister. She began to work in the civil service but eventually moved south to Hastings, where she met and married a local grammar school master. Although she was originally acclaimed as a regional writer, her readership quickly spread throughout the world and her many bestselling novels have established her among the best loved of contemporary writers. After receiving an OBE in 1985, Catherine Cookson was created a dame of the British Empire in 1993. She died in 1998 at age ninety-one.